DISTANT MEMORY

Also by Alton L. Gansky in Large Print:

A Ship Possessed

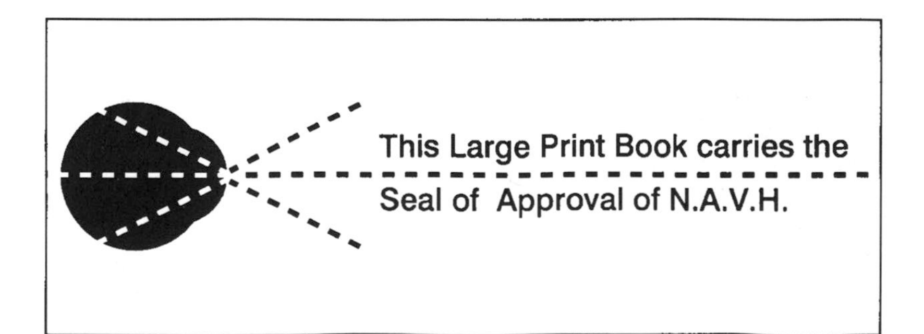

DISTANT MEMORY

Alton L. Gansky

Thorndike Press • Thorndike, Maine

Published in 2000 by arrangement with WaterBrook Press,
a division of Random House, Inc.

Scripture quotations are taken from the *King James Version.*

Thorndike Press Large Print Christian Mystery Series.

The tree indicium is a trademark of Thorndike Press.

The text of this Large Print edition is unabridged.
Other aspects of the book may vary from the original edition.

Set in 16 pt. Plantin by Al Chase.

Printed in the United States on permanent paper.

Library of Congress Cataloging-in-Publication Data

Gansky, Alton.
Distant memory / Alton L. Gansky.
p. cm.
ISBN 0-7862-2915-2 (lg. print : hc : alk. paper)
1. Amnesia — Fiction. 2. Truck drivers — Fiction.
3. Women — Crimes against — Fiction. 4. Large type books. I. Title.
PS3557.A5195 D57 2000b
813′.54—dc21 00-060766

To my son Aaron,
who taught me the meaning of courage
and the power of perseverance

Prologue

Monday, 10:40 P.M.

The tires released an anguished scream like an animal caught in the steel jaws of a trap. The car slid several feet into the oncoming lane. A truck, a behemoth on eighteen wheels, careened past, just inches from the vehicle. Half a foot closer and it would have ripped the side mirror from its base and sent it tumbling along the asphalt highway.

Instead of slowing, the driver pressed the gas pedal to the floor and the engine growled loudly. A glance in the rearview mirror showed the piercing high beams behind her fall away into the night. Seconds later, the lights began once again to gain, slowly pulling closer and closer.

The lights — stabbing, burning, brilliant lights — were still there, like tiny suns pushing back the cold black of space. Pursuing. Tracking. Hunting. Tears formed in her eyes, as much from the reflected brilliance as from the fear within her. The pursuer was closing the distance. The speedometer read ninety-five, and the needle was still moving up.

"Leave me alone!" she shouted and slammed her fist on the steering wheel. The headlights behind her were higher off the ground than those of a passenger car — a van, a truck, or maybe a sport utility vehicle. Whatever it was, it was big and, worse, it was fast.

Ahead she could see the lights of a town. That was her hope — her only hope. There would be people, and people meant safety. Perhaps there would be a highway patrolman or sheriff or someone else who could help.

Something brown shot out of the desert and into the bright white of her lights. A coyote — a young one judging by its size. Instinctively she hit the brakes. It was a mistake. The car lurched forward, and she was thrown back into the seat as the vehicle behind rammed her bumper. The tires lost traction, and she turned into the swerve. She found herself in the oncoming lane. A horn blared with painful intensity; the high beams of an oncoming car blinded her. Her heart pounded like a piston, and she cried out in fear. Yanking the wheel hard to the right, she accelerated and once again missed a head-on collision by mere inches.

The vehicle behind her rammed her

again, and she struggled to keep the tires on the road. Once more she pressed the accelerator to the floor in a desperate attempt to get to the town ahead.

Desert landscape rushed by as she willed the car to go faster, praying that she did not lose control. The coyote had almost been the death of her. If she had hit it, she would have done so at nearly one hundred miles per hour and she would certainly have crashed.

Slam! Her head rocked back, hitting the headrest behind her. A scorching pain raced down her neck. *Slam!* The sound of crumpling metal reverberated through the metallic skin of the car.

She was losing the race. She would die, they would see to it. They knew about her, and she knew about them.

The attacker was just a yard or two behind her. One more hit would certainly put her off the road. Another pair of lights, higher than those of her attacker, caught her eye. These were farther back but closing the distance rapidly. *Great,* she thought. *He has a partner with a bigger truck.*

There was another bump, but more gentle than the previous ones. For a second she was thankful, but then she felt herself drifting to the right. The car behind her was pushing her left rear bumper, causing the car to veer. If she hit the brakes, the car would slip into a wild spin. She had to stay on the road, had to keep the tires on the pavement.

It was impossible. The right front tire of her car left the firm surface and dug deeply into the soft, sandy shoulder of the highway. The steering wheel twisted out of her hand as the car flipped into the air. The horrific sounds of tearing and crunching metal, of breaking glass and racing motor, blended in a crescendo of destruction. One moment she was staring into unforgiving desert floor, the next into stygian night. The car rolled and flipped. The windshield blew inward, showering her with a thousand pieces of safety glass.

The two-second eternity ended with the car upright on all four deflated tires. Seconds later, another symphony of twisting metal pierced the night. She did not care. She could not think.

Her head lolled to the side, resting on the driver's window. Blinking several times, she let her eyes look up at the black velvet night sky. Stars sparkled like sequins — all but one. A tiny light moved slowly across the backdrop of stars. The sight terrified her. "No," she said softly. "No, no, no."

The black of night filled the car; the black of unconsciousness filled her eyes. She took a ragged breath and waited for death.

Chapter 1

Tuesday, 9:45 A.M.

The dark of unconsciousness swirled at the edge of her mind like black coffee. She first became aware of a sound, small and distant, barely perceptible. It was a chirp, made by a bird near a window. It chirped again and then fell silent, its small cry replaced by the louder, harsher noise of rubber wheels, like those of a shopping cart, being pushed along a concrete walk. A wobbling wheel released a rhythmic slapping sound. The noises of distant cars and trucks traveling quickly along a remote road filtered through the fog of oblivion, from which she was slowly rising like a bubble from the bottom of the ocean.

She tried to swallow, but her mouth was dry as sandstone and her tongue was slow to respond. Her lips hurt. They were dry and cracked. Inhaling deeply, she winced as an ice pick–like pain stabbed her side. The air that passed her lips tasted bad. It was thick with cigarette smoke and the smell of stale beer. Sleepily moving the fingers of her right hand, she felt the coarse fabric of a cheap bedspread beneath her. The material felt rough and old, and the dirty threads that formed the yet unseen pattern were stiff to the touch. The bedcover felt alien, unknown. She was sure she had never before touched it.

The darkness began to call her again. The bliss of oblivion beckoned and tugged at her mind, but she resisted it. Several times she had come close to waking, to opening her eyes to see what surrounded her, but each time she had surrendered to the hypnotic chant of dreams, to the warmth of unconsciousness. Tempting as sleep was, she knew that the time for sleeping had long passed. By an act of determined will, she forced opened her eyes and blinked back the foggy dregs of slumber. She was staring at a ceiling that had once been white but was now tobacco brown from neglect and age. A cobweb swayed in a lazy waltz, moved by an air current too subtle to feel.

She raised a hand to her face, and pain raced through her body like a thousand tiny bayonets. Her right side burned, her head throbbed percussively, and the skin of her face was painfully sensitive to touch. She groaned. Things were out of place, something was wrong, but her mind was muddy and slow. Full consciousness eluded her.

Bits and pieces of rational thought spun wildly through her brain like confetti in a strong breeze.

"What did you do last night?" she asked herself. Her voice sounded muffled and unfamiliar. She gently eased her legs over the side of the bed and let her feet touch the floor. A deep, aching pain tightened in her back. Looking at her feet, she saw an old pair of Nikes. She had gone to sleep with her shoes on. Beneath her feet was a thin pile, gold carpet with brown stains that looked as old as dirt itself. She had no memory of the stains. For that matter, she had no memory of the carpet or even the shoes she wore.

Raising her head she stared at the off-white drapes that hung limply from a gaudy curtain rod, which looked as if it had been pulled from an old, dilapidated Victorian. The unfamiliar curtains were thin and threadbare, and clearly they had not been cleaned in the last ten years.

The heavy blanket of wooziness began to recede only to be replaced by questions. *Where am I? Why am I here? How did I get here? Why is there so much pain?*

She forced herself to stand. The room began to spin, and a sea of nausea raged within her, forcing her to steady herself by placing a hand on the mattress. At first she wanted to lie down again, to crumple onto the bed and wait for a better time to rise, but she resisted the urge. She had no idea how long she had been asleep, but she knew it had been too long.

A marred wood nightstand stood next to the bed. On it was an inexpensive clock radio which appeared new, as if it had just been taken out of its box. Blue numbers shone weakly: 9:45. That seemed late, although she was uncertain why. Closing her eyes, she waited for the spinning to stop. She took a deep breath, but this time she inhaled slowly to avoid another stab of pain. Holding the air in her lungs for a moment, she released it in a long, steady exhalation through pressed lips that made a soft whistling sound. She repeated the act several times before her stomach calmed and the dizziness evaporated.

Standing erect again, she wondered if she had spent the night drinking and was now hung over. But that thought seemed misconceived. She had no memory of drinking last night or any night. What then? The flu? If so, it was the worst case she had ever experienced. Her body was weak and sore; her mind muddled and foggy. It was hard to remember anything.

Unconsciously, she licked her lips and

was again reminded of her parching thirst. Rounding the bed with deliberate steps, she made her way to an open door at the back of the room. As she had guessed, it was a bathroom. She flicked on the light switch. Inside were a scarred and heavily scratched fiberglass tub and shower, a white toilet with chipped enamel and a rust-streaked bowl, and a freestanding sink. Turning on the water, she watched as brown-tinged liquid flowed from the faucet. After a minute, the water ran clear. There were no plastic cups from which to drink, so she cupped her hands, filled them with the cool water, and brought them to her lips. The water had an odor to it and tasted like copper. She drank it anyway, and then splashed the liquid on her face. It stung. "Ouch," she cried softly.

Taking a yellowed towel from a plastic holder mounted on the wall between the sink and toilet, she dried her hands and dabbed at her face. The towel felt sandpaper rough against her flesh. Pulling the towel away, she looked into the cracked, oval mirror that hung precariously over the washbowl. She gasped loudly, faltered back, and dropped the towel.

The woman in the mirror was a stranger. Nothing about her was familiar. In utter disbelief, she pushed a wavering hand against the cold glass until her fingertips gently touched the image. The strange woman in the mirror did the same. Pulling her hand back, she touched her own hair. The woman in the mirror mimicked the action. She was seeing a true reflection. The woman was certainly her, but why didn't she recognize her own face?

She studied the image. The hair was shoulder length and raven black with a part on the right side. Her eyes were green and rimmed by smudged mascara and eyeliner. Her skin was clear but reflected a pale yellow. As she stepped closer to the mirror, she realized that the yellow hue was from the weak fluorescent light over the sink. The more she examined the reflection, the more puzzled she became. How could she not know her own face? And the face was a mystery in other ways. It was pretty, on the young side of middle age. But it was also — damaged. The lower lip was slightly swollen and creased by a small cut. A tiny rivulet of blood had dried on her chin from where the cut had bled. The skin of her face, which had at first appeared yellow, now paled in the glow of the dim light. Still there was some discoloration; a slight, uneven pink stippled the tissue. It reminded her of a windburn she would occasionally get as a child when . . . when . . . She closed her eyes and tried to recall when she had been a child, but no memories surfaced. Focusing as hard as she could, she tried to raise the spectral memories of her past. Surely she had had parents, gone to school, made friends, but no images came to mind — no names, no recollections.

Panic seized her as realization crashed down on her. The sick, burning nausea returned in a hot flood. Ironically, an icy chill ran down her spine. Her brain fired confusing questions that she could not answer. Her eyes danced around the drab little room. "Tub," she said, pointing at the fiberglass bathtub. Then in rapid, staccato words she uttered: "Toilet. Sink. Mirror. Floor." She turned and continued her frenetic inventory. "I know these things. Door. Hinges. Screws." She touched the jamb and then crossed the threshold into the motel room. "Bed. Carpet. Television. Radio alarm. Fire alarm. I know all these things. Why don't I know who I am?" The last words came out choked and uneven.

The pounding in her heart increased geometrically, thudding so fast that she was sure it would explode violently and she would drop dead to the floor. Turning, she took in the room again with its dirty carpet and moldering walls. A cheap painting of an old California mission hung crookedly from a nail. An aged Zenith television sat on a battered dresser. A thin film of dust covered the furniture.

Another bolt of pain, inflamed by her rapid respiration and agitated motions, ripped through her side. "I know everything in this room, but I don't know the room," she said to herself. But that was wrong, she realized a moment later. She could identify everything in the room for what it was, but it all lacked familiarity. The clock radio was easy to identify, not because she had seen it before, but because it was like all other clock radios.

Staggering to the bed, she slumped down on its edge and laid her head in her hands. She calmed herself, willing her heart to slow and her breathing to settle. "Think," she commanded herself. "Think. Panic can only make things worse. Logic works; fear hinders." The last phrase seemed familiar and brought a small degree of comfort. Rising from her perch on the bed, she began to pace the small space.

"Let's start with what we know," she muttered as if she were talking to a close friend. "I'm in a motel room. But where?" No answer came. She looked around the room again, this time more carefully. Then she saw a key with a dark blue plastic tag attached to it. The dull and washed-out lettering read:

PRETTY PENNY MOTEL
HIGHWAY 58 & 3RD
MOJAVE, CALIFORNIA
ROOM 110

"Mojave? Where on earth is Mojave?" She clutched the key tightly. It was a clue — a solid, concrete connection to reality. "Okay," she said in a whisper. "If I'm in a motel, then there must be a record of my having checked in. The desk clerk must have a receipt for the room." That thought made her stop. If she had checked into the motel, then she must have paid for the room. That meant that she must have money or a credit card. Either would mean that she had a purse or a wallet. But where was it?

Still clutching the key, she walked back to the bed and looked over the nightstand. Nothing. Slumping to her knees, she searched the floor and even under the bed, but found nothing. "The closet," she said, rising to her feet. The act of standing from a kneeling position hurt and she groaned deeply. *What has happened to me?*

The closet was empty. No clothing hung from the hangers, no handbag rested on the floor. She searched each drawer in the dresser and found only a thin and worn telephone directory. At the top of the phone book were the words: PACIFIC BELL YELLOW PAGES 1999. 1999? Was that the year? The book looked old and well used. Most likely it was out of date like everything else around her. That would mean that it was sometime later than 1999. How much later, she could not tell.

Why could she find no purse? Why was there no wallet with identification? Why . . . ? She froze as the most obvious possibility broke the surface of her mind. Her body was sore, her lip was split, and she had no money or credit cards. Had she been robbed? It was logical and it would answer many questions, including her physical condition. A robber might have attacked her and in a struggle beat her and —

The last thought was unwelcome and sickening. Had it been more than a robbery? Had more than her money been taken? Had she been — ? A cold finger ran up her spine, and she shuddered. Surely she would remember that. If nothing else, she would have to remember being attacked, being violated. Or would she? Wasn't it just such a thing that could push a woman into a psychological hole — a place to hide from something so horrific, so appalling? In such cases, it wasn't just the body that was raped. The rapist also violated the mind, the character of the woman, the fragile psyche of a human, and that often took much longer to heal than any bodily wounds.

Returning to the mirror in the bathroom, she once again studied her image. This time she removed the white cotton T-shirt she wore. Pulling the garment over her head caused her side to ache and her head to throb. She continued disrobing, removing her loose-fitting jeans and undergarments. She studied herself in the mirror and was shocked to see a large, narrow, bluish bruise that ran from her left shoulder to the bottom right of her rib cage. In addition, a deep purple discoloration covered the upper part of her left arm and shoulder. Another bruise ran across her hips just behind where the elastic band of her underwear would be. Her right arm bore no marks. Raising her hands, she studied her wrists. They too were unmarked. If she had been in a struggle, there would have been bruises on her wrists and upper arms. An ache in her foot caused her to look down. She was still wearing the Nikes. She had tugged the jeans over her shoes. Placing a foot on the edge of the toilet, she untied the laces and removed the sneaker and white sock. She repeated the act with the other foot. It had been her right foot that ached and she examined it closely. It too was bruised, and the skin at the top of her foot was broken.

She continued her self-examination until she had checked every part of her body. Finally, she dismissed the idea of a physical attack. The markings seemed wrong. But something had happened to her, and she was at a loss to explain what.

She dressed again, washed the blood and makeup from her face, and exited the bathroom. The unsettled feeling of panic rose in her again. Nothing made sense. Once more, her eyes traced the room, looking for any clue that would help her to discover who she was. If there were any clues, they were well hidden. Maybe there was something out there, outside the room.

The thought made her uncomfortable, although she could not tell why. Walking to the drapes, she pulled them aside and peeked out the window. The white sun shone down through a cloudless sky. Just outside her room was an asphalt parking lot in grave disrepair. Small but persistent weeds had pushed up through cracks in the macadam. Walking across the lot was an elderly Hispanic woman. She was pushing a maid's cart. The cart had a wobbly front wheel. Only two cars were parked on the lot: an old, heavily dented, beige Volkswagen Beetle and a yellow Ford Pinto with oxidized paint and a cracked windshield. An eighteen-wheeler was parked curbside, where the lot met the road that ran along the front of the property. The road itself was wide, with two lanes of traffic going in each direction. Cars and tractor-trailer rigs drove noisily by the motel.

The surrounding terrain was sparse and foreboding. Thick-limbed trees, their pointed leaves aimed skyward like upraised organic spears, dotted the empty field across the road. The ground was a depressing brown. She was in the desert, that much was clear.

Closing the curtain, she stepped away from the window and waited for her eyes to readjust to the dark room. "What now?" she asked herself. She wondered about the two cars out front. Could one of them be hers? If so, then there would surely be a DMV registration form that would have not only her name, but also her address. And maybe she would find more, a datebook or piece of luggage. Maybe her purse or wallet was in the car, left there as a result of her amnesia.

Amnesia! The word struck her hard. She had not thought of her failed memory in that way before, but it was the only word that would do. "Amnesia," she said tentatively, as if some evil magic were associated with it, as if its very mention could summon dragons or demons.

She forced aside her rising sense of fear and focused on the cars outside. How could she tell if one of them belonged to her? She had no car keys, and neither car looked familiar. The front desk would know. She had stayed in motels before and had always been asked to leave the license number of her car with the motel clerk. For a brief moment, a picture of her hand filling out a form flashed across her mind. A half-second later, a maddening fugue replaced the image. Still, the memory gave her something to work with. Grabbing the room key from the dresser, she shoved it into her pocket and stepped outside.

The air was hot and dry, and the heat stung her face. Remembering the time on the clock, she knew that it was no more than a few minutes after 10:00, but the temperature was already scorching, causing her tender face and chapped lips to hurt all the more. Waves of heat rose around her feet as she stepped from the cracked concrete walk in front of her room onto the black pavement. It was as if she were walking through an oven.

The motel complex's L-shape bordered two sides of the parking lot. To her right, one leg of the L ran at a right angle to the side of the building her room was on. At the end of the leg was an office. The building was a one-story structure covered with marred and cracked stucco. Its red clay tile roof reflected the midmorning sun back to the bright sky. Overhead, a hawk circled in lazy loops. The starkness of the terrain, the heat of the day, and the dilapidated condition of the building gave her a sense of otherworldliness, as if she had been transported to a distant desert planet.

It took less than forty steps for her to cross the lot and reach the office, but it seemed like a trek of several miles. Her stomach was upset again, and her head throbbed. Grabbing the worn brass handle on the glass door that separated the outside from the office, she pulled it and quickly entered. The office was air-conditioned, and the cool air enveloped her in a cold caress. At first it felt wonderful, but the sudden change in temperature made her woozy. She stopped just inside the door and raised a hand to her forehead, as if doing so would push away the darkness that threatened to flood over her.

"Hey, you all right?" someone asked.

She looked up to see a young man no older than twenty-one standing behind the counter that divided the small lobby from the front desk. His hair was red and cut short, and he wore two earrings in each ear. "What?"

"I asked if you were okay. You look sick or something."

"The heat . . . the air conditioning . . ."

"Ah," he said matter-of-factly. "It happens all the time. People don't realize how hot August gets around here."

August. It is August. "I'll be fine in a minute. I just need to catch my breath." She took a couple of deep breaths, wincing with each inhalation. The wooziness subsided, and the room stopped spinning.

"You want some water or something? I got good water back here. Not the junk that comes out of the tap."

She recalled the brown fluid from the faucet in her room. "Yes, that would be nice. Thank you."

"No sweat, lady. I can't have you passing out in the lobby." He stepped into a side room, then reemerged with a small paper cup in his hand. "Here you go," he said, holding the cup out over the counter. She walked forward and took it, slowly sipping the clear, cold fluid. It tasted wonderful.

"More?"

"No, thank you," she replied and handed the cup back. As she did, she looked up into the young man's face. It was pimpled and unshaven; thin, reddish peach fuzz covered his chin. His appearance was rough, but there was kindness in his eyes. As he stared back, his expression showed concern. "Are you sure you're okay?" he asked.

"I'm fine," she said. *At least for the moment.*

"If you say so," he replied. "What can I do for you?"

At that moment, she realized that she had given no thought about what to say. "I'm . . . I mean, I was —" She stopped abruptly, wishing she had given this more consideration. What should she say? *Hi, I have no idea who I am or how I got here. I'm beat up and confused. Got any ideas?* That seemed unwise. Another concern crossed her mind. What if she owed him money for the room? She had no way of paying. He could become angry and call the police. But then, maybe that would be good. Maybe they could help her figure out who she was. She decided to start slowly. "I'm in room one-ten and I can't seem to find my receipt. Do you have one for me?"

"They're supposed to give you one when you check in," he said. "Did you come in last night?"

She had no idea, but that seemed right. "Yes."

"Let's see. Here it is. I'll have to make a photocopy of it. We have to keep a copy for our files."

"Thank you."

"Sure you don't want more water?"

"I'm sure."

Again he disappeared into the side room. When he returned he had an 8½-by-11-inch piece of paper with him. He handed it to her. She took it with a shaky hand. The paper was a reproduction of a small note. The receipt had the name of the motel and its address in block letters at the top. Underneath was a barely legible scrawl. She found the line that read *Name*. Next to it was printed *Nick Blanchard*. She was nonplussed. "Are you sure this is the right receipt?"

He looked at the original. "It's the one for room one-ten. The night manager could have screwed things up again. That happens sometimes. It's easy to write down the wrong room number or switch a couple of the numbers around. I've done it myself. If you tell me your name, I can go through the receipts and —"

"There's no need for that," she said quickly. She studied the paper again. The check-in time was listed as 11:30 P.M. One night was paid in advance. *That's a relief. At least I won't be reneging on a bill*. It also meant that she was out on the street.

"Did you want to check out now?" the clerk asked.

Nick Blanchard. She mulled the name over, ignoring the question. Did she write that name? That seemed unlikely. The night clerk would have thought it strange. Did she arrive with someone else? A husband? A boyfriend? Who was Nick Blanchard?

"Lady, do you want to check out or not?"

"Sure she does," came a new voice. She spun around and saw a man standing in the doorway. His eyes were fixed on her. "No one wants to stay in this dump two nights running." He released the door and walked into the lobby. He held out his hand. "Hi, I'm Nick Blanchard."

In silence, she took his hand.

Chapter 2

Tuesday, 10:15 A.M.

"I went to your room, but you weren't there," Nick Blanchard said. He was tall with a medium build. His hair was dark brown and touched with gray at the sides. It was his face that struck her. It was heavily lined around the eyes, and two deep creases ran vertically along his cheeks. Smiling made the creases deeper. Yet his face was neither old nor harsh, but was simple and ruggedly attractive.

"I'm . . . um," she began shakily, wondering what to say.

His dark eyes flashed as he offered another smile while holding up his index finger. "Hold on a minute," he said smoothly. Reaching into his pocket, he removed a key identical to the one she had just surrendered to the clerk. In a fluid movement, he tossed the key to the earring-decorated employee. "Room one-eleven," he said to the young man. "I'm ready to check out too. Do you need anything else from me?"

"No sir," the clerk said. "I mean, I don't think so. Let me check." Once again he stepped back into the adjoining office and reemerged with a receipt. "It looks like you're all paid up and you made no phone calls. So we're square."

"I made no phone calls because the phone doesn't work," Nick said bluntly.

"Oh. Sorry."

"Where can we get some breakfast?" Nick asked.

"There's a McDonald's next door. They serve breakfast. There's also a café two blocks down." He motioned north with his thumb.

"Is it any good?"

"Not even close. You won't catch me in there."

"McDonald's it is." Turning to her again, he said, "I don't know about you, but I really could use some coffee."

Did she drink coffee? It sounded good. "I'm afraid that I don't have —"

"My treat," he said before she could finish. "I eat alone all the time, and I hate it. It will be nice to have some company for a change. Shall we?" He motioned to the door with a gallant gesture.

Uncertainty welled up in her like a geyser. This was absurd. She didn't know him. At least, she didn't think she did. Maybe he was responsible for her condition. Maybe he wasn't a white knight coming to her rescue. But he had arranged for her room the night before and had even come looking for her this morning. Certainly an attacker would not do that, would he?

"I don't bite," he said softly. "I imagine you're a little confused. I know I am. Let's go somewhere where we can talk. It's a public place. You'll be safe."

Unable to think of any alternative, she nodded slightly and started for the door without a word.

The fast-food restaurant was crowded with travelers, locals, and children. The small dining room was a cacophony of laughter and conversation. She was sitting at a cartoon yellow booth. Before her was a large cup of black coffee and an egg-and-biscuit sandwich. Blanchard sat opposite her, eating a pancake-and-egg breakfast from a thin plastic foam platter. He ate quickly and with gusto. She raised the sandwich to her mouth and took a bite, then winced.

Nick noticed the expression of pain. "I'm sorry," he said softly. "I should have realized that your lip would be sore. Let me get something you can eat with a fork."

"No, that's all right, Mr. Blanchard. I'm not really hungry."

"Nick," he said. "Call me Nick. Mr. Blanchard makes me think you're speaking to my father."

"You don't like being called Mister?" she asked, hoping to direct the conversation away from her. She was still trying to make sense of everything around her and was failing.

"Much too formal."

"Okay," she agreed. "Nick it is."

"Now what about you? What's your name?"

This was the question she feared. Perhaps blurting out the truth might be useful, but she was uncertain. Breakfast notwithstanding, Nick was still a stranger. For that matter, everyone was a stranger to her, including herself. "I didn't tell you last night? I mean, when you arranged for the motel?" She was hoping he would fill in the blanks about how she had come to be in a motel just one room away from him.

"No. You didn't say much at all. In fact, the only word that came out of your mouth was *no*. I could tell that you were hurt and disoriented. I offered to take you to a hospital or the police, but you went ballistic.

Threatened to jump out of the truck if I tried. I figured that was the last thing you needed. And I couldn't leave you on the side of the road. A lot of wackos drive the 14 and the 58."

"Truck?" She had no memory of a truck.

"Yeah, my tractor-trailer rig." He took a sip of coffee. "It's parked in front of that lousy excuse for a motel. I suppose I should apologize for that too. There's not much choice around here, and it was the first place I saw. At least you agreed to stay there."

He's a trucker. "Do you pass through here often?"

"Sometimes," he answered. "I'm an independent. I own my own rig and work for whomever I want."

Whomever. Not whoever. He knows the difference. He has some education. Her mind was desperately grasping for facts.

"Do you like it?" It was an inane question, but she knew of nothing else to say or do.

"Yes, and I think you're stalling."

She sat back, uncertain what to say.

"I don't mean to be rude," he said apologetically. "I have no right to ask you any questions. I just want to help, that's all."

A sense of guilt washed over her. He had been kind enough to pick her up and see that she had shelter for the night. He could have just passed her by, leaving her to wander on the road. That was what he'd said, wasn't it? That he had found her on the roadside. "You found me on the road-side?"

"That's right. You were just wandering along the highway like you were in a trance. Lucky for you it's summer; in winter you would have frozen. Most people don't realize how cold it can get up here."

Why would she be walking along the side of a desert highway? "And I didn't say anything to you?"

"Not a thing. You got in the truck easy enough. All I had to do was open the door and you crawled right in, although I could tell it hurt you to do so. That's why I wanted to go to the highway patrol or to a hospital, but you made it clear that wasn't going to happen."

"I'm sorry if I've caused you trouble."

He waved a dismissive hand. "What good is it being a knight errant if I can't help the occasional damsel in distress?" He motioned courteously with one arm and, since he was seated in a booth, bowed as best he could. She smiled and then, touching her sore lip, said, "Ouch." She scowled. She had grown tired of hurting.

Nick frowned. "Is the rest of you as sore as your lip?"

At first she hesitated, all the fears resurfacing in her mind. But she needed help; she needed a friend. Alone, penniless, lost, she had to have help even if it meant taking a risk. "Yes," she said with a sigh. "I'm damaged but not broken."

"You sound like you're talking about a piece of furniture or something. What else hurts? If I'm not being too personal, that is."

"Bruises, and my side hurts. My head aches some too."

"Bruises?" He looked thoughtful for a moment. "May I ask where the bruises are?"

This was uncomfortable. Should she tell a total stranger about the marks on her body? She decided that she had nothing to lose. "Besides what you see on my face, there is a bruise on my shoulder and —"

"Which shoulder?"

"What difference does that make?" she asked, puzzled.

"Maybe nothing; maybe everything."

"My left shoulder. And there is a long diagonal bruise from my left shoulder to my right hip." She felt her face turn hot.

"Don't be embarrassed," he said softly.

"What about the lower abdomen? Is it bruised too?"

She nodded.

"How is your chest? Is it sore?"

This time she didn't answer. The questions were getting personal.

"I'm not a pervert. I'll explain why I ask in a moment. Now how about it? Is your chest sore?"

"Yes, and my left side."

"I wouldn't doubt your right foot is pretty banged up too. Maybe the ankle."

"How did you know?"

"I was in an auto accident once. Flipped my car several times. Your bruises mean that you were in a wreck of some kind."

"I don't get it."

"It's simple. Your split lip and chapped face came from the airbag. That's also why your chest is sore. Air bags save thousands of lives, but they leave their mark. The diagonal bruise on your chest is probably from the shoulder harness. That would also explain why your left side is sore. You were driving."

"How can you know that?" she asked with disbelief.

"The direction of the bruise. You said it ran from your left shoulder to your right hip. That's the direction of the driver's shoulder strap. It would explain the bruise across the lap area. I'd bet money that you were in an auto accident. Probably rolled the car, hitting your shoulder on the side window as well as your head. That's where the knot on your forehead came from. As far as your foot goes — well, that just proves that you were driving. Most likely you hit your foot on the brake pedal when the accident happened. You're lucky, really. I had a friend whose foot was broken that way."

She reached up and touched the sensitive lump on her forehead.

"An auto accident. That might explain . . ." she trailed off.

"Explain what?"

She didn't answer.

"Okay, then. Let me guess. You seem quite confused, and you've been hesitant to say anything about yourself or what has happened to you. You're fearful, even paranoid. No offense intended."

"None taken."

"That's good," he leaned back and took a long sip of coffee, his eyes darting over her as if he could see into her very being, peering through each layer of emotional defense like an x-ray machine through flesh. "You don't know who you are, do you?"

"That's ridiculous," she snapped defensively. “Who could forget something like that?”

“Accident victims for one. The traumatized for another.” His words were steady yet soft, devoid of any accusation. “Am I right?”

Tears began to brim in her eyes, and she lowered her head. This nightmare was real. This was no dream from which to awake. She was sitting in a strange restaurant in a strange little desert town talking to a strange man who might be the only person she could trust.

Leaning forward, Nick reached out a hand and gently touched her arm. His hand was warm and smooth. It felt good, reassuring. “I didn’t mean to upset you. I just want to help.”

“I don’t know who I am,” she said in a soft but forced whisper. “I have no memory. I don’t remember a car accident. I don’t remember you picking me up on the road. I don’t remember going to the motel. My past, even my name, is a mystery to me.”

“No identification?”

She shook her head. “Not that I could find.”

“That makes sense,” he said flatly, leaning back in the booth.

“How does that make sense? It sure

doesn't make sense to me."

"You're a woman. Women often carry their identification in a purse, seldom on their person. Men are just the opposite. We tuck our wallets in our back pockets. If you were indeed in an accident and sufficiently stunned by it, it is quite possible that you wandered away from the wreck leaving your purse behind."

"If I was in a collision, why didn't the other person help?"

"Maybe it wasn't a collision. Perhaps you fell asleep at the wheel and went off the road. It was late when I found you. It's possible that you veered off and crashed and that no one saw you."

"I suppose." She thought about that. It made some sense, but it didn't sit right. Something was missing. "I'm very confused," she admitted. The words were inadequate to describe her consternation. She was far more than confused — she was bewildered, disoriented, and panicky.

"I can imagine. Would you like me to take you to the hospital?"

The thought frightened her and she tensed. "No."

"What are you afraid of?" he asked softly.

I don't know. "I'm all right."

He cast a doubtful look.

"Physically, I mean," she said. "I'm sore, but I don't think anything is broken. If only . . ." she trailed off.

"If only what? If only you knew who you are?"

"Yes."

"That's why I want to take you to a hospital. Let the doctors take a quick look. Maybe they can fix you right up."

"No," she insisted without knowing why.

Nick sighed and rubbed his eyes. "Okay, you win. But what am I supposed to do with you? You have no money, no direction, no transportation, and no one you can call for help."

The cold summary of truth that Nick had just spoken made her stomach ache again. "I don't know. I'll figure something out."

They fell silent. She could tell that he was thinking, mulling over some unspoken thoughts. A few moments later, after swallowing the last of his coffee in a single gulp, he said, "I guess you'll come with me."

"With you?"

"I can't very well leave you sitting in a McDonald's in a small town out in the middle of nowhere, can I?" Before she could respond, he continued. "I'm headed home. My truck is empty, so I don't have any deliveries to make. All I have to do is check my messages and then we can be on our way."

"But —"

"But what? Do you have a better idea?"

She tried to think of an alternative, but none came. If she didn't go with Nick, she would be alone and penniless in a desert town that she knew nothing about. Eventually she would have to trust someone. "No, but I don't want to be a bother to you. You've already done enough."

He smiled broadly. He was a handsome man, she decided again. Not movie-star handsome, but good-looking in a unique way. His deeply lined face gave him the look of a rugged outdoorsman, yet his kind eyes and broad smile made him friendly and approachable. "I'm going to check my messages. You sit here and relax. There's no phone in here, so I'll use the public phone in front of the motel. I'll be right back." He rose from the booth and walked away.

As he exited the restaurant, a sudden sense of abandonment stabbed her. What if he didn't come back? What if he was lying? He could walk straight out to his truck and drive off before she knew he was gone. Then what would she do? She fought back a compulsion to rise and chase after him. What good would that do? If he wanted to leave, that was his business. He owed her nothing.

If anything, she owed him for picking her up and providing her with shelter for the night.

The noises of the room seeped into her consciousness. Husbands were talking to wives, children were calling out to each other. The sound of people ordering food filled the air. A young, brown-haired woman in a McDonald's uniform wiped down empty tables and picked up trash. Outside, she could see cars passing, and she wondered who was in them. People everywhere, and each person had a name. The clammy hand of fear gripped her. Did she have a family? Was she a mother? A wife? Tears welled up in her eyes again. Sadness and uncertainty enveloped her. Alone, she was so very alone.

"Well, I'm off the hook. No messages and —" He paused as he studied her face. Then he said softly, "You thought I was leaving without you, didn't you?"

"I guess. It's silly, I know. I have no right —"

"It's not silly," he interrupted. "It's going to be okay. Things are going to work out. I'm sure of it."

"That's pretty optimistic," she said as she removed a napkin from the tray in front of her and dabbed at her eyes. She remembered the image she had seen in the mirror. "I must look horrible," she said.

"All easily remedied. Why don't you use the ladies' room to freshen up? I'll throw away our trash and get us a couple of large coffees to go. Unless you prefer something else."

"Coffee will be fine."

"Great. Now only one piece of business remains."

"Business?" she asked with apprehension.

"Yup," he replied with a smile. Turning he called out to the young uniformed woman cleaning tables. "Miss? Miss, do you have a moment?"

The woman stopped her cleaning, studied Nick for a second, and then walked over. She had a damp towel in one hand and a tray of plastic foam containers and paper wrappers in the other. Like many teenagers, she was having trouble concealing her emotions. Clearly she didn't like being interrupted. "Yes?"

"I was just wondering what your name is," Nick said with a smile.

Frowning the woman looked down at her nametag. It read, LISA.

"Oh, I see," Nick said. "Thanks. That's all I needed."

The employee looked puzzled then annoyed. She walked away, shaking her head.

"Lisa it is, then."

"What?"

"You need a name," Nick said. "I can't go around saying, 'Hey, you' all the time. If you can't remember your name, then let's pick one for you. At least until your memory comes back. I vote for Lisa."

She mulled the name over. It seemed foreign to her, but then any name would. "Lisa," she said to herself.

"If you don't like Lisa, then how about Drusella? She was a famous movie star."

"Movie star? With a name like Drusella?"

"Okay, she was a cartoon."

"Lisa will be fine," she said with a laugh. The laugh felt good.

Carson McCullers felt lousy. He was bruised and battered, and his head pounded with pain. He was also angry, furious with himself and with the situation. But most of all he was angry with *her*. This whole thing should have been executed flawlessly. Finding her had been easy. Disposing of her should have been equally easy, but she had surprised him. Instead of responding with terror, instead of being frozen by fear, she had become assertive and nearly killed him and herself.

"I see you're back with us," a voice said from nearby. Turning his stiff neck to the right, he saw a nurse standing at the threshold of a door. "Any idea how long you've been awake, Mr. McCullers?"

He cut his eyes back to the clock on the wall opposite his bed. "Twenty-two minutes." During that time he had quickly assessed his situation. The woman he had been tracking had been found in Bakersfield. He had followed her east over the Tehachapi Mountains and down the other side into the desert. Knowing the road well, he had waited for just the right moment to begin his attack —

"You're a precise one, Mr. McCullers," the nurse said as she stepped to his bedside. She had an electronic thermometer in her hand. She slipped a thin, sterile plastic shield over the wand and deftly inserted it into his mouth. "This will just take a second."

McCullers waited patiently, wondering if the fierce anger that boiled inside him would somehow show on the thermometer. The device beeped, and she removed the wand. "Right on target. That's good. How are you feeling?" She worked as she spoke, removing a blood-pressure cuff from its mounting on the wall next to the bed and wrapping the black band around his arm. She began squeezing a small, black plastic bulb, and the cuff began to swell with pressure. Slipping the stethoscope into her ears, she placed its business end in the crook of his elbow.

He wanted to say, "I'm great. No problems whatsoever, so I'll be leaving now," but he knew that might raise suspicion. Instead he replied, "I feel pretty good. Sore, and I have a little headache. Nothing too bad." He wondered if she could hear him with the stethoscope stuck in her ears.

"That's good," she said, her gaze fixed on the dial, its indicator dropping as she released the pressure. A second later, she finished the reading and returned the cuff to its hanger. "BP is a little high, but not much. Is your blood pressure normally high?"

"No."

"Are you on any medications?" she asked perfunctorily.

"No. Where am I?"

"You're in Saint John's Hospital in Bakersfield. You were airlifted here last night. Your medical report says that you were admitted at 10:30. Do you remember that?"

"Not really." *Bakersfield.* They had brought him back to Bakersfield. That was a setback.

"I'm not surprised. The night nurse said you were pretty out of it when you arrived. Do you know what happened?"

She was testing his memory. "I was in an auto accident on Highway 58 near Mojave."

"That's right." She reached down and placed two fingers on his wrist. He waited until she was done taking his pulse before he spoke.

"I assume you learned my name from my driver's license." The license was a fake like all of his identification. McCullers was as good a name as any in his line of work.

"I wasn't here when they brought you in."

"Is there a problem I should know about?" He wondered if he was worse off than he felt, and since he felt horrible, that would be bad.

"The doctor will be in to examine you shortly, but the file says that you're in good shape overall. No broken bones, no internal bleeding. We kept you overnight since you were unconscious when you arrived. We couldn't have you slipping into a coma, now could we?"

"I'd prefer not to have that experience."

She laughed. "Well, at least your sense of humor isn't broken."

He returned the smile, but he was loath to do it. He had a question, but he wanted to phrase it right. First he asked, "When can I leave?"

"The doctor will decide that, but assuming he finds nothing new to be concerned about, you can probably go home this afternoon. You will need to call someone to pick you up. You shouldn't drive for a few days. Also, there is some paperwork we need from you."

"I see." *I'll be driving before the day is out, lady.* "What kind of paperwork?"

"There is always paperwork in a hospital. Is there anyone you want me to call for you? A wife, maybe?"

"No, thank you," he replied quickly. "I'm not married. But thank you."

She smiled, as if the revelation of his marital status pleased her. He had seen the look many times. His dark wavy hair, square jaw, and hard, chiseled physique had caught the attention of many women. There was no doubt that he could have any woman he wanted. She turned to leave. "Wait, before you go." She stopped and turned to face him.

"Yes?" There was something in her glance, a message of availability.

Wanting to appear nervous and concerned, he licked his lips and then lowered his head. "Um . . . was . . . was anyone else hurt in the accident?" His voice oozed with a childlike apprehension.

"There was another car," she said softly. "I don't know if they were hurt or not. I do know the CHP wants to ask a few questions. Maybe they can tell you more."

The California Highway Patrol. That's all he needed. "I see," he said just above a whisper. "I'm not sure what happened. I'm hoping that no one else is hurt."

It was a lie. He knew everything that had happened, and he hoped that she had been more than hurt. He hoped she was dead. The scene played across the screen of his mind: her Lexus speeding down the highway, his Dodge Ram pickup truck behind, closing the distance between them. She had spotted him and floored the accelerator, but her car was no match for his enhanced V-eight. The road at the base of the Tehachapi Mountains narrowed and was bordered by a soft sand shoulder. The darkness of night, an oncoming car, and a narrow lane had made it impossible for her to avoid him, despite her best efforts. He rammed her car hard from the rear, accelerating as he did. There was the sound of buckling metal and squealing tires, and then the Lexus flipped. Its right front wheel had left the pavement and slowed when it hit the sand shoulder. The car spun, then flipped through the air as if it were a toy thrown by a child. It landed hard on its side, then flipped end over end again.

McCullers lost sight of it as he shot past. Slowing, he had intended to turn around, to go back and make sure she was dead. But before he could negotiate the U-turn, he saw two pairs of headlights behind him burning hot and bright. Before he could utter an exclamation of fear, he was hit. His truck had spun wildly, then flipped once and landed on its roof. The dark of night had flooded his mind, and his eyes closed. When he opened them again, he was in the hospital.

"Is there anything I can get you?" the nurse asked.

"No, thank you. I'm fine for now. When did you say the doctor would be in?"

"Probably within the hour," she replied. "I was asked to let the highway patrol know when you awoke. I'll call the investigator and let him know that you're back among the living." She smiled again.

One hour. It was doubtful that the CHP investigator would arrive before the doctor. One hour. That was enough time to get his story straight in his mind. It would have to be enough time. He looked to the stand next to his bed. "Can I make a call out on this phone?" he asked.

"Sure, but don't make too many calls, you need your rest."

"I'll try not to overdo it," he said.

As the nurse left, McCullers pulled the phone from the stand and set it on his lap. Again he looked at the clock. It was nearly 10:30, which meant his report was nine hours late. His employers would be concerned, maybe even angry. That would have to be his first call. He preferred not calling from a phone in a hospital since the phone recorders would document the time and number he called, but that couldn't be helped. Not that it mattered in the end. The phone he would be calling could not be connected to his employer. The phone number, like the business under whose name it was listed, was a front.

Now all he had to do was make his report, bad as it was, lie his way past the doctor and CHP investigator, and then find out what had happened to his target. If she was dead, then he could go home; if she wasn't, his job was just beginning.

Chapter 3

Tuesday, 11:02 A.M.

"Need any help?" Nick asked.

Lisa was looking up at the broad, white door of the semi that he had opened for her. In front of her was a pair of flat, knurled steps, and mounted to the side was a smooth, vertical, chrome handrail. To enter the truck, she would have to place her tender right foot on the step, reach up with her left hand, extending the sore muscles in her side, and pull herself up. The thought of pain caused her to hesitate. Nick moved to help. Taking a deep breath, she said, "No, I think I can do it."

"I don't mind."

"I'm sure you don't," she responded, "but let me give it a try."

"Okay. I'll catch you if you fall. It's the gallant thing to do."

"So chivalry isn't dead," Lisa quipped.

"No, just wounded."

Raising her arm, she grasped the tubular handhold, placed her foot on the first step, and hoisted herself up. Pain fired in every direction. Spots of light flashed in her eyes, and spasms erupted in her back. She winced and muffled a cry.

"You all right?" Nick asked with concern.

Lisa took another deep breath. "Give me a second," she whispered. Resting her weight on one leg, she clung tightly to the rail. Taking quick, shallow breaths, she felt the pain slowly subside. A few seconds later, she climbed into the cab of the truck. A thin gloss of perspiration covered her face. She felt woozy and tired, as if she had run a mile instead of merely stepping into the high cab of a diesel truck. She licked her lips and closed her eyes. The pain continued to recede, like the tide from the shore. "I'm . . . I'm okay now."

"You sure? That looked pretty tough."

"It was, but I'm fine." She looked down from her perch in the cab and saw Nick standing next to the open door. His face was a portrait of fretfulness. "You can't drive this truck from down there."

He laughed lightly, but his concern was still evident. "I guess you're right. Can you take these?" He held up the two cups of coffee he had purchased at McDonald's. "There's a cup holder just to your left."

Taking the cups one at a time, she placed them in a black plastic holder situated between the passenger's and driver's seats. Gently Nick closed the door and then entered the cab through the driver's side. "Welcome to my home away from home."

"It looks new." She let her eyes trace the inside of the cab. The seats were leather and showed no sign of wear. The dash was free of dust, and its components showed no scratches.

"It is," he said with obvious pride. "My old one finally gave up the ghost, so I purchased this one just a few months ago. It's a Mack CH with an in-line six-cylinder diesel engine and an eighteen-speed transmission that delivers 460 horsepower —" He stopped abruptly. Lisa was smiling at him. "Sorry, I tend to get carried away."

"You sound like a proud papa."

"She's my baby, all right. I spend as many nights sleeping in here as I do at home."

"You sleep in here?"

"Sure. Look behind you. That's the sleeper cab."

Stiffly Lisa turned and looked over her shoulder. She saw a small compartment with a neatly made bed, a small counter, a shelf, windows on the side, and a television. "Wow."

"There's a refrigerator with soft drinks and sandwich makings if you get thirsty or hungry. And if you want to lie down, you can use the bed. There's a television, but it's hard to get anything while we're on the road. I have a video player if you want to watch a movie."

"What, no cable television?"

Nick laughed. It was a hearty, deep laugh that came easily to him. She sensed that he was a man who enjoyed humor. Just hearing his guffaw made her feel better. Evil men didn't laugh, did they? At least not like that.

"That would have to be one long cable."

Lisa looked around the cab. It was immaculate. No discarded candy wrappers, no newspapers lying in a pile on the floorboards, no empty coffee cups. She had a feeling that she was not so neat.

"There is also a tape player and a CD player here," Nick said, pointing to the dashboard.

"You seem to have everything," Lisa said. "Why did you sleep in the motel last night? Your truck is cleaner than those rooms."

"That's for sure. What a fleabag. That place gives *roach motel* new meaning. I feel bad putting you in that room. But I stayed in the motel for two reasons: I wanted to be able to hear you if you needed anything, and

I wanted to take a shower. I've been on the road for quite a while and was getting a little . . . ripe."

The thought of Nick listening through the night for her cry was touching. All he needed was a suit of armor and a mighty steed. "It looks like you keep your truck in perfect condition."

"It was perfect," he said solemnly. "I need to have the front bumper replaced. Some kid was carting his friends around in his mother's minivan, playing the radio loud and goofing off. They were trying to pull into a parking lot for pizza or to buy CDs or whatever kids do these days, and they cut in front of me. Next thing I know, *smash*. The front end of their car is crumpled and my bumper is trashed."

"Was anyone hurt?"

"No. I had just pulled out of the back lot where I had made a delivery, so I was going slowly. Still, their mother's car is going to need a lot of work."

"Where did this happen?"

"Sacramento, two days ago. It's no big deal. My insurance will cover it. But it irritates me."

"I can imagine. It's easy to see that you love your truck."

"There are more important things in life,"

Nick said philosophically.

"Oh? Like what?"

"Love, friends, family, purpose. Things like that."

"A truck-driving, philosophical, good Samaritan. Is there some deep, dark secret about you that I should know about? You're not an axe murderer, are you?"

"Nope. I like axes. I can't imagine hurting one."

Lisa laughed. It hurt her to do so, but it also made her feel good inside. Nick reached over and turned the ignition key. The diesel engine came to life with a deep, guttural roar.

An annoying tone filled the cavernous office.

"Turn that off," Gregory Moyer snapped without turning his attention from the view from his seventieth-floor window. He heard the speakerphone click off. Below him traffic crawled along the surface streets, the late morning sun sparkling off windshields and chrome bumpers. In the distance he could see the San Francisco Bay shimmering green in the summer light. A long tanker slowly plowed through the water. Double-decker ferries plied their way along courses they had traveled countless times.

But his mind was fixed on a far more compelling image that filled him with fury. He fisted his hands and clenched his teeth. His neck muscles tightened, his back went rigid, and his eyes narrowed. "Incompetent. Idiot. Inept fool. I thought you said he was the best, Raymond."

Raymond Massey sucked in a long breath, then said, "He is, sir. He came highly recommended."

"I'm unimpressed," Moyer said icily, turning to face his employee. "If he's so good, then what is he doing in a hick-town hospital."

"Bakersfield is hardly a hick town, Mr. Moyer, and —" Massey stopped short, cut off by a look from his boss that said, *Don't you ever contradict me*. He cleared his throat and looked down at the highly polished walnut conference table. "What I mean, sir, is that our man did track her down and make an attempt to eliminate the threat."

"Bottom line, Raymond," Moyer said. "What's the bottom line? I'll tell you what it is. Your man is snuggled down in a hospital bed while the woman who can destroy a forty-billion-dollar project is still out there somewhere. Do you understand why I don't care how valiant his attempts were? He failed. He failed his mission and he failed me. How he played the game doesn't matter." He studied his longtime aide. He was a husky man of forty with a thick mustache. Despite his size, he never looked slovenly or rumpled. Moyer would not allow it. His top aides spent more on suits than most men made in a year's salary. That was the way he wanted it, and that was the way it had been for the last decade.

At fifty-two, Gregory Moyer was trim, fit, and one of the most respected men in the nation. He was also the fifth richest in the country, tenth wealthiest in the world. Had things gone as planned, had it not been for *her*, he would have been number one in less than eighteen months. That possibility was now in danger, his plans teetering on an uncertain precipice. His whole empire could crumble, and he could find himself locked up in some white-collar prison, passing the time with businessmen who thought they could beat the system. Moyer had no intention of beating the system; he had designs to do away with it.

"I'm sure Mr. McCullers will be back on the job before the day is over," Massey said softly. "He doesn't strike me as one to let a setback dissuade him from his commitments."

"Still have confidence in the man, do you?"

"Yes sir. I've made many good decisions on your behalf and that of Moyer Communications. I believe this is another one. We just need a little more time."

That part was true. Raymond Massey had been with the firm for fifteen years, climbing through the ranks and proving himself to be an exceptional executive. He could hold his own in any boardroom in the world and was comfortable dealing with the media or with less gentlemanly people like Carson McCullers. Massey was a strong man, emotionally and physically, possessing a powerful bulk, which the unenlightened assumed was merely a weight condition. It wasn't. His body had been hardened by summers spent on fishing boats during his high school and college days. He maintained his strength with daily workouts in the company gym. And he was as loyal as he was strong. If the building were to collapse, in the "big one" that every resident in the Bay Area feared, around Moyer's ears, Massey would be there to dig him out with his bare hands. Then, if he had time, he would check on his family.

"I'm glad to hear of your assurance," Moyer said. His anger was subsiding a little, tempered by his respect for the man at the conference table. Returning his gaze out the window, Moyer studied his thin reflection in the tinted pane and brushed back a stray hair. His hair was a flat gray, combed straight back; his eyes were an icy blue. He tugged the lapels of his expensive three-piece suit and turned to face his associate. "I want you to join Mr. McCullers in Bakersfield."

"You want me to go to Bakersfield?"

"That is exactly what I want, Raymond. This is too important. I know that Mr. McCullers just assured us that he would be out of the hospital within the hour, with or without the doctor's permission, but he may be more injured than he has let on. If so, then his progress would be impeded. This matter must be taken care of as expeditiously as possible. You understand that, don't you?"

"Yes sir, I do. But I don't —"

"There is no one I trust more than you. You know that. Together you and I have faced many challenges and won many victories, not to mention having made a great deal of money." Moyer turned from the window and approached the table. "We're on the verge of ruin. If she gets away, then all our plans, all our goals, will be lost, and no amount of money or conniving will be able to save us. She is a bomb in the hold of our ship, Raymond. A very big bomb."

"I understand, sir."

"Frankly, she has me scared. I've spent twenty years building Moyer Communications. I started with an idea and a few thousand dollars drawn against credit cards. That was a long time ago, and I had to ford a lot of financial streams and cut through even more government red tape. I'm not willing to let all that I worked for, all that *we* worked for, go down the drain with her."

He paused, straightened himself, and clasped his hands behind his back. The posture was one of control, of discipline, but he could feel the fury building like a balloon inflated to the breaking point. "You go, Raymond. You make sure that our Mr. Carson McCullers finishes the task he was hired to perform. Pay him more if you must, but I want this taken care of as soon as possible."

Massey pursed his lips for a brief moment and then stood. "I'll leave immediately."

"Excellent. Take the company jet. I imagine you can be in Bakersfield in short order. If the doctors down there lag, you might even catch him in the hospital. Take whatever equipment you need. We have the best there is; use it. If you need anything more, call. I'll make sure you get what you need."

"I should let him know I'm coming so we don't miss each other. He won't like it."

"I'm not concerned with what he likes," Moyer snapped. "I'm concerned with what I want and with what is best for this company. The devil can have everything else."

Massey nodded his understanding, turned, and marched out of Moyer's opulent office. Before he could close the door, Moyer spoke again. "Don't come back until it's finished. Understood, Raymond? I cannot tolerate failure on this."

The large man closed the door behind him.

McCullers was furious, but he had to contain it. It was like holding a dozen angry bees in a jar with nothing except his hand for a lid. He wanted to shout obscenities, to punch someone, anyone, but he couldn't. An assault charge was the last thing he needed, especially with a California Highway Patrol investigator on the way in to grill him about the accident. The concerned, cooperative patient act would have to be played out a little longer before he could get back to work. Assuming that his new "partner" arrived sometime soon. *Partner*. He hated the thought.

A tall, lanky doctor, who looked like he

had just graduated from high school, stood before him. McCullers wondered if the man was old enough to shave. Now that he had crossed middle age, everyone looked young to him.

"I'm Dr. Wadell, Mr. . . ." He paused as he looked at the chart. "Mr. McCullers. How are you feeling?"

"A little sore, but not too bad," he answered as friendly as he could manage. "It looks like you guys took good care of me last night."

"It was a busy night," the doctor said, pulling a silver cylinder from his pocket. He flipped a switch, and a small, bright light came on. Wadell bent over the bed and peered into McCullers's eyes. "Any trouble with your vision?" His breath smelled of coffee.

"No."

"Dizziness? Nausea?"

"No. Really, Doctor, I feel fine. Just a little bruised."

"Uh-huh," the doctor said perfunctorily. Returning the penlight to his pocket, he held out both hands to McCullers. "Squeeze my hands."

"What?"

"Take my hands and give them a squeeze."

"What for?" A bit of pent-up anger tainted his words.

"It's a little complex, but it helps me judge the symmetry and response of your muscles. It's a simple test to verify that each side of your body is getting the same message from your brain."

McCullers smiled. He liked the idea of squeezing the doctor's hands. He was strong enough to easily break the bones in the medical man's fingers. Then where would the doctor be? It would be hard to practice medicine with two or three crushed fingers on each hand. Despite the nearly overpowering urge, McCullers decided to play nice and comply. The exam continued with the doctor asking questions, examining his patient's ears, poking bruises, and scribbling words on the chart.

Ten minutes later, Dr. Wadell delivered his judgment. "Well, Mr. McCullers, I think we can let you go. Your test results and x-rays are all negative, and you seem to be in pretty good shape. You'll be sore for a few days. I suggest you take some over-the-counter pain medication if you need to. No driving for the next week and get plenty of rest. Should your vision change any — double vision, blurriness, that sort of thing — then you should see your doctor immediately or come into emergency. The same goes for sudden bouts of nausea, difficulty in waking, and dizziness. Those could be signs of trouble."

"Will do, Doctor," McCullers said with a broad smile. One part of his complex situation had just got easier. He would have no trouble checking out of the hospital. That saved him the trouble of sneaking out. "Thank you. I appreciate your help."

"You're welcome," he said. "The nurse will be in soon to start some of the paperwork for dismissal. I understand the CHP wants to talk to you."

"That's what I hear, although I don't know what I can tell them."

"I wouldn't worry about it too much. It is all pretty routine. Unless you were purposely trying to run someone off the road, they shouldn't bother you." He chuckled.

McCullers tensed and then caught himself. The doctor was only making a joke.

"Thanks again, Doc."

"Good-bye, Mr. McCullers." Five quick strides later, the doctor was gone and McCullers was planning his next move.

The bed in the sleeper cab was more comfortable than Lisa had imagined. The thin mattress wedged in the closet-size area provided a soft, cozy rest. Just fifteen minutes into the trip, a heavy blanket of weariness had covered her. Nick had noticed and suggested that she nap on the bed.

"If the highway patrol pulls me over for any reason," he had said, "I would greatly appreciate it if you would return to your seat. California requires that everyone in a vehicle wear a seat belt. The bed has no seat belt."

She had chuckled at the thought and promised that she would move as quickly as she could. Once on the bed, she was fast asleep. There had been no dreams. Now she lay on her back, peering through the curved skylight that made up half of the sleeper cab's ceiling. Outside was an azure sky with a single wisp of white cotton cloud. A hawk seemed to hover overhead for a few moments before the truck moved from beneath it.

The cab bounced lightly as it moved down the road. The droning of the tires and her physical exhaustion, coupled with a profound emotional weariness, had proved to be a powerful sedative, lulling her to sleep within minutes of lying down. Lisa felt slightly refreshed, but her memory was still gone.

She yawned and gently stretched.

"She lives," Nick said jovially from his seat behind the steering wheel. "I was starting to think you had slipped into a coma. Except people in comas don't talk in their sleep."

"I was talking in my sleep?" Lisa asked, sitting up.

"Well, not really talking," Nick said. "It was more of a yodel."

"A yodel? I did not."

"It was really quite good. Maybe you should consider a yodeling career."

Leaning forward, Lisa could see the broad smile on Nick's face. "I think you're having a little fun at my expense."

"Me?" Nick said with flourish. "I speak nothing but the truth. You yodel nicely."

"I don't know how to yodel. I don't even sing."

"Are you sure?" Nick asked. A hint of seriousness had tinged his voice. "I mean, how do you know?"

That is a good point. "I guess I don't know, but I'm pretty sure that I don't yodel. I don't think I sing either, but I don't know why I think that." The darkness of uncertainty that had cloaked her when she had awakened in the motel room returned.

Nick seemed to notice the return of her gloom. "I'm sorry. I was trying to cheer you up. I seem to have had the opposite effect."

"That's all right. You did nothing wrong."

"Thirsty?"

She was. "Yes. My mouth feels like I've been sucking on cotton."

"It's the air conditioning. It keeps the air cool, but it also removes the moisture. Not that there is much moisture out there." He nodded forward. The desert stretched out before them. "There's soda in the refrigerator."

"How big is this desert?" she asked as she opened the small cooler and removed a root beer.

"The Mojave? It's huge, but we'll be out of it soon. We're on the 14 and headed south. Pretty soon all this open space will be replaced with wall-to-wall buildings."

"How long was I asleep?"

"Not long really. Half an hour, maybe."

"It seemed a lot longer," she said. "Do you want a drink too?"

"Please. I think there's a Squirt in there. That's my favorite."

Lisa removed a green can of citric soda and handed it to Nick. She then returned to the passenger seat and buckled her belt. It pressed on her bruised hips. "I feel foolish asking this now, since I should have asked before I agreed to go with you, but where are we headed?"

"To the coast. I have a home just south of Santa Barbara. It's a nice place. I think you'll like it."

"You're taking me to your house?"

Nick nodded. "I'm taking the next few days off. I have some paperwork to do, forms to fill out for my business, that sort of thing. Besides, you wouldn't let me take you to a hospital or to the police. I don't have many other choices."

Lisa was uncomfortable for reasons she could not determine. Maybe it was going to a man's house when she knew neither the man nor the city in which he lived. "I see."

"I'm open for other ideas," he said kindly. "Actually, I'm at a loss. I certainly can't leave you on the street somewhere. At least at my place you will be warm and comfortable and have a place to stay."

The logic was unassailable. Nick really did have his hands tied, and she was the cause. He seemed trustworthy and honest, but how could she really tell? Did evil men walk around with tattoos on their foreheads that read, BEWARE? How much different would a criminal look from a saint? She had no idea.

"You can make yourself at home," Nick

continued. “The guest room is clean and available. It doesn’t get much use.”

“Then what?” Lisa asked. Confusion had mixed with her uncertainty to form an amalgam of apprehension. It had been crazy of her to get into a truck with a man she didn’t know, but she had no other choice, at least that she could see. Besides, if Nick had wanted to harm her, he wouldn’t have taken her to a hotel. There was nothing in his words or manner to suggest evil. He was the only help on the horizon, so she had agreed to his offer.

Nick shrugged. “Hopefully, you get your memory back. Maybe there will be a news report or something to help us identify you. Somebody must know you. Maybe you have a family, a mother, a neighbor, or an employer. Sooner or later someone is going to miss you and make a report. That would be the easiest solution.”

“I don’t know if I have a family,” Lisa said sadly.

“There’s no wedding ring on your finger,” Nick observed. “I doubt you’re married.”

“Maybe I lost it, or it was stolen.”

“Perhaps, but the skin tone is uniform on your fingers. The skin shows no sign of having been hidden beneath jewelry. It’s not conclusive, of course, just interesting. Do you think you like jewelry?"

"I have no idea."

"Check your ears."

"What?"

"Are your ears pierced?" Nick asked.

Lisa placed her soda in the cup holder and touched her earlobes. She felt nothing. "I don't think so."

Nick glanced at her. "They don't look pierced. Most women I've known have pierced ears, but I've known some who don't. In general the ones who don't have pierced ears don't wear much jewelry."

"And just how many women do you know?" Lisa asked.

"Not many," he admitted. "I spend too much time on the road."

"I see," she said. She felt suspicious. It seemed odd to her that Nick was not married or at least serious about some woman. He was attractive, had a sense of humor, was concerned for others, and was well-spoken. Somehow she had thought a truck driver would be the opposite of that.

"I suppose the thing to do is let you rest up and get over your injuries. In the meantime we can keep our ears to the ground. If you were in an auto accident, then the CHP is probably looking for you. The best thing would be for you to call them."

"I don't want to do that."

"Why?"

"I don't know, I just don't." Her heart began to beat faster. The thought of the police bothered her.

Nick fell silent, and Lisa knew she was putting him in a difficult spot. Her refusal to seek help from the police made her look guilty, as if she were running. It amazed her that he would be so willing to help, given the circumstances.

As they passed through Palmdale and continued down the grade, the terrain changed from the high desert with its spotty juniper, scrub brush, and Joshua trees to rolling hills made brown by the summer heat. Highway 14 led them through Soledad Pass and into Soledad Canyon. Large tract houses sprouted out of the ground like trees, their red rooftiles shimmering in the harsh daylight. The number of houses increased as they continued southward into Santa Clarita.

"We're about halfway there," Nick said. He had not spoken for the last half-hour. "In a few miles we'll start toward the coast. The road through Fillmore and Santa Paula is narrow and always under construction, but it's pretty. If you want, I can show you where they filmed a few movies."

Warmth of recognition filled her. Nick noticed. "Do you like movies?" he asked.

"I think so. I mean, I feel like I do — like it is something I enjoyed doing." She closed her eyes and tried to remember a movie she had seen, any movie. None came, just the comfortable feeling of familiarity. "I can't remember ever seeing one, but I know that I have. Surely, I must have."

"Don't try to force the memories to return," Nick advised. "Let them come back on their own. The harder you try, the more difficult it will be to recall anything. At least that's the way it is with me when I can't remember where I put my keys."

"This is more important than keys," she said harshly. She immediately felt remorse at her words. "I'm sorry. Apparently I'm not a very nice person."

Nick laughed. "That's a little extreme, don't you think? I'm amazed how controlled you've been. I don't think most people would be as calm and reasonable."

"Reasonable?"

"Exactly," Nick explained. "You haven't been overly emotional, you haven't panicked, and you haven't dissolved into depression. I'm impressed. I bet you're a pretty smart cookie."

"Cookie? Chauvinist."

"I'll have you know that I'm a reformed chauvinist. I'm only mildly superior in my attitude."

A smile crept across Lisa's sore lips.

"Do you like music?" Nick asked.

Lisa shrugged. "It's like the movies. I think I do, I just don't know for sure."

"I like show tunes," Nick offered. "That's not a popular thing to say, but I can't get enough of them. Ever hear of Andrew Lloyd Webber?"

"No bells are ringing."

"He writes great stuff. *Joseph and the Amazing Technicolor Dreamcoat, Cats, The Phantom of the Opera, Evita, Jesus Christ Superstar* —" Lisa cringed, an action noticed by Nick. "That got a response," he said.

"I don't think I like that last one," she said with a frown.

"Interesting. Very interesting. That means you've heard it or, at least, heard of it. That makes sense. You would be about the right age. It was popular in the early seventies."

It was an odd sensation. At least on a subconscious level, Lisa could recall emotions that were tied to events that were too deeply buried in the debris of her mind to be excavated. *What is it about a musical named* Jesus

Christ Superstar *that I find so unappealing?*

"Let's try something else and see what you think." Nick reached into a small case near his seat and removed a CD and placed it into the player. "This is *Cats*."

The overture filled the cab with the rich orchestration. Violins blended with horns, percussion, and piano. The music was simple yet emotionally complex. Lisa listened closely, hoping that some series of notes would open the floodgates of recollection. Perhaps she would recognize the songs when the performers began to sing; perhaps she would even know the words. That would be encouraging. It would mean that her memory had not been erased, just sequestered by whatever had happened to her.

As the music played, Lisa watched the scenery pass. Cars of every type passed them, each filled with someone who knew who he was, where he was going, and what his future held. Looking out the windshield, Lisa noticed the dashed white line of the multilane highway. There were a great many more cars on the road now, and the traffic was getting thicker.

A song began to play, "Memory," and the sweet melodic voice of a woman sang in sad and haunting tones.

The words were insidious: "Has the

moon lost her memory?" She was lost. She was alone without even the company of her own memories or the companionship of her own self. No loneliness could be so deep, none so desperate. Lisa's eyes burned as tears fought their way to the surface. Turning her head so Nick wouldn't see, she stared from the lofty perch of the cab at the road that raced beneath her.

As the song droned on, Lisa sank deeper and deeper into depression. The fugue pulled at her like a tentacled monster from the cold gloom of a deep ocean. She felt that she might die right there in the leather chair of the commercial truck as it bounced down the wide ribbon of asphalt. Her heart seemed to be breaking and her soul withering like a petal detached from its flower.

"I love the way this artist pours her heart into the music," Nick was saying, but Lisa continued to stare out the side window. "It's a great play. I got to see it once in Los Angeles. This is one of my favorite songs. Some think it's sappy, but I —" He stopped abruptly. "Are you okay? Was it something I said?" He paused. "It's the song, isn't it?" Lisa heard him click off the CD player. "I'm an idiot," he said animatedly. "I've heard that song so many times, I no longer hear the words, just the music. I'm sorry if I upset you. I feel horrible." His words rang with concern.

Lisa dragged a finger under her eyes wiping away tears. "There's nothing for you to feel bad about. I'm just being emotional. That's not your fault."

"Sure it is. It was callous of me not to realize how the song might affect you."

"You can't go changing your life for me, Nick. You've done enough all ready."

"Nonsense," Nick said. "I've done very little." Then with soft but firm words he coaxed, "It will all work out. I promise. Somehow, someway, we'll get it all figured out. Trust me."

Trust him. At the moment, she had no other choice.

Chapter 4

Tuesday, 1:05 P.M.

The high-backed leather chair squeaked in protest as Gregory Moyer leaned back and placed his feet on his custom desk. He rubbed his temples as he spoke into the speakerphone. "I don't know who your source is, Senator, but I suggest you get a new one." His words had an edge to them.

"He has never been wrong in the past," Sen. James Elliot said firmly. Unlike the cheap phones on the market, Moyer's was state-of-the-art, as befitted the CEO of the country's largest communications development firm. Senator Elliot sounded as if he were seated across the desk instead of in Washington, D.C.

"He is wrong now. I have told you that there is nothing to worry about, and there isn't. Are you going to take your man's word or mine?"

Elliot was slow to reply, and Moyer knew why. The senator owed Moyer a huge debt, one that was counted in millions of dollars of indirect gifts to the man's campaign fund.

Losing badly in the polls four years ago, Elliot had made a personal appeal to Moyer and the CEO had responded quickly and generously. The election was won handily, thanks to the sudden infusion of talent and money — all of it hidden, of course — from Moyer Communications. A score of smaller companies, all indirectly controlled by the strong hand of Moyer, laundered the money. Election officials suspected nothing. Even if they did, it wouldn't matter. The money trail was too well concealed, too intricate to follow.

"This isn't about loyalties, Moyer," Elliot said in softer tones. "I have the highest level of confidence in you. This is such an important matter, however, that errors can be made if we are not careful."

"All diligence is being maintained," Moyer said dryly. "Nothing is going to go wrong. I have everything under control. I always do."

"And the girl?"

Moyer cringed. Elliot should not be mentioning that over the phone. Although his office was safe from any surveillance, he couldn't be sure that was true for the senator. At least the man had had the good sense not to use a name. "She's fine," Moyer said, hoping that Elliot would catch his unspoken meaning. "I'm sure she will be back with us and doing her job just as before. I'll tell her that you were asking about her. I'm sure she'll be honored."

"Um . . . ," Elliot began. "I'm glad to hear that. I would hate to hear that anything bad had happened. She's vital to your good work."

"That she is," Moyer said. "That she is. We miss her but hope to see her again soon. In the meantime, relax. There is no problem for you to be concerned with. All goes as planned."

"I see," Elliot replied. Moyer could tell that he had gotten the message. "Well, keep me posted."

"Good day, Senator," Moyer said, reaching forward and punching the button that would hang up the phone. Lowering his feet, he turned to face the desk that formed a semicircle around him. A quick touch of the keyboard brought the computer monitor, which was capable of being lowered out of sight or raised when needed, to life. A few keystrokes more and the Moyer Communications logo — a blue planet orbiting a communications satellite — was replaced by a live, digital image of Pad 3 at Vandenberg Air Force Base in California. Pointing upward was a sight familiar to most Americans: a Titan 4B rocket. A powerful thrill washed over him as he studied the image. Anyone could recognize the craft, but only a handful of people knew what was in its payload; fewer still knew its purpose, and he had complete control over them — all but one. Prickly anger arose within him and he clenched his teeth tightly, grinding them as he spoke. "I'll find you," he said in a growl. "I'll find you and you will die. That is a promise."

"What a mess," McCullers said bitterly. He was staring at what used to be his Dodge Ram pickup. The once new truck was now twisted and bent at awkward angles, its windows broken. The metal skin was a mass of dents and folds. Scratches ran deep into the metal. "Do you know how much this truck cost me? I added five thousand dollars worth of personal improvements."

Raymond Massey nodded in sympathy. He had taken the Moyer Communications private jet to the Bakersfield Municipal Airport and then rented a car. Thirty minutes later he was standing at the bedside of McCullers, who was already dressed. He had been dismissed by the hospital staff and was eager to leave. Massey had watched him carefully as they walked down the hall of the small hospital, into the lobby, and out to the rented sedan. McCullers moved stiffly but made no complaints. Massey watched the man, not out of concern for McCullers's health, but out of concern for McCullers's ability to complete the job for which he had been hired. If the determined, angry look in his eye was any indicator, he was well capable of doing the work.

From the hospital, Massey had driven south along Highway 99 to Highway 58 east. Sixty minutes later he and McCullers had pulled into the small desert town of Mojave and found the impound yard where the Dodge pickup had been towed.

"From the looks of it, you're lucky to be alive," Massey said, meaning every word. It seemed unimaginable that McCullers was not as battered and broken as the truck.

"I don't believe in luck," McCullers said flatly. "I'm alive because I've trained myself to survive. That . . . and I have yet to fulfill my destiny."

"Destiny?" Massey was astonished. The man was a hired criminal and assassin, not a humanitarian.

"You think I have no destiny?" McCullers asked harshly. "You think I'm some kind of thug? Fair enough. I've done the work of a thug, but I've done much more. At least I don't sit at some desk waiting for the lead dog to bark. I'm my own man."

"Really?" Massey said, annoyed at McCullers's arrogance. "You would do well to listen when Mr. Moyer, as you say, barks. He is very powerful."

"Moyer doesn't scare me," McCullers snapped as he walked around to the front of the truck. The radiator bled green fluid on the ground from its fractured grill. He bent over and studied the damage. He sighed loudly. "This is hopeless. It's a total loss."

"Moyer doesn't scare you?" Massey laughed. "Then you are a fool."

Slowly McCullers straightened and faced him. "What did you say?"

"You heard me. Anyone who underestimates Mr. Moyer is a fool. That includes you." Massey watched as McCullers tightened his jaw.

"I would be careful if I were you, Mr. Massey. I will finish my job because I'm a professional, but I don't have to put up with the likes of you."

"Actually, you do," the company man replied coldly. "I am your new partner."

"I told you on the way down here, I don't work with a partner," McCullers snapped. "I never have, and I never will. You got that?"

With a sigh, Massey walked toward the hired killer. Most men would have been frightened out of their skins if they knew what he knew about McCullers. He had been a streetwise orphan, bounced from foster home to foster home until finally he was institutionalized in an orphanage. Having never experienced love, having been deprived of any nurturing, he had grown cold and heartless. He started small, stealing change from other children, but he soon graduated to bigger things. He stole his first car at the age of fourteen and was arrested for battery when he was sixteen. While other boys his age were dreaming of their first date and driving their own car, McCullers fantasized about money and power.

The road to crime was not easy. He took his share of beatings, including one that left him lying close to death in a gutter in downtown Los Angeles. The drug dealer who, with the help of three "associates," had pummeled McCullers had taught him important lessons: Trust no one, suspect everyone, make no attachments. So his life of crime had been solitary. No partners meant he could never be betrayed.

Strong-arm robbery was sufficiently lucrative to keep him housed and fed. There was money to be made and excitement to be had. By the time he was twenty, however, McCullers knew that he did what he did not for money alone but also for the thrill. Strong-arm robbery led to home burglary and then to office burglary, which required new skills to deal with locks and alarm systems. His activities also put him in touch with other criminals, including some who were willing to hire a young and upcoming man. McCullers accepted the jobs, but he neither made attachments nor revealed much about himself. He learned tricks that could be learned no other place except prison, and he was determined not to go to that school.

On his twenty-first birthday, McCullers killed his first man, an elderly security guard who had stumbled upon him in the act of a commercial burglary. Assuming the guard was armed, McCullers shot him in the chest with a .25-caliber pistol. The guard had crumpled to the ground in a lifeless heap, a crimson circle of blood puddling around him. McCullers had waited for the guilt, waited for the wave of nausea to sweep over him. Neither came. McCullers finished his work and left, being smart enough to toss the gun down a nearby storm drain.

Killing came easy to him, and it was far

more profitable than simple theft. And more people than he had ever imagined were quick to hire a man without a conscience to clean up the "difficulties" in their lives. Of all the things he did, he enjoyed killing the most. Some killings were direct and simple; others required planning, patience, and genius. His genius was what prompted Massey to hire him in the first place.

"I asked you a question," McCullers was saying. He stepped forward and put his face close to Massey's. His breath was sickeningly sweet. He poked Massey sharply with his index finger. Astonishment registered in McCullers's eyes. He had assumed that the portly man was a soft, flabby desk jockey who would get winded walking up a single flight of stairs. McCullers was learning that Massey's dark gray suit concealed a stone-hard body.

Massey smiled, conveying a very clear message: He, too, had secrets.

"Just stay out of my way," McCullers snapped. Massey recognized the hint of weakness in his voice, the chink in his armor. "Why don't you get whatever you need from your truck and let's go. Every second we stand here is another opportunity for her to put more distance between us."

"I know that," McCullers said bitterly.

Another sigh escaped Massey's lips. He was not going to enjoy his time with Carson McCullers.

"Feeling better?" Nick asked as he raised his cup of soda and sipped from the straw. Before him lay the paper that had once wrapped three tacos and the cardboard that had contained a healthy helping of nachos. In front of Lisa was a half-eaten burrito.

"Yes," she said softly. "Thank you."

"Well, you should feel better," Nick said with a broad, teasing smile. "After all, I have taken you to two of the finest restaurants in the state."

"McDonald's for breakfast and Taco Bell for lunch?"

"Absolutely. This should prove to you my gentlemanly nature and superior tastes."

Despite the pall of depression that threatened to envelop her, Lisa smiled. "I am honored to have accompanied you."

"Ah," Nick said jovially. "You do have a sense of humor. It suits you well."

"Thanks," she replied. "Can I ask you a question?"

"Sure. Fire away." He took another sip of soda.

"You don't strike me as the truck-driver

type," she said. "You seem too . . . refined."

Nick erupted with laughter. "Why thank you, Lisa. It's been a long time since anyone called me refined."

"You know what I mean," she said defensively.

"I do. I'm not laughing at you. Your comment just caught me off guard. I thank you for the compliment."

"See, that's what I mean. I expect truck drivers to be rough and uneducated. You seem just the opposite."

"Thanks again," Nick said. "People drive trucks for different reasons. Some like the travel, some like handling a big machine, some like the freedom. I like the solitude."

"Solitude?"

"Some people can get up each morning and drive to an office or cubicle, put in their eight hours, then go home. That's not for me. I'm not the office type. I'd go crazy just sitting and looking at four walls. Driving lets me move from place to place, meet interesting people, and I don't have to answer to an employer. At least in my case, I'm my own boss. I can think what I want, eat when I want, listen to whatever music I want. What could be better than that? Besides, I do more than drive a truck."

"Oh," Lisa said with curiosity. "Are you

an artist? An impressionist, maybe?"

"I know nothing about art," Nick said. "I own four other trucks. It's not a big fleet by any stretch of the imagination, but it's a start. I hire others to drive them. Especially for the long hauls. The cross-country stuff doesn't leave me enough time for the paperwork. I suppose I could hire a secretary, and she could e-mail whatever I need to wherever I am."

Something stirred in Lisa, an uncomfortable sense. She furrowed her brow.

"What?" Nick asked. "Did I say something wrong?"

Lisa shook her head. She had no idea how to answer. Something he said had triggered a response in her, but what? Secretary? Cross-country driving? E-mail? The thought of e-mail was disturbing.

"Talk to me, Lisa. Speaking your thoughts may help."

"Your comments about e-mail made me feel uneasy. I don't know why. Why would e-mail make anyone uneasy?"

"That is curious." Nick scratched his chin in thought. "Maybe someone sent you some disturbing messages. Maybe even threats. Does that seem possible?"

"I'm so mixed up, anything and everything seems possible."

"Okay, don't try to force it, that will just bury the memories deeper."

"How do you know that?" Lisa said sharply. "You're a truck driver, not a medical doctor."

Nick held his hands up as if surrendering. "Okay, okay. Don't bite my head off. I just know that the harder I try to recall something, the more difficult it is for me to remember. But if I just relax and let the thoughts come, I do much better."

"I'm sorry," Lisa said. She felt sick about snapping at Nick. "That's twice I've snapped at you. Now I'm certain the real me is not a very nice person."

"I doubt that," Nick said softly. "I imagine you are a wonderful person. Losing your memory doesn't change who you are, it just changes what you can recall. And I like what I've seen of your personality."

Warmth ran up her cheeks as she began to blush. "I hope you're right."

"I'm sure of it." He reached forward and touched her arm. The caress was gentle, warm, and unassuming. It felt good. A second later, as if checking himself, he removed his hand. "Well, it's time we got back on the road. We can't spend our lives eating Mexican food."

"I can think of worse things," Lisa said.

Nick rose and said, “I’ll be back in a minute. I need to use the little trucker’s room.”

Lisa chuckled. “Okay.” She watched Nick work his way through the crowded dining area and down the hall that led to the rest rooms. Turning her attention to the window, she watched as cars drove by and pedestrians strolled along the concrete sidewalk. Nick had called the town Fillmore, and it looked like a sleepy bedroom community with a four-lane highway through the middle of it. Oak trees lined the street. There was a certain charm to the neighborhood, and some of the buildings looked like throwbacks to the early fifties.

A structure across the street caught her eye. Its dilapidated condition struck her. Then something visceral moved her. The building was an old, whitewashed clapboard church with a towering steeple. Even from her position in the restaurant she could see that the building had been unused for years. It was a token of a different time, a monument to a different era.

A scene began to play across her mind: Women dressed in bright, flowery dresses, white gloves, and broad-brimmed hats stood outside the church door; men in suits chatted with each other; children scampered across the lot in a playful game of chase. In the doorway stood a tall, gray-haired minister, dressed in a long black robe. He was holding a Bible and talking to a young couple. It was a happy scene, a peaceful portrait that beckoned to her. Emptiness welled up within her, a longing to be in that place at that time and surrounded by those happy people.

Massive waves of sorrow washed over her. Missing. Her past was all gone, having disappeared in an event she couldn't remember for a reason she couldn't recall. In her mind's eye the minister looked up, across the street, and through the window where she sat. He smiled and raised a friendly hand.

Lisa started for the door.

Chapter 5

Tuesday, 1:45 P.M.

Lisa didn't know how she had got to the other side of the street from the Taco Bell, but she had somehow crossed the busy avenue without being hit. She was vaguely aware of a car horn and shouted insults. She stood on an ancient, fractured macadam parking lot where thick-stalked weeds had pushed their way through the cracks in the pavement. It had been years since any vehicle filled with worshipers had parked here.

The building in front of her was in a similar condition of disrepair. Paint peeled from the wood siding, dust covered the stained-glass windows, and spiders had built elaborate webs at the base of the building and around the windows and doors. A series of five wooden steps bridged the distance between the lot and the floor of the church building. Lisa took them carefully, listening as they offered squeaky protestations. To her relief, they held her weight.

A pair of doors at the top of the stairs had

been carved with the image of a cross. Carelessly nailed to them was the sign: CONDEMNED. UNSAFE. NO TRESPASSING. Lisa was unable to turn and leave. The song "Come, Thou Fount of Every Blessing" began to play in her head. It was as if she could hear the long-missing congregation singing inside. She closed her eyes and listened: ". . . tune my heart to sing thy grace! Streams of mercy, never ceasing, call for songs of loudest praise."

Looking down, Lisa saw a tarnished bronze doorknob. She touched it and turned the knob. Locked. She turned it again, as hard as she could, but the lock held. Then she pushed, and the door rattled on its hinges, giving a little. She pushed again, this time harder, and the door sprang open, the tongue of the lock tearing through the rotting wood of the jamb. An eerie squeal erupted from the rusted hinges and echoed through the empty narthex. Inside the small entry was a wooden slat floor covered in undisturbed dust. A piece of yellowed paper lay in the dirt. A cockroach ran across it, and Lisa shivered. Old posters for Sunday school and mission offerings hung on the walls. A modest chandelier danced in the new breeze that flowed through the open doors. Opposite her was another pair of double doors, but unlike the entrance doors, they had no lock.

Lisa pushed past the doors and into the worship hall. It seemed familiar, yet she was certain that she had never laid eyes on it before. Maybe any church might have seemed familiar.

Closing her eyes, she tried to summon distant wisps of memory. But the only emotions that answered her call were diaphanous. Nevertheless, she felt a free-floating peace associated with the church.

The more she tried to connect the abstract sensations, the more nebulous they became. The greater the effort she expended, the keener her failure. A new sadness filled her, a concoction of despair, frustration, and anger. She felt weak, and her battered body reminded her of her injuries. Seizing the side of one of the old oak pews, Lisa steadied herself and took several deep breaths. Dust and detritus of years of gradual decay filled the air.

Lisa sat down, ignoring the thick coat of dust. Once there had been a purpose in her life, a reason for doing whatever it was that she used to do. She knew that instinctively. What she didn't know were the particulars.

Imagination began to take over. As she tried to calm her raging spirit, she heard the sounds of people. With her eyes closed, she could imagine them sitting around her: children fidgeting in their seats; women fanning themselves with paper fans; men, uncomfortable in coats and ties, facing forward, listening to the gray-haired minister standing in the pulpit. She could almost hear the organ begin to play a sweet, melodious hymn. What a wonderful illusion, what a magnificent vision — peaceful, honest, open, welcoming. Her anxiety began to recede like an ebbing tide, and the darkness that had covered her began to flee, giving way to an inexplicable light. She wanted to stay in the pew; she wanted to forever embrace the newfound warmth.

"What are you doing here?"

The voice startled Lisa, and she jumped to her feet with a gasp. Nick's concern was etched deeply in his face. "You frightened me," she said.

"I could say the same thing. When I came back from the rest room, you had disappeared. I was afraid that something had happened to you. Luckily one of the workers had seen you walk out and cross the street."

"I'm fine, really." Lisa felt off balance. "I just . . . just wanted to get some fresh air."

"In here?" Nick said, his voice softening. He smiled. "It seems a little musty, but then most sermons I've heard are old and dusty, so I guess it makes sense."

Lisa didn't find the joke funny. "I don't know why I came in here, I just —"

Nick cut her off with the wave of his hand. "You don't need to explain yourself to me, Lisa. You're a big girl, and I have no claim on you. I was just afraid for you. I'm sorry if I frightened you."

"That's all right. I shouldn't have run off. It wasn't fair to you."

"Well, let's get out of here," Nick said. "This place is condemned. The floor may be rotted away for all we know. Not only that, we're trespassing, and I don't want to spend another night in jail."

"What?" Lisa said with surprise.

Nick's face parted into a wide smile. "I'm joking, Lisa. I've never spent a minute in jail. My life is pretty dull."

"That's good news," she said as she started for the door. "I don't think I could drive the truck myself." It was a vain attempt at humor, but it was the best she could do.

"I wouldn't be surprised if you could," he said lightly. "Now let's get out of here before my allergies kick in."

"Used to be a nice car," Bill Hobbs said

flatly as he studied the crippled remains of the gold Lexus. As an investigator for the Kern County Sheriff's Department and a twenty-year veteran of police work, he had seen many mutilated cars.

"Not anymore," CHP officer Jay Tanner said. "It's nothing but twisted metal. I'm amazed that anyone lived through this."

"That's the way it is, isn't it?" Hobbs said, walking around the car. "I don't know how many wrecks I've seen where the occupants should be nothing more than grease stains on the seats, yet they're walking around waiting for the police to arrive. Then there are the little fender benders that send people to the hospital. It never makes sense to me."

The CHP officer raised an eyebrow. "You were a traffic investigator? I thought you were missing persons."

"I spent time in traffic," Hobbs said. "I've spent the last five years doing criminal investigation. I assume you've run the plates and VIN number."

"Yeah," Tanner said. "But something's wrong."

Bending over, Hobbs peered into the car. He wanted to open the door, but the caved-in ceiling and the jammed-shut doors prevented him. The windshield was broken out, as were all the other windows. Hobbs was thankful the CHP had left the car in situ. Seeing the vehicle where it had come to rest would help him to understand the chain of events.

"Wrong? What do you mean wrong?"

Tanner seemed uneasy. "There is no owner assigned to the plates or to the vehicle identification number."

"How can that be? Are the plates bogus?"

The patrolman just shrugged. "They look genuine, but even if they're fakes, that wouldn't explain the VIN being unassigned. The car doesn't belong to anyone."

"Stolen from a car lot?"

"If it was, no one reported it. But even that wouldn't explain the plates. New cars don't leave the lot with license plates."

"Used ones do," Hobbs said. Then he rethought his words. "Of course, that would mean that a record of the previous owner would be on file. You're saying that there's no record at all? Do I have that right?"

"That's the sum total of it," Tanner said.

"How can that be?" Hobbs was puzzled. Every car had some owner on the record, even if was just the manufacturer.

"It can't," Tanner replied. "I double-checked the numbers too. I thought maybe someone messed up and transposed a number or something, but it all checks out. You can run them yourself if you want."

"No need," Hobbs said with a polite smile. "I believe you." He paused, his smile melting into a frown. "Someone wanted the car to be invisible. I've seen lots of cars with plates stolen from other vehicles, but never one with counterfeit plates, not to mention a counterfeit VIN number."

"Not something one whips up in the garage, is it?"

Hobbs shook his head. "Hardly. It makes this a little more interesting: no witnesses, no identification, no registration, no proof of insurance, and now no valid, traceable numbers. Not to mention, no driver. Didn't you say that there had been another accident around here?"

"Yeah. A truck went off the road a quarter-mile south of here. The driver was taken to a hospital in Bakersfield. Says he fell asleep at the wheel. We had an officer interview him. Record is clean. I doubt they're related."

"Why?" Hobbs asked.

"This is a heavily traveled road. Not a week goes by without some kind of auto accident. During the three years I've worked out here, I've seen several accidents happen within minutes of each other and none of them be related. Too many cars going too fast result in accident after accident."

"Get me the info on the other wreck anyway. You're probably right, but I might as well take whatever information I can get. I'd rather check it out now than be asked later by my superiors why I didn't."

"Will do," Officer Tanner said. "Anything else?"

"I'll have some lab techs go over the car for any forensic evidence. I see a few spots of blood on the airbag. It may not tell us who was at the wheel, but it may provide some clues. In the meantime, we start searching for the driver."

"Where?"

"Hospitals, doctors' offices, motels, restaurants. I'll have a few officers assigned to work those places. Someone, somewhere has seen something. We just have to find the right person."

"Yeah, that's her all right," the redheaded desk clerk said. He was holding a photo in his hand.

"You're sure?" Carson McCullers said, taking the picture back. It was his only copy, given to him at the beginning of the assignment.

"Oh yeah, man. Who could forget a face

like that? She's a fox." He paused. "She was also a little weird, man."

"How so?" McCullers asked. He was standing in the tiny, dingy lobby of the Pretty Penny Motel. Massey stood next to him.

"I dunno," the clerk replied with a shrug. "She seemed lost, confused, like she didn't know where she was. And she looked kinda busted up. Like she had been in a fight or something. Her lower lip was split, and she had a big bruise on the side of her head. Looked like someone might have worked her over pretty good."

"Where is she now?" McCullers asked.

For a moment, the clerk became suspicious. "Are you sure you're cops?"

What an idiot, McCullers thought. *Are you sure you're human?* "I showed you my badge, didn't I? I can take you down to the station for a few hours if you need more convincing." His words rumbled heavily with threat.

"Okay, okay, don't get shook up. I'm just trying to be careful. You know, do my job and all that."

"Right now, your job is answering my questions. You can understand that, can't you?"

"Yeah, yeah, I got it. What more do you want to know?"

"You said she left. How long ago?" McCullers snapped.

The clerk turned to the clock. "Three, maybe four hours ago."

"Where did she go?"

"How should I know?" the clerk said irritably. "I check people in and out. That's it. People don't file travel plans with me. They just come in, settle up their bill, and then bail."

McCullers closed his eyes and inhaled slowly, willing his temper to step down. He had spent the last hour asking the same questions of waitresses and other motel clerks. His feet hurt, and the rest of his body reminded him that he had been in a bone-rattling accident the night before. What he really wanted was to find a stiff drink and a soft bed, neither of which he would see until he found the woman. "Was she alone?"

"How am I supposed to know?"

"Was she alone?" McCullers shouted, letting his temper slip.

The clerk's eyes widened. "She came into the lobby alone," he said rapidly, his words oozing fear. "A man came in, a truck driver, and introduced himself. He was the one that paid for her room."

"They shared a room?"

"No. He paid for a room of his own. I

thought that was strange. I mean, I didn't check them in, the night manager did, but if it was me, and she looked as good as she does —"

"No one asked you that," McCullers said, cutting him off. "You say he was a truck driver? Can you tell me the make, model, and license number of the truck?"

The clerk shook his head. "Just the license number. He put that on his registration. Do you want to see it?"

Of course, I want to see it, McCullers thought, but he said only, "Please," in forced tones of courtesy. The clerk disappeared for a moment then returned with a copy of the registration.

"Can you describe the man?" McCullers inquired.

"Tall, maybe six-one, older guy, maybe forty-five."

Older? Forty-five? That was McCullers's age, and he considered himself anything but old. "Go on."

"He looked like he was in pretty good shape."

"What about his hair?"

"Brown with some gray. I didn't look at his eyes. I don't usually look at another man's eyes."

McCullers looked down at the registration in his hand. Nick Blanchard had been penned on the line marked "Name." Everything else but the license plate number was blank. Apparently the motel didn't care who stayed there — any name, any number would do as long as you had cash or a credit card.

Nick Blanchard. He let the name percolate in his mind, committing it to memory. A passerby? A good Samaritan? McCullers doubted it. He didn't believe in fate, and he was willing to wager a large sum of money that this Blanchard fellow was more than he seemed. If that was true, then McCullers's job had just got harder.

The image of burning bright headlights bearing down on him and the sensation of being rammed from behind came back to him. He was certain that it had been a big rig that plowed into him, pushing him off the road and into the gritty desert. Coincidence that this Nick Blanchard had a truck? No such thing, McCullers decided. Blanchard had to be the one who had run him off the road. There was a score to settle.

"You got any more questions?" the clerk asked with a cracked facade of arrogance.

"Yeah. Lots of them."

"Not much on civility are you, Mr.

McCullers?" Raymond Massey stated. The two men were parked on the motel lot, sitting in the rental car.

"I got what I was after," McCullers snapped.

"And made both of us as memorable as possible in that young man's eyes. There's no way he's going to forget us now."

"So?"

"So if the real police come by later — and they are certain to do that — he'll be able to give a full description of us."

"He would have done that anyway."

"Perhaps, but by bullying him as you did, you fixed the event more deeply in his mind. He will be very motivated to tell everything he knows."

"So what do you want me to do? Go back in there and apologize?"

"You can't unscramble an egg, Mr. McCullers. I suggest a more evenhanded approach in the future."

"Why don't you just let me do my job?"

"Because your job is now my job. I don't like it any better than you do, but that's the hand that's been dealt us."

"You can quit anytime you want."

"No, I can't. And I wouldn't if I could. Mr. Moyer has given me a mission. I will fulfill it."

"The loyal servant," McCullers said with disdain. "A worker bee mindlessly doing as he's told. You're no different than that kid in the lobby."

"You have no loyalties?" Massey asked. If McCullers's jabs angered him, it didn't show. McCullers found that unsettling.

"Sure I do. I'm loyal to myself. That's all I've ever been loyal to."

"I'm not surprised."

Backing out of the stall, McCullers directed the car to the street and turned south on Highway 58. Two blocks later, he was at the intersection that split 58, which ran to the east, and Highway 14, which ran south toward Lancaster and Palmdale. He went south.

"Do you have any idea where you're going?"

"I'm going to find my target and this Nick Blanchard. I owe them both a little visit."

"How do you know they didn't go east?" Massey asked.

"I don't."

"So you're guessing."

"It's more than a guess, Massey; it's instinct. My instincts are never wrong."

Massey let loose a little laugh. "Never?"'

"That's right. My life is special. Things tend to go my way. I've learned to trust my instincts. That's why I'm still alive."

"Did your instincts tell you that your truck would be flipping end over end last night?"

McCullers turned a hard face toward the man in the passenger seat. Much more talk from him and he would kill him and enjoy the process. That would cost him the sizable fee that Moyer had agreed to pay, but McCullers had limits. Massey was pushing those limits to the breaking point.

"My instincts made me look up just in time to save my life. Anyone else — say you, for example — would have died in the wreck. As you can see, I'm still on the job. A little battered, but greatly motivated."

"Your instincts tell you she went south," Massey said. "You had better be right, or we'll be wasting time that we can never get back."

"You can always go home."

"I think I'll stay awhile longer. Mr. Moyer is very interested in seeing that your work gets carried out as promised."

"Whatever," McCullers said, accelerating. "Why don't you get on that fancy phone of yours and see if you can't get someone to run that plate and name. If he's a truck driver, he must have a base. At least that will give us some place to look. And keep an eye out for a new, white tractor-trailer rig."

"There must be a thousand trucks that fit that description."

"Only one with that license plate."

Massey sighed, pulled a cell phone from his coat pocket, and dialed his administrative assistant. Moyer Communications had ways of getting private information.

Chapter 6

Tuesday, 3:10 P.M.

The Joshua trees and scrub brush of the high desert had yielded to the manicured lawns, concrete-block walls, and industrial and mercantile sections of Valencia, which had in turn given way to the oak trees of Fillmore and Santa Paula. Now the large truck motored north up Highway 101. To Lisa's left was the deep blue of the Pacific Ocean, which glimmered in the bright sunlight like a sequined blanket. To her right were hills of green dotted with expensive homes that overlooked the freeway and the wide expanse of ocean. In a few hours, she had left behind the starkness of the desert to be surrounded by verdant hills and azure water.

"I never get used to it," Nick said.

Lisa snapped her head around to face him. "I'm sorry?" she said, uncertain of his meaning.

"The ocean," he answered. "No matter how many times I see it, it still captures my attention."

"It's beautiful. Serene."

"I grew up by the ocean. I'm convinced that the worst day by the ocean is better than the best day anywhere else. That may be an exaggeration, but not much of one."

"Did you grow up around here?"

"Oceanside," Nick said, his eyes fixed on the traffic before him. "My father was an officer in the Marine Corps. We spent a lot of years on different bases around the country, but my early high school years were spent in Oceanside. After my father retired, he took a civil-service job and moved us to a place just south of Santa Barbara. That's where we're heading now."

"We're going to your father's house? I thought you said that you worked out of your home."

Nick smiled. "Well, at least your immediate memory seems to be intact. You're right. I did say that. The house belongs to me now. Well, it belongs to my sister and me. But she's seldom there."

"I don't understand." Lisa was struggling to make everything fit. Understanding was crucial to her sanity. Every fact was a peg of reality that reminded her that all she had lost was a hunk of her memory, not her senses. She was still lucid, still thoughtful, still able to reason.

"My father passed away about five years

ago. My mother died two years later. There's just my sister and me, so everything was willed to us, including the house."

"You live with your sister?" Lisa said, then quickly added, "Not that there's anything wrong with that."

Nick laughed. "No problem. My sister and I own the house together. But she lives on the East Coast and works for a large corporation there. She's a vice president or something like that. She comes out to California two or three times a year. She keeps a few things in the house, but other than that, I have the run of the place."

"Oh, I see."

"I think you'll like it."

"I'm sure I will, but I feel like I'm imposing."

"Not at all. You're good company." He paused as he changed lanes to pass a slow-moving car. "Traffic gets kind of squirrelly around here. At least it's moving nicely." Once the maneuver was completed, he asked, "How are you feeling?"

"Better," Lisa said. "My brain seems to be clearing."

"You're starting to remember things?" he asked with interest.

She frowned. "No, but my thinking seems less . . . fuzzy."

"Your memory will come back in time."

"I hope you're right." The dark sense of doubt surfaced again. Her emotions were a churning pot of depression, fear, and perplexity.

"I'm sure that I am," Nick said reassuringly. His voice was smooth, easy, the kind that kindled trust, the kind that was familiar with laughter. She liked the sound of it. "Do you know what kind of car you were driving?"

"No. Why?"

"I was wondering if a small memory might trigger a larger one. I mean, if you could remember the kind of car you drove, then other things might fall in place."

"I don't recall my car. I don't even recall ever having driven. My oldest memory is the motel."

"Had I known that was going to be the case, I would have searched for a nicer place. Motels like that are best forgotten."

She gazed out the window and studied the cars, hoping that one would seem familiar. Maybe Nick was right; one memory could launch an avalanche of others. She had nothing to lose. She looked at the passing autos, studying each one, visualizing herself behind the wheel. An old Ford van followed a Cadillac, which was followed by a shiny black Mercedes. Pickup trucks, Volkswagens, commercial vehicles, sports cars, luxury autos made up an endless parade, and none looked familiar. "There are so many cars," Lisa said. "What are the odds that the kind of car I was driving will pass us?"

"Who knows? I suppose the odds are pretty good. If nothing else, you're exercising your brain, jogging your memory. It can't hurt to try."

"You didn't see my car when you picked me up?" she asked, her eyes still following each car she saw.

"No. Like I said before, I found you walking along the side of the road in a daze. I have no idea where your car is . . . or was."

"Was?"

"I'm sure the CHP have found it. That's why I wanted you to go to the police. Technically, you've left the scene of an accident. They won't like that."

Dread flowed through her like an icy stream. The mention of the police unnerved her, and she had no idea why. She wondered if she were a criminal. Why else would she feel such apprehension?

A pearl-colored Lexus sedan rolled by and caught Lisa's attention. Suddenly her mind was filled with strobelike flashes of memory. Visions of the car's interior flooded her consciousness: walnut wood trim, leather seats, leather-wrapped steering wheel. Her heart pounded, and she caught her breath.

"What?" Nick said with concern. "What's wrong?"

"The car," she said pointing. "I know that car . . . or a car like it."

"The Lexus?" Nick said. He whistled in admiration. "SC 300. Nice piece of work. You have good taste. Those things go for more than fifty thousand."

Lisa nodded. "Fifty-eight thousand."

"You remember the price? What else do you remember?"

Closing her eyes, Lisa tried to organize the bits of memory that had splashed on her mind like raindrops on a windshield. "Gold," she said. "My car was gold. Leather seats. Music. I remember music." Bits and pieces of a tune drifted into her thoughts. "Beethoven. I think it was Beethoven." Bright lights. Impact. Crunching metal. Spinning, spinning. Blackness. The car was in the air, then on its side, in the air again, rolling, rolling. Pain. Fear. Scorching terror. Silence. Glass everywhere. Fire in her ribs, stabbing in her chest. Powder, fine and gray, filling the front seat. The steering wheel collapsing upon its column, a white airbag hanging flaccidly in her lap.

"Lisa . . ."

She was still alive. The pain meant she was alive, but for how long? Would he come back? Would he make sure that the job was done? Run. Move. Hide.

"Lisa!"

It was Nick's voice, strong, concerned. Lisa snapped her eyes open. It was day, not night. She wasn't in the desert, sitting in a mutilated car; she was in the cab of a Mack truck on Highway 101. Her heart had gone from thundering to tripping, fluttering in fright. Her breathing was ragged and harsh. Hot tears steamed down her cheeks.

"Are you back with me, Lisa?" Nick asked. "Are you all right?"

She wiped the tears from her face and took a deep breath. "I'm . . . I'm okay, I think."

"Wow," Nick said with obvious relief. "You scared me there. One moment we're talking about cars, the next you're trembling like someone cut a hole in the ice and dropped you in."

"Then why am I sweating?"

Nick shook his head. "I take it you remembered something. Want to talk about it?"

What was there to talk about? She still knew nothing. "I was reliving the accident. I still don't remember anything except being pushed off the road."

"Pushed? You were pushed?"

"Yes, I think so. I remember headlights and a bump from behind. The next thing I knew . . ." She took another ragged breath. "The next thing I knew, my car was flying through the air."

"Did you pull in front of someone? Is that how the accident happened?"

Accident was no longer the right term. Of one thing Lisa was now certain: What had happened to her was no accident. Someone intentionally ran her off the road. "Someone tried to kill me," Lisa said softly. The words seemed to stick in her throat.

Nick fell silent, gazing out the window into the distance. He seemed disturbed. "Do you know what you're saying? That's a strong accusation. Are you sure that it wasn't an unintentional collision? I spend a lot of time on the road. I see them all the time."

Turning her head, Lisa gave Nick a hard look. "I was there. I may not be a professional truck driver, but I know when someone rams my car." Her words were even yet heavy with barely controlled anger.

"Okay, okay," Nick protested. "I'm just trying to get a feel for things."

Closing her eyes, Lisa said, "I'm sorry. I've snapped at you again. It's becoming a habit."

"No, you're right. You were there and I wasn't. I shouldn't be questioning your judgment. But that does put a new twist on things, doesn't it?"

"What do you mean?"

"It's good that you came with me. After all, if what you say is true, the killer is still out there."

Lisa felt sick.

Bill Hobbs drew a circle on the yellow legal pad in front of him. It was one of many such circles he had drawn in the last half-hour. Doodling was therapy for him, a way of allowing his mind to free-associate miscellaneous bits of facts that, for the moment, seemed unrelated.

He knew that the uninitiated might see him and think that he was just daydreaming, wasting time and the taxpayer's money, but no one in the Kern County sheriff's office in Bakersfield thought that. Hobbs's record was impeccable. The only fault to be found in his personnel jacket was his profound hesitancy to take vacations. He was a bachelor who loved his job, and it was not uncommon for him to continue working on his own time.

The phone on his desk rang, startling him from his thoughts. He quickly answered it. It was the third call for him since he had returned from Mojave. The first was about the VIN and license plate number. Even though the CHP officer had told him that both numbers were phonies, he had run the numbers himself. He didn't doubt Tanner's work, but there was little else he could do at the moment. He had compared the number on the dash with the one in the engine compartment. They matched. He then ran a check on the number itself. Nothing. Not only was there no match, there was no such number recorded anywhere. Calling for a wants-and-warrants check on the license plate was just as futile.

The present call was different. He had taken one of the license plates to the forensics lab to have it examined for authenticity. He wanted to know if the plate was a genuine California Department of Motor Vehicles issue or a counterfeit. The caller, a technician in the lab, told him it was real. His frustration mounted.

How could a car, a new car, have an illegitimate VIN number and unassigned plates? And that was not all that was out of place. The wreck had been severe, but where was the injured driver? He had seen many cases where drivers had lived through impossible crashes, but they never just walked off — not unless they had something to hide. Was that what he was dealing with? A drug runner fell asleep at the wheel, wrecked the car, and then fled to avoid police? Possible, but no drugs were found in the car.

The vehicle was missing other things, too. There had been no registration and no proof of insurance form; state law required both to be carried in the car. Even more suspicious were the facts he was hearing now. Tanner had examined the car again, and this time he noticed something strange.

"You heard right," Tanner said. "Once we had the car at the impound lot, I took a closer look. It has a global positioning navigation system in it. You know, one of those things that tell you where you are and where you're going. It can even give you directions to the next gas station."

"I'm familiar with the GPS, Tanner. What about it?"

"It was disconnected."

"Maybe the connections were broken in the accident," Hobbs suggested.

"No way. The wires were cut, neat and clean. Someone wanted the system disabled."

"But why?"

"I have no idea, but there's more. The car comes with a cellular phone. It mounts in the dash for hands-free use. It was deactivated — big time. Someone yanked the whole system out."

"What?" Hobbs couldn't believe his ears. "Both the GPS and the cell phone were disabled?"

"You got it."

"This is too weird," Hobbs confessed. "No driver, no way to trace the car, and now this. Got any ideas?"

Tanner sighed into the phone. "I was hoping you could tell me something."

"Who spends fifty grand on a luxury car and then guts it like that?"

"Promise me that you'll let me in on the secret when you figure it out," Tanner said.

"I will. And thanks. It means something. I just don't know what."

"Maybe the fingerprints will help us," Tanner offered. "Hold on."

Hobbs could hear Tanner talking to someone in his office. The CHP officer came back on the line.

"We may have something," he said. "One

of our officers found a clerk says that a woman who looked pretty beat-up stayed at his motel. He said two men had come looking for her. They had a picture and — get this — they said they were cops."

"I'm on my way down," Hobbs said quickly. "I want to talk to this guy. I'll see about getting a police artist to join us. Maybe the clerk can describe the woman well enough for us to get a composite picture."

"Sounds good."

Hobbs hung up and grabbed his coat. Mojave was a good hour's drive from Bakersfield, and he didn't want to waste time. He picked up the phone again. A few moments later he was out the door and headed to the airport, where a sheriff's helicopter would be waiting for him.

"Got it," Raymond Massey said, then switched off the cell phone and placed it back in his suit coat pocket. "That was Mr. Moyer," he added.

McCullers grunted with feigned nonchalance. Things were getting out of hand. Having Massey along was annoying. Now Moyer was getting involved. Soon, he was sure, the UCLA football team would be offering suggestions.

"We've got a break," Massey said flatly. "He followed my suggestion and ran down Nick Blanchard's name. There's no record of him anywhere. No one by that name has a license to drive a commercial truck."

"That you can find, you mean," McCullers said.

"If Mr. Moyer says that there is no Nick Blanchard that fits the given parameters, then there is no Nick Blanchard."

"Fits the given parameters?" McCullers laughed loudly. "That's a good one, Massey. You sound like you're talking about stock options or a business merger. We're tracking a man. The parameters change constantly."

Massey sighed loudly. "Once again you're missing the point. Why would a man rescue a damsel in distress, put her up in a motel room, and then lie about his occupation and name?"

"Lots of reasons," McCullers snapped, "and it's you who's missing the point. That kind of behavior is what I'm talking about. You can't feed a man's name into a computer and have some database kick out a picture of how the guy thinks. Maybe the guy is one of those antigovernment fanatics who hoard guns and food and who refuse to get a driver's license or to pay income tax."

"It is almost impossible to conceal an identity. Maybe he is something more challenging."

"Like what?"

"Like a government operative, you idiot," Massey snapped. "Maybe he's something worse."

"What could be worse?"

"A competitor." Massey said it as if the word were dirt in his mouth. "Our business is highly competitive, and a dozen firms would like to know what we know . . . would like to know what *she* knows."

"That's hard to swallow."

"Well, try harder. This may be difficult for you to understand, McCullers, but at the level of business that Moyer Communications operates, there are a great many shady practices. Some firms retain their own circle of industrial spies and operate with a sophistication that rivals the CIA. If those firms knew about her, they would stop at nothing to bring her on board. It would be a grave mistake for us to underestimate them."

"That's all very interesting," McCullers said sarcastically, "but it doesn't help very much, now does it?"

"I'm changing our approach," Massey said. "Stay on the 14 until we reach Lancaster, then take the G Street turnoff."

"Why?"

"Because that's where the Gen. William J. Fox Airfield is. Mr. Moyer has arranged for a helicopter. We'll never catch a truck with a three- or four-hour lead. We can cover a lot more ground this way."

"I like the idea, but the truck could have gone so many different directions, not to mention the number of trucks on the road."

"Mr. Moyer is sending up other helicopters. He has one from Bakersfield that will follow Highway 58 east; another will lift off from Riverside and check out I-15, I-215, and I-10. There will be others, too. We're to follow the 14 and cut over to I-5."

"That's a lot of helicopters. You guys must have pretty deep pockets."

"You don't know the half of it."

"Yeah, whatever," McCullers said flippantly. "And how are we supposed to find our man from the air?"

"The motel clerk gave us a few clues," Massey answered with a tone that did nothing to hide his disgust. "You really make a living at doing this?"

"Cut to the chase," McCullers snapped, resisting the urge to backhand the man next to him.

"The clerk said Blanchard's truck was

white, looked brand-new, and had no markings on the doors. Almost every commercial truck has some kind of signage on it that identifies the company and even the name of the driver. The clerk thought it was unusual that the truck had no markings at all."

"So we look for a brand-new semi without markings?"

"And two people in the cab."

"Not a very technical approach."

"I'm working on that. Hopefully, that will all change soon."

"It galls you to have to do this without all Moyer's technical gizmos, doesn't it? Well, welcome to my world, Massey. Some things have to be done the old-fashioned way. That's what I'm good at."

"We'll see," Massey commented dryly. "We'll see."

Chapter 7

Tuesday, 3:10 P.M.

Gregory Moyer was angry. He could bring down any man in the country and had done so when it suited his purposes. Generals turned to him for information on world leaders. He could pinpoint almost every dignitary on the globe, but now he faced the possibility of failure. This one woman had slipped through his fingers. The woman was smart.

He paced his cavernous office, his hands clasped firmly behind his back. She was headed south. She could lose herself easily in Los Angeles or San Diego. Eight million people lived in the greater L.A. area, and more than two million lived in San Diego County — ten million people in just those two cities. She could hide indefinitely. She knew all the tricks, things to avoid and things to do to disappear without a trace. Armed with her knowledge, she could drop off the face of the earth and still destroy him and Moyer Communications.

Her first step would be to go primitive, eschewing technological luxuries. No cell phone, no e-mail, no GPS, no ATMs, no credit cards, no bank accounts. Nothing. By leaving no records, she would become invisible. She could easily obtain false identification if she knew where to look and had sufficient cash. And she could borrow an identity. A few cycles of new identities would make her impossible to find.

He had to find her. Every hour made the task more difficult; it was time to call in a few favors, time to pull out all the stops.

He walked back to his desk. His phone, unlike most phones, had no handset. Microphones in his desk and around his office could pick up his voice and speakers relayed the words of the person on the other end of the line. The phone was voice activated. "Phone," he said.

Ready, a synthetic voice replayed.

"Security high, encrypt, priority one."

Ready, the computerized system said. Moyer knew that his voiceprint had been compared to the one stored in the system. No one could use his phone but him.

"Gen. Lawrence Scott, Pentagon number."

There was a pause, but no dial tone. Moyer hated noises.

Ringing, the synthetic voice offered.

A moment later: "Scott, here."

"General, this is Gregory Moyer. Sometime back you said you owed me a favor. Do you remember that?"

The general laughed. "Not much on pleasantries, are you? I believe I owe you several favors. I count a dozen just from Desert Storm. You had the capability to find my son after he was shot down when no one else could. Yeah, I'd say I owe you a favor."

"I'm in need of your help."

There was a short pause and then General Scott said flatly, "Name it."

Bill Hobbs, who would rather have a root canal than fly, released a sigh of relief as the McDonnell Douglas 500E helicopter set down on the concrete pad at the Mojave Civilian Flight Test Center. He had flown only once before in the Kern County sheriff's helicopter, and he had hated that too. His relief was tempered by the fact that he would soon have to strap himself in for the return flight home.

A short distance away, just out of the rotor blast area, was a CHP cruiser. Tanner was standing next to it, his arms folded casually in front of him. Hobbs exited the craft and jogged to the car.

"You look green," Tanner said bluntly.

"Yeah, well, it's nice to see you, too. Is our man ready?"

"Unhappy, but ready. I have him at the substation. I ran his record, and he's clean. One shoplifting charge when he was sixteen, but nothing since."

"Did he give you a description of the men who were impersonating police officers?" Hobbs slipped into the passenger seat.

Once inside the car, Tanner answered. "Yes. I put an APB out on them. He saw their car, a dark sedan. That's the best he could do. A dark sedan."

"Not much help there. Let's see what else he has to say."

"I'll have you there in five minutes. The substation is just a couple of miles away."

"Good, the less travel the better. Helicopters and me don't mix."

The motel clerk sat in a small examination room, a cup of coffee in front of him. His head was down and his shoulders slumped. He looked miserable when Hobbs and Tanner breezed in.

"Good afternoon, Mr. —" Hobbs paused to looked at the clipboard he carried. "Webber. I'm sorry to keep you waiting. Can I freshen that cup of coffee for you?"

Webber looked up. Hobbs thought he

looked like the kind of kid who causes parents to grow gray prematurely, but that was a prejudicial opinion. For all he knew, the young man was the best son a mother or father could have. "No," Webber said. "You can let me go home."

"That is exactly what I plan to do. I just have a few questions."

Webber frowned and shook his head. "I don't know anything more than what I told him." He pointed to Tanner.

"Officer Tanner said that you have been very cooperative. We appreciate that." Hobbs was being as nice as he could. He wanted the clerk to trust him. "We're very concerned about the two men who came to you asking questions. They told you they were police officers?"

"That's right."

"Did they show you any identification?"

"Yeah, one did. The one in the suit didn't, just the other guy."

"One was in a suit and the other was not?"

"Right. He wore jeans and a dress T-shirt. You know, like a polo shirt that some of the older guys wear."

"He showed you a badge? Did the badge have a number on it?"

"I don't know. I didn't look that close."

"Was it a shield or a star like mine?"

Hobbs pulled his leather wallet with badge out and showed it to Webber.

"Shield, I think."

"They didn't say who they worked for? FBI? INS? Secret Service? ATF?"

"They didn't say, and like I said, I didn't look that close. No offense, but I don't like cops coming to my work. It makes me look bad in the eyes of the boss."

"No problem," Hobbs said. "We'll square things with him and make sure he knows that you didn't do anything wrong." He smiled. "Were the men asking about a woman who stayed at your motel?"

"Right."

"Did they say why?"

"No. They showed me a picture, and I recognized her. I told them all that I knew, which wasn't much." He told the story of the woman's confusion, of her injuries, and of her association with Nick Blanchard. "I gave a copy of the registration to your friend there."

"I appreciate that," Hobbs replied. "We need your help. The people who spoke to you are not cops. We don't know who they are, but they're not cops. I want to ask you a few more questions, and then another officer is going to join us. Do you like computers?"

"Yeah, I guess."

"Well then, you'll like this. He's going to use a laptop to assemble a composite image of the two men, the woman, and this Nick Blanchard."

"That's a waste of time."

"Why?" Hobbs asked.

"It would be easier to copy an image off the security tape."

"Your motel has a security camera?" Tanner said with surprise.

"Look, I know the Pretty Penny Motel is a dive, but we're right off the highway. We could get robbed just like the other places. The boss put up a camera a few weeks ago."

"I'll go get the tape," Tanner said. "You ask your questions."

"Tanner," Hobbs said, "see if you can get the tape from the previous night, too, the one where Blanchard and the woman check in."

"Got it," the officer acknowledged as he left the room.

Hobbs turned back to Webber. "Did you tell the others about the videotape?"

"No. The guy in the jeans was pretty rough. I didn't like his attitude, so I only answered his questions and didn't offer anything more."

Leaning back, Hobbs smiled broadly. "You, Mr. Webber, have just made my day."

★ ★ ★

Gregory Moyer stood before the closed security door and swiped his smart card through the electronic reader next to the right jamb. A green light came on. He punched a six-digit PIN into the keypad, and a second green light came on. Then, looking straight ahead, he said, "Gregory Moyer." A small camera had already analyzed his face and was now matching his biometric data with his voiceprint and his PIN, which were recorded on a small electronic chip embedded in the smart card. A third green light signaled acceptance, and the door slid open with a whoosh.

Inside resembled a NASA control room. A dozen large monitors shone in the dim light of the center. They were set in a doughnut-shaped console of molded Formica, plastic, and metal that was twenty feet in diameter. A holographic globe hovered above the "hole" at the center of the doughnut and glowed a ghostly yellow-green. The sphere rotated in perfect coordination with its real-world counterpart.

Moyer studied the scene. No matter how many times he visited the Communications Control Center, he was always amazed. This was one of four interlinked centers throughout the world. Moyer's black wingtip shoes thudded softly as he strolled across the black marble floor. The floor was an unnecessary expense, but one he thought worthwhile. Twenty employees and twenty employees alone had access to the chamber, each young, enthusiastic, and extremely gifted. They were not only the best at what they did, but they knew the benefits of loyalty. Moyer paid them three times what they could get anywhere else in the world. Each, through wise financial effort, could become a millionaire in less than five years. Money bought their best effort and assured their silence.

Several strides later, Moyer stood behind Bernard Cox, a young man in his midtwenties. His hair was the color of amber and cut close to the scalp. Everything about him was casual. He wore slip-on loafers, a yellow T-shirt, and brown chinos. His attention was riveted to a monitor that showed a long black ribbon of asphalt that ran through brown-green hills. Moyer could see cars and trucks moving along the road.

"Which road is that?" Moyer asked.

"U.S. 101," Cox answered after a brief glance at his boss. Cox was the project manager for the MC2-SDS system that was providing the picture on the monitor. Roughly the size of a school bus, the Moyer Communications Satellite Data System was one of thirty such reconnaissance platforms designed and built for the military. Most were placed in strategic positions above global hot spots. Part of an intricate network that combined communications satellites, the kind that made Moyer a wealthy man, and existing SDS systems, MC2 was the latest state-of-the-art surveillance satellite. Like its big brothers, Keyhole and other secret observation platforms, MC2 was an eye in the sky — a very keen eye. MC2 was also movable, able to change altitude and orbit parameters. While most satellites either hovered over a fixed area in a geosynchronous orbit or passed over an area at regular intervals, MC2 was more flexible. It could reposition itself at a thousand kilometers from its designated orbit and, using its powerful telescope, could define objects less than a meter across at a distance of fifteen hundred kilometers off its track. For objects directly under its track, it could read the headlines of a newspaper on the ground.

Cox was responsible for all that and for what Moyer was seeing. "We repositioned as you asked and began a moderately wide search of the area."

"And?" Moyer prompted.

"So far so good, although we haven't

found the test target."

Moyer had seen no need to let Cox or anyone else in on his plan. He had enough problems to occupy his mind. As far as the young scientist was concerned, this was a drill whose results would be sent to the Pentagon. He had even been cryptic with General Scott whom he had called earlier. The general believed, because Moyer had told him so, that new software was being uploaded to the MC2 and tested. The general had been all for that.

"You haven't found the truck?"

"Oh, I've found trucks all right," Bernard answered casually. "Over six hundred in the first ten minutes. There are a lot of trucks on southern California freeways. But you want a specific truck. That would be impossible if not for the software we developed."

Moyer nodded. The MC2 satellite system used a digitized photo system that allowed a computer to do the actual searching. Since it was a teraflop system, the computer was capable of doing a trillion operations per second. By year's end, that system would be updated to a petaflop, capable of doing a thousand times more work than the teraflop. The tightly integrated system was now tracking the only clue Moyer had to the whereabouts of the woman who threatened to bring down his empire.

The computer monitor flashed from one scene to another as the satellite acquired each new image of a semitrailer, compared it to the database of information that Bernard had fed into it thirty minutes before, and dismissed it if it did not match. In some ways the MC2 was similar to a program called People Spotter that had been developed in the late nineties. That program had been designed to enable a computer to read a video image of a person, analyze the individual's facial features, and compare its findings to a database of criminals and terrorists. If it made a positive match, it notified the authorities automatically. People Spotter had been used with some success in Europe, but politicos in the United States, fearing a backlash from privacy rights groups, were slow to move on it. Moyer chuckled to himself. If the privacy do-gooders knew what he was up to, their hearts would seize in their chests.

"We'll be done with Highway 101 in ten minutes, then we can —" A short, sharp beep cut Cox off. Simultaneous with the alarm, ACQUISITION flashed on the computer screen. "Bingo!" he shouted, tapping the screen with his finger. "You gotta love this, bossman! We score a hit fifteen minutes after you started the test. The Pentagon is going to love you."

"They already love me." Moyer was transfixed by the tiny image of the truck. Even though he understood the principles involved, he was having trouble believing that a satellite hung in space fifteen hundred kilometers away could recognize a specific vehicle. "Let's not get ahead of ourselves, Bernard. Pull in tighter."

Cox snapped the commands into the keyboard. The image of the tiny truck suddenly became large, filling the screen. The satellite tracked the moving vehicle smoothly. "There you have it," he said with pride. "A white truck, single trailer, two occupants, no markings on the vehicle."

"Show me the license."

"Okay, boss." Cox entered more commands, and the image of the truck got larger. It took him nearly a full minute to adjust the angle to show the front license plate.

"It's too blurry to read," Moyer complained.

"Give me a sec," Cox replied with confidence. After a few keystrokes he tapped the enter key. "I'm sending it through digital enhancement." The moving truck on the monitor was replaced with the still image of a California commercial truck plate.

A smile slipped across Moyer's face as he read the number of the plate. It matched the one that had been on the motel registration under Nick Blanchard's name. Even though when he'd had both Blanchard's name and license checked they both proved bogus, that didn't matter right now. He had the right truck.

"Give me a position," Moyer demanded.

A single keystroke brought the information up. Cox grinned like a father who has just seen his son take his first few steps. "Twenty miles south of Santa Barbara on the 101. Oh, he's also northbound."

"Let's take a look in the cab."

"Will do, but it won't be real clear. It looks like we're getting massive sun reflection off the windshield."

"Try."

Again the image changed. Through the man-made miracles of technology, Gregory Moyer peered through the windscreen of the truck. He saw a man at the wheel and a woman in the passenger seat. Their faces were not clear, but they were clear enough. "So we meet again," he said softly.

"Excuse me?" Cox said, turning to face his employer.

"Nothing, Bernard," Moyer answered,

placing a hand on the man's shoulder. "When your shift is over, take your crew to Zilli's for dinner on the company. Order what you want; drink what you want. I'll have them set up the banquet room for you. Until then, you stay on this vehicle. I'll let you know when you can pull off."

"Thanks," Cox exclaimed. "That's very generous."

"Nonsense. You've earned it. In more ways than you realize, you've earned it."

"Almost there," Nick said, leaning forward over the steering wheel and stretching his back. "Want to hear some more music?"

Lisa declined. Already in their short trip she had heard enough musicals to last her the rest of the year. She was content to listen to the sound of tires on the road and the dull rumble of the diesel engine. "No thanks," she said.

"You've been quiet for the last hour. Are you feeling okay?"

"Pretty good, I guess. Still stiff."

"That will take weeks to get rid of," Nick said. "Muscles take awhile to get over what you've been through. Actually, I was asking about you . . . otherwise. I know this is rough on you. Remembering the accident had to be tough."

"I'm okay now," she said softly. "I just don't know why anyone would want to kill me." She laid her head back against the headrest and released a long, troubled sigh. "For all I know, I could be married to the mob or be president of the United States."

"You're not the president," Nick said lightly, "and that's a plus. I also doubt that you're married to the mob. You don't seem the type."

"I didn't know there was a type," she said.

"Well, if there is, you're not it."

Lisa chuckled. "That's a rather circular argument, isn't it?"

"See? Would a mob moll know about circular arguments?"

A muted ringing interrupted the conversation. Lisa unconsciously stiffened, her stomach constricting. "What's that?"

"Relax, it's just my phone." Nick reached down by his seat and pulled a cell phone from the door pocket.

Exploding into action, Lisa turned in her seat and reached across the space between them. "Give me that!" she shouted, snatching the phone.

"Hey, what are you doing?" Nick responded with surprise.

Lisa had the phone in her hand. She found the power switch, a tiny black rubber button marked PWR, and quickly pressed it. Turning the phone over she fumbled with the battery compartment release. The phone dropped to her lap and then fell to the floor.

"Lisa! Stop! What are you doing to my phone?"

Icy fingers of fear ran over her body and dug into her mind. Panicky, she released her seat belt and grabbed for the device. She flipped the phone over, pressed the release switch, and removed the battery. Then, as if they were covered with vile slime, she threw the dead phone and the battery into the sleeper cab, wiping her hands on her jeans. After several deep inhalations, she turned to face Nick. His lips were tight, his face red, and his jaw clamped shut. She thought she could hear his teeth grinding.

"I had to do that," Lisa said weakly, not even sure herself why. She felt like a child who had just broken her father's favorite radio.

"You *had* to do that?" Nick said, his voice barely above a growl. "That's not some inexpensive phone you pick up at a mall kiosk. I paid good money for that. A lot of good money."

"It's not broken, just deactivated."

"You couldn't just turn it off?" he snapped. "That's what most people do.

They just turn it off."

"No. It had to be separated from its power source. They can trace phones, especially cell phones."

"What are you yammering about?" Nick's anger was percolating to the top. "They? They? Who are they?"

Lisa didn't know.

"The CIA? The FBI? The IRS? If I hit any letters you like, let me know." His voice had turned sarcastic.

"I . . . I don't remember," she admitted. "I just know that phones like that can be traced."

"Wouldn't they need to know the number? Wouldn't they need to know me?"

"Yes . . . no . . . I don't remember."

"That's convenient," Nick said harshly.

"Fine," Lisa said loudly. "I didn't ask for a ride. I didn't ask you to be a white knight. If I'm a problem, then stop the truck and I'll get out."

"And do what? You can't make a living tearing phones apart."

"I'll figure something out." Lisa felt anger mix with her fear, forging an explosive mixture.

"I can see it all now. The newspaper headlines will read, 'Angry woman attacks cell phones.' "

"Stop the truck and let me out."

"No," Nick said flatly. "That's not going to happen."

"If I'm such a big problem, then you should be glad to get rid of me."

Silence.

"Well?" Lisa asked.

Nick's reply was softer. "I'm sorry. I don't want to be rid of you. I'm just taken aback. Grabbing the phone the way you did shook me a little. I overreacted."

Nick had every right to be angry, Lisa thought. She had acted rashly and without explanation. Anyone would have been put off by her actions. "No, I should be the one apologizing."

Nick's tight jaw, pursed lips, and flushed face melted into a small smile. "Next time, just talk to me. I promise to listen."

"Okay," she said, her terror beginning to ease.

"Great," Nick said. "Now what was all this talk about *them* tracing my phone?"

"Cell phones are wonderful tools, but they're not secure," Lisa explained, wondering how she knew this. "If the phone is on, it can be easily traced. As we drive, we pass relay towers. Your phone registers each time it passes one. It's an easy matter to triangulate a position. Police use the technique all the time. And it's now possible to do that even if the phone is off."

"You're kidding."

"Not at all. What happens when you turn your computer off or there's a power failure? When you turn it back on, does the clock show the correct time? Of course it does. Cell phones work the same way. A little power is used even if the phone is turned off."

"Okay, I believe you, but so what? Who would care about where we are? I mean —" He stopped short. "You said someone tried to kill you by running you off the road."

"Right."

"But you still don't know who?"

Lisa shook her head. "I'm not sure which is worse, knowing or not knowing."

"Knowing is always better. At least then you can make plans and fight back."

"Maybe," Lisa said. "Maybe." Once again she felt lost and confused, but most of all she felt frightened.

Raymond Massey spoke into the microphone of the headset he wore as he adjusted the helicopter's collective. "Did you get that?" he asked McCullers. McCullers looked ill.

"Yeah, I got it," he replied. "When you

said that we would be taking a helicopter, I didn't know you'd be the pilot."

"One of the many things the military gave me," Massey said. He made a sharp bank to the right, changing his course west. "We should be able to cut over to the 101 and be there in short order. We'll have the truck in our sights in twenty minutes or so."

"Great, just see if you can smooth the flight out a little. This is like riding a roller coaster."

Massey made another sharp bank. "First we verify the truck; then we follow it. We'll have to be cautious. We can conceal ourselves from them, but not from the other motorists. It's also possible that other helicopters will be in the area, and they'd be sure to notice us. If we're lucky, we'll find the truck quickly and can then decide on our next move."

"How did Moyer know where the truck was?" McCullers asked.

"He is a resourceful man," Massey said cryptically.

"That doesn't answer the question," McCullers complained.

"You're right." Massey said nothing more.

Chapter 8

Tuesday, 3:10 P.M.

Copying frames from the motel video was easy. By using a video capture device and program, Bill Hobbs soon had several photos of the woman and the man. The clerk had identified the man as the one who registered for the rooms using the name Nick Blanchard. The clerk didn't know the woman's name.

"Let's get this out with the APB," Hobbs said to Tanner. The men were in the conference room of the sheriff's substation. The black-and-white photos taken from the video were on the conference table. "Let's make sure that the border patrol gets copies too, just in case our couple want to make a quick trip to Mexico."

"They could be there by now," Tanner opined.

"Maybe, maybe not. A semi is not the best vehicle to make an escape in — if they're escaping anything."

"Something's up," Tanner said. "Useless VIN numbers and license numbers tell us that."

"That is exactly why we're pulling the stops out on this." Hobbs studied the photo. The picture was gray and slightly blurred, a testimony to the motel owner's frugal approach to business. But some simple computer enhancement made the pictures useful. He had watched the tape several times. "She looks frightened," Hobbs said thoughtfully.

"Frightened or guilty?" Tanner asked.

"Frightened. She seems uncertain of her surroundings. The question is why."

"Do you think she was abducted by this Blanchard?"

Hobbs shook his head. "Not from what the clerk said. He said that she seemed lost but that she left under her own power and by her own choice. He didn't think she was coerced."

Hobbs studied the photos again. The lobby of the motel had several large windows that looked out over the main road. A white semitrailer was parked at the curb. Hobbs had quizzed the clerk about the truck, but the man couldn't be sure that it was the truck Blanchard and the woman had left in. He guessed that it was. "Let's do this," Hobbs said. "Let's get a blow-up of the truck." The motel camera was set to record events in the lobby, not on the street.

The image was blurry, but it was all he had.

"Why?" Tanner asked.

"I want to have it distributed to all the weigh stations in the area."

"There are a lot of trucks on the road," Tanner said pessimistically. "It's going to be hard to find one."

"There are a lot of cars on the road too, but we still put APBs out on them and make plenty of arrests because we do. We have a few things in our favor. One, the truck looks new, and two, there is no logo, company name, or anything else on it. That makes it unique."

Tanner nodded. "Makes sense. I'll make sure the aerial crews know about it. The CHP has a few helicopters and airplanes in the area. They may be able to spot it from the air."

"Good idea," Hobbs agreed. He sighed. "Now comes the hard part — waiting."

They had passed over Pyramid Lake and were now pressing on over the San Ynez Mountains, Massey pushing the small helicopter as fast as it would go. He wished for a faster craft, but he knew wishing would change nothing. At least he could travel in a straight line, unhindered by traffic and road conditions. Every few minutes he received a communication from Moyer with an update about the truck's position. Each time Massey adjusted his course slightly, aiming not at where the truck was, but where it would be in the near future. The tactic dramatically cut down airtime and course corrections.

McCullers had settled into an uneasy silence in the passenger seat. He was not enjoying the ride, and Massey knew that he wasn't enjoying the company.

"Look," he said, nodding forward. "See that hawk?"

McCullers looked where Massey was indicating. "Yeah, I see it. So what?"

"Have you ever wondered how a hawk can find its prey?"

"No. I usually have better things to think about."

Massey shook off the cold response. He was going to make his point whether McCullers liked it or not. It was important for him to remind McCullers that he was no longer in charge. "Most people think that it's because the hawk has superior eyesight, which it does. But its prey is small. A field mouse is only a few inches long. No matter how keen its eyes, it would be difficult for the hawk to locate a brown mouse scampering on brown ground underneath brown shrubs. Look down, do you think you could spot a mouse with binoculars?"

"Probably not."

"You couldn't. No one could. At least not well enough to spot it, track it, and then capture it. The hawk has an extra advantage."

"Like what?" McCullers was beginning to show interest.

"The hawk not only has keen eyesight, but he can see in the ultraviolet. Most of its prey are burrowing animals like field mice, small rabbits, and the like. Many of those animals mark their territory with urine."

"How nice," McCullers said sarcastically.

Massey ignored the comment. "Urine glows a pale blue under ultraviolet light."

"You really need a different hobby."

"Shut up and listen," Massey snapped. "The hawk doesn't just look for a mouse on the move, he looks for the pale blue glow that indicates a burrowed community of animals. The animal's markings alert the hawk to their home. In a sense, it acts like a fast-food sign."

"And?" McCullers prompted.

"In most ways, humans are inferior to animals. We've got big brains, but they have better physical senses. Technology is changing that and changing it fast. Because of advanced technology, we can now see farther than ever before and see in new and revealing ways."

"That's great, teach. Thanks for the lecture. But what's it got to do with my mission?"

"*Our* mission," Massey corrected. "Once again, you're missing the point. The hawk has the advantage because he knows how to read the signs. Once he knows that, he can fly over large areas, find the distinctive blue glow, and know that lunch is nearby. He still has to catch the mouse, but at least he knows where to look. That's what we're doing right now, McCullers. We've used technology to look for our prey, but we still have to catch it."

"You get me close, Jeeves, and I'll do the rest."

"I'm not your chauffeur or your butler, but at least you understand the division of work. My job is to make sure you do your job. You're being paid a great deal of money for this."

"This has gone beyond money. Someone ran me off the road, put me in the hospital, and destroyed my truck."

"Not to mention, prevented you from doing your job."

"Yeah, that too," McCullers conceded.

"But it's more than business now; it's also personal. I have a score to settle with both of them."

"That's what I'm getting at," Massey said. "The hawk does not kill out of some need for vengeance. It kills for food. You need to kill because that's what you've been hired to do. Not for revenge, and not to prove anything except that you can do what you say you can do. If you make revenge your motive, you may make mistakes, take too long, or be too emotional. That can't be allowed."

"Don't worry about anything," McCullers said coldly. "I'll do my job, and I'll do it just right. The killing will take place, and it won't be traced back to your boss. But no one — not you, not Moyer, not anyone — is going to keep me from enjoying it."

Massey frowned. He had the distinct feeling that he was flying with a bomb on board — a bomb named McCullers.

The traffic was thicker now, and Nick had fallen into silent concentration. Lisa gazed out the side window at the green hills that were separated from the azure ocean by the wide asphalt strip of U.S. Highway 101. The diesel engine droned on, its subtle vibration throbbing through the cab. Sleep threatened to take hold of Lisa, to pull her into its inky blackness, and although sleep would be good for her recuperation, she refused to give in. The past was just as elusive as it had been when she first awakened in the strange motel room that morning. She had no new memories, but her mind was clearing.

The amnesia was odd in several ways. As a test, Lisa had run the day backward in her mind. She could easily recall their lunch in Fillmore and her strange attraction to and excursion into the old, dilapidated church. The events at the McDonald's in Mojave were clear and crisp, as were her sensations in the motel room. Her current memory seemed to be unaffected by the events that had led to her amnesia. She found comfort in that. While she could not summon her name, her occupation, the images of her parents, or the events of her childhood, she was, at least, not getting worse.

Questions swirled in her mind. Why had she reacted the way she did when Nick picked up the cell phone? Her actions had been fueled by an unknown fear. Even more troubling had been the words that had poured from her mouth, dire warnings about "them" and "their" ability to track a cell phone. Could such a thing be true? Yes.

She knew that. What she didn't know was how she knew it. Who was the collective "they" she instinctively feared?

A nearly overpowering urge to look behind her, to study the side mirrors of the truck to see if they were being followed, made her wonder if she had other problems than amnesia — such as paranoia. Could she be schizophrenic, seeing and fearing what was not there? Were there really pursuers? Or was she having some psychotic event, some fire of delusion fanned and fueled by demons unknown to her? Out of the fog of her thoughts came an unbidden quotation: "Even paranoids can have enemies." She said the words aloud. To her surprise, she remembered the source: Henry Kissinger.

"What?" Nick said.

Lisa turned to face him. "Huh?"

"You said something about paranoids."

"Oh," she said, realizing that she had uttered her thoughts aloud. "I was just thinking about a quote I read. 'Even paranoids can have enemies.' Henry Kissinger said that."

"You remember Henry Kissinger but can't remember your name?" Nick said, shaking his head. "That must be frustrating."

"It is."

"Well, I've got a quote too: 'I envy paranoids; they actually feel people are paying attention to them.' "

Despite her gray mood, Lisa chuckled. "You made that up, didn't you?"

"No, I'm not that clever. I think a writer said that. Susan Sontag or something like that."

"I was thinking about the phone. I feel like I should apologize again. That was an irrational act."

A broad smile spread across Nick's face. "Everyone should be entitled to a little irrationality now and then. Otherwise, how would we know when we were being rational?"

"I suppose," Lisa replied. "Is it much farther?"

"My place?" Nick shook his head. "We're almost there. I imagine you're ready to get out and move around some."

"Yes. I'm getting stiffer."

"When we get to the house, you can take some ibuprofen and lie down. That will help some. It will be more comfortable than sitting in a bouncing truck and gazing out the window."

"Nick," she began. "Can I ask you a question?"

"Sure."

"Back at the McDonald's in Mojave, when we were having breakfast, you told me you had to make a call and then you said you knew where a pay phone was. Remember?"

"Yes," Nick said with uncertainty.

"If you had a cell phone in the truck, why would you use a pay phone?"

Nick was silent; his smile evaporated. Then he said, "Because the phone was in the truck, and I wanted to give you a few more minutes to finish your breakfast. If I said I was headed to the truck, you might have felt the need to hurry."

"But I wasn't really eating breakfast. My mouth was too sore. Still is."

"I know, but it's not a big deal. I was just trying to be courteous, like my mother taught me." The smile returned. "Besides, I have a calling card. I often make calls from pay phones when my cell phone isn't handy."

"Oh," Lisa said. Something was gnawing at the back of her mind.

"Look," Nick said suddenly. "You see that sign that says CARPINTERIA?"

"Yes."

"The next exit is ours. Ten minutes on surface streets, then it's home, sweet home."

Lisa felt awkward. "Are you sure you

don't mind putting me up?"

"Don't mind at all. It will be my pleasure . . . unless you start tearing up my phones." Nick laughed.

Lisa joined him . . . for a moment.

Moyer studied the image on his office computer screen. He had ordered that the direct, real-time image from the MC2-SDS satellite be channeled to his monitor. The image was clear and amazing to him, even though it was his company, under his direction, that had created, launched, and maintained the satellite. The technology was light-years ahead of the old surveillance platforms. He could clearly see the truck, bogged down in traffic, traveling in the far right lane of the highway. As he watched, a new image came on the screen — a helicopter. Moyer felt like a Greek god looking down on his puny subjects. Even aircraft were not hidden from his near-omniscient view. What he didn't know was if that particular helicopter was the one with his men.

His phone rang. A good portent, he decided, as he spoke the command, "Answer." It was Massey. Moyer listened for a few moments. "No, stay in the area, but don't be obvious about it. I think we can track him from here. Once we have a position, do a flyover and then set down at the nearest airport. I'll have a car waiting for you." He hung up, leaned back in his thickly padded leather chair, and watched as the white truck pulled from the freeway to an off-ramp.

"It's just a matter of time now, dear," he said to the image on the screen. "Just a matter of time."

"We got a break," Tanner said, pulling a chair up next to Hobbs.

"So soon?" Hobbs was astonished.

"Hey, you're dealing with the CHP here. You work with the best, you get the best."

"Pride in one's work is a noble thing," Hobbs said dryly. "What have you got?"

"Two things. Our truck may have been seen in Fillmore by a motor unit. It was parked near a fast-food place. The officer hadn't received the APB yet. When he returned it was gone."

"And second?"

"One of our air units spotted a white truck with no logos on U.S. 101."

"So our duo travels south on the 14 until the 126, crosses east from there until they reach the 101. Which way was it going on the 101?"

"North, toward Santa Barbara." Tanner

leaned back in the chair with a self-satisfied look. "We've dispatched another helicopter to the area and assigned a few ground units."

"What happened to the other air unit?"

"Low on fuel. He had to pull off. He should pick up again after he refuels."

"So there's a limit to our luck. I have to hand it to you, Tanner. You guys are the best."

"Is that what you'll tell all your sheriff buddies?"

"No, I'll deny it at every turn, of course." Both men laughed. Hobbs rose from his seat. "I'm going to see if I can't get another helicopter ride, not that I like it. I want to be on the scene when the truck is located."

"Mind if I go along?"

"You'll have to clear that with your superiors," Hobbs said, "but it's fine with me. A little interagency cooperation can be a good thing."

"I've already cleared it," Tanner replied. "There's more to this case than there appears. I can feel it."

Hobbs nodded. Tanner was right. He could feel it too, and it was a cold, unsettling feeling.

Chapter 9

Tuesday, 3:40 P.M.

"This is your home?" Lisa said with surprise. She was staring out the window at a wide, expensive-looking two-story house. The home was nestled between the lushly landscaped front yard and the ocean behind. Nick had directed the large truck off the freeway and down several side streets until they were on a frontage road that ran parallel to the shore. More than a dozen other houses were on the street, forming a tiny, tidy seashore community. Each large home was set in a well-manicured yard. The single row of houses looked like a picture of a Maine fishing community lifted from a chamber of commerce brochure. Except these houses were much larger than the quaint cottages of the East Coast. "The trucking business must pay great."

"My parents bought it, remember?"

"I remember that you told me your father was an officer in the marines. He bought this house with what he made in the service?"

"That and his work after retirement. My dad made some money in the stock market. He had a knack for recognizing emerging companies. He started small, then kept at it. When he retired twenty-two years later, he had built up a little nest egg and bought this place."

"It's gorgeous," Lisa said. "And right on the beach too."

"It's a private beach," Nick explained. "There are fifteen houses in the association. The beach is limited to the members of the association."

"Which includes you?"

"Which includes me," Nick said. "Come on, I want you to see the rest of it."

"Will the truck be okay parked on the street here?"

"For a while. I can't leave it very long or the neighbors will start complaining. They're fussy about such things."

Nick slipped out of his seat and quickly made his way around to Lisa's door, which he opened with a flourish, offering his hand as an escort might offer his to a noble lady in a carriage. Lisa took his hand and slipped from her perch in the high cab to the step. Her body was stiff, and her ribs reminded her of her sensitive condition. Her face registered the discomfort. She took a deep breath, held it for a moment, then released it.

"Do you want me to carry you to the house?" Nick asked with a sympathetic smile.

"That would probably hurt more. Does the ibuprofen offer still stand?"

"Absolutely. It's the gentlemanly thing to do." Lisa let Nick help her down. Once on the ground, she stretched gingerly, keenly aware of every bruise and ache. Despite her stiffness, the short walk from the truck to the house felt good. She had spent the better part of the day in the cab of the truck, getting out only for lunch and her little excursion into the dilapidated church.

A large pair of double doors opened into a wide, hardwood-floored entrance hall. A few steps later she stood in the living room. Everything looked new — the white leather furniture, the glass top coffee and end tables, the charcoal gray carpet. The impression was more like a model home than a house in which someone regularly lived.

"Wow," Lisa said with genuine surprise. "You keep a clean house."

"Since my sister makes only the occasional visit, it's just me here, and I spend most of my time on the road. I also have a maid who comes in to vacuum and dust once a week. She would have been in yesterday."

"It's certainly better than the Pretty Penny Motel," Lisa said.

"You won't get any argument from me on that," Nick said as he crossed the living room. Cobalt blue drapes hung along the wall. Nick went to the left end of the curtains, found the drawstrings, and pulled the drapes back. The thick curtains parted to reveal a magnificent view of the ocean that surged and sparkled in the August sun. "Tada!" he pronounced holding his arms out and striking a dramatic pose.

"Amazing," Lisa uttered softly. The deep blue of the ocean, the azure sky, and the white rollers churning toward shore painted a striking picture. Sea gulls, their white and gray bodies in contrast to the crystalline sky, danced their waltz of flight, balancing in the wind, hovering over the water as if suspended by invisible strings. "It's beyond beautiful."

"It is, isn't it?"

"You actually leave this view to drive around the country in a truck? I would stay here forever, gazing out the window."

"Tempting as that is, I enjoy my work. There are other beautiful things in the world besides the ocean." His voice trailed off, and Lisa caught him staring at her. An unwanted sense of discomfort stirred in her. A second passed like an hour before Nick said, "Let me show you where you can rest. I bet you're exhausted."

Lisa nodded quickly. "I am. All I've done is sit in a truck, but I feel like I've been working all day."

"Riding can be tiring, especially after all you've gone through. Can you make it up the stairs all right?"

"I'm sore, not crippled," Lisa said more sourly than she meant. She quickly added, "But thank you for your concern."

"Shall we?" He motioned toward a set of stairs that separated the living room from the dining room.

Lisa followed him, trying not to show how much pain the climb was causing her. At the top of the stairs was a balcony that looked down on a portion of the lower floor. From it she could see the room she had just left as well as the dining room and a breakfast nook.

"The bedrooms are split," Nick said. He pointed to the left. "That's my room. It's the master bedroom. I'm going to put you in my sister's room, over here. It's a good size room with a hall bath right next to it. You should be comfortable."

The bedroom, like the rest of the house, was large and nicely decorated. Art hung from the walls, and a large bed made of oak dominated the room. A dresser was on the far wall, and a window looked out over the rear roof and the ocean. Lisa could imagine herself sitting in its cushioned window seat and gazing hour after hour at the captivating ocean.

She felt again the sadness that had plagued her since awaking that morning. This was not her home. Worse, she didn't know if she even had a home of her own. Surely she did, but where? What was it like? Did it have a beautiful view too, or was it sandwiched in the midst of identical looking cookie-cutter houses? A vague sensation of memory wafted through her subconscious, but it left as quickly as it had arrived. It took a moment for her to realize that Nick was still speaking.

"And over here is the closet." Nick opened a pair of louvered bifold doors. "Help yourself to any clothing you find in here. My sister is about your size, so everything should fit."

"She won't mind?"

"Not at all," Nick said quickly. "She is one of the kindest people on the planet. If she knew you were here and thought that I hadn't offered these things to you, she would fly out and kick me around the block — and this is a big block. So help yourself."

"Thank you."

"I'm not sure what she has in the dresser, but you can look. The same offer stands for anything else you find in there."

Lisa just nodded. The thought of wearing another woman's clothes made her uncomfortable, but she had little choice. At the moment, she was wearing her only possessions.

There was an awkward silence.

"If you need anything, there is a store nearby. We can get you whatever you want."

"I'm okay for now," Lisa said. Nick seemed embarrassed.

"Well," he said quickly. "The medicine cabinet has some pain relievers in it and whatever else my sister may have left. Use what you need."

"When was the last time your sister was here?"

Nick shrugged. "About six months ago I guess. Why?"

"Just wondering."

Turning toward the door, Nick said, "I have some calls to make, then I'm going to take a little nap." He thought for a moment, and then said, "There's not much food in the house. We'll go out for some dinner later . . . if you feel up to it, that is."

"That would be nice. I think I'll rest, then shower."

Nick nodded and left, closing the door behind him. Lisa found herself once again utterly alone.

"We're losing time," McCullers complained.

"It couldn't be helped," Massey countered sternly. "Landing a helicopter in the middle of the road might have been a little obvious, don't you think?"

McCullers ignored the snide remark. Massey was a royal pain, but he had been able to do what McCullers could not — find his target. That fact alone bothered him. He was supposed to be the professional, and here he was manacled to a man in a three-piece suit. If McCullers cared about what others thought — which he didn't — he would feel embarrassed. Instead all he felt was a growing annoyance with Massey and a rising anticipation of connecting with the woman once again. This time she wouldn't get off the hook so easily. She was going to die at his hands even if he had to take out an entire city block to do it.

"They will be there," Massey said. "They didn't spend that much time on the road only to stop briefly at some house."

What was it about Massey? McCullers wondered. At first, he had assumed the man was just a suit, a guy who lived his life between home and the office. Yet there was something different about him. He had secrets, deep secrets. Under that Brooks Brothers was a man who knew more than he was telling, had seen more than he was willing to share. McCullers was a good judge of character. He had to be. His life often depended upon it. Still, he couldn't get a read on the man who sat next to him in the rented Mercury. Although he would never admit it, McCullers found the man unsettling. Massey was too smart, too calm, too self-assured. Men like him could cut your throat before breakfast and forget that you ever existed by lunch.

"We may need this equipment," Massey said. "We don't know what we're going to face, and I want us to be prepared."

McCullers thought of the equipment in the backseat. All of it fit into two regular looking briefcases, and he had no idea what they contained. Massey played his cards close to his chest, never offering more information than necessary. McCullers didn't care. He knew everything he needed to know: the nature of his mission and the paycheck he would receive. Everything else was superfluous.

The briefcases had been waiting for them when they set down in Santa Barbara. Massey had explained that Moyer had arranged for the equipment. How Moyer had been able to have the cases available so quickly, McCullers couldn't even guess, but if anyone could arrange it, Moyer could. A man had been waiting too — a stiff-looking older man with silver hair. The helicopter had barely settled on the pad when the man approached, handed the rental keys to Massey, and took charge of the helicopter. They had spent less than five minutes at the Santa Barbara Municipal Airport.

"How much longer?" McCullers asked as he gazed out at the ocean. Massey was driving the car south at the precise speed limit. It was driving McCullers crazy.

"Ten minutes," he answered.

"Can't you drive faster? At this rate she'll die of old age. Where's the fun in that?"

"I don't want to draw attention."

"Cars are racing past us, Grandma. That makes us stand out. At least keep up with the flow of traffic."

"Speeding gives a police officer just cause

to stop us. That would slow us down all the more. Is that what you want?"

"I just want to get there."

"We're almost there. Just sit back and enjoy the view."

"You enjoy it," McCullers snapped. "I've got a job to do."

"*We* have a job to do," Massey corrected.

"I told you, I work alone."

"Not on this, you don't. You're stuck with me until our mission is accomplished. Then you can run off and do whatever it is you do."

Massey turned off the freeway, directed the car through an intersection, and continued down the frontage road that ran along the coastline. The two-lane street they were on was lightly traveled. A minivan drove slowly in front of them. McCullers could see the driver pointing to the ocean and jabbering. "Tourists," he said angrily. "Pull around that guy."

"Just sit back and take it easy."

Swearing, McCullers reached over and leaned on the horn. A loud, obnoxious tone bellowed from the front of the car.

With a motion so quick that it surprised McCullers, Massey knocked his hand away. "Are you nuts?"

The driver of the van looked in his rearview mirror and threw up an obscene gesture. McCullers swore again and returned the sign. The van came to a sudden stop, its tires squealing on the pavement. A second later, the driver was out of the vehicle and approaching the car.

"Great," Massey said, but McCullers didn't respond. He had something else on his mind. Popping loose his seat belt, he swung open the door and exited the car.

"You gotta problem, buddy?" the driver said. He was a tall, athletic man in his late twenties. He stood several inches taller than McCullers, and his fists were clenched. McCullers knew he was a hot-tempered fighter, a road-rage warrior. A woman's voice yelled, "Steve, Steve. Stop it. Don't fight."

"Yeah, I got a problem," McCullers said loudly. "You're my problem."

"Aw, poor baby," the man taunted. "What are you going to do —" The man's words were cut short.

McCullers had continued to approach as the man spoke, then, like a rattlesnake striking, McCullers landed a hard right to the man's mouth. Blood splattered as the man brought his hands up in a belated effort to ward off the blow. McCullers hit the man again, ignoring his victim's upraised hands.

He felt the bone in the back of the man's hand break as McCullers's knuckles found their mark. The man screamed, but McCullers wasn't done. He was having fun. This time he struck a vicious kick to the stomach that dropped the man to his knees.

"Stop it! Stop it!"

McCullers turned to see a thin woman running toward him, her face marred by the terror of seeing her husband pummeled.

"Stop. Please stop. You're killing him."

"That's the idea, lady," McCullers sneered. She charged him in a heroic effort to protect her husband, who lay in agony on the steaming hot asphalt. Raising her hands in tight fists, she tried to deliver a punch of her own. It was a wasted effort; McCullers easily blocked the punch and grabbed her arms, picked her up, and pushed her out of the way.

"Mommy!" a little girl screamed.

"Get back in the car," she cried, tears streaming down her cheeks.

McCullers took a step forward. All of his pent-up frustration and anger surfaced in a rush — the time spent in the hospital, the time confined to a car or helicopter with the annoying, self-righteous Massey. This was fun.

Instead of advancing, McCullers found himself in a sudden, unexpected retreat not of his own making. Someone had grabbed him by the collar, and he flew backward. Before he could turn to defend himself, he felt a sharp pain in his back. It took a second before he realized he had been thrown onto the front of the rental car.

Massey stepped in front of him, his eyes flashing with a burning, searing rage. McCullers stared in confusion. Massey's mouth was pulled tight, his shoulders set, and he wore an expression that could freeze water. McCullers had seen expressions of fear, terror, uncertainty, and anger, but nothing like what he was seeing now. For the first time in his life, he felt the chill of terror.

Raising a thick finger, Massey spoke loudly. "If you move, if you bat an eye or say a word, I'll tie you to the back of the car and drag you to death. Got it?"

McCullers was enraged. With a loud roar, he charged, swinging his large fist at his companion's head.

Again McCullers landed hard against the car. He straightened himself and charged, throwing punches. Massey easily deflected each attack. Screaming obscenities, McCullers renewed his futile attack with kicks and punches. Massey blocked and deflected them all, then threw a rocket-fast fist. McCullers saw it too late.

Everything went dark.

Chapter 10

Tuesday, 4:50 P.M.

She knew it was a dream, yet it frightened her. Her subconscious would allow neither logic to take control nor reason to assert itself. Instead a series of hot emotions poured through her mind, shaking her, drawing her, abducting her into a world of bizarre images, garish colors, and uncontrollable sensations.

Lisa was floating above the earth, circling it in a rapid, wild, and erratic orbit. Below her a blue, green, and white orb spun on its axis like a child's top, spinning, spinning. It wobbled as it plied its course through space. The sight was terrifying. All those countries, all those people would certainly die if the earth did not correct itself.

The detail she could see amazed her. At first the globe, then layers of clouds, land formations, cities, buildings, trains, buses, cars. And still her vision continued to focus. People were walking on the streets: A mother held the hand of a young girl; a father played catch with his son; a small group gathered in a circle, each holding and studying from a book. This last one struck an emotional chord with her.

The bitter cold of airless space began to seep into her body, passing through her skin as if it were but tissue paper. With each passing second, she became colder. The chill of absolute zero pressed in invasively until it froze the marrow of her bones. Still she lived, she saw, she experienced all that was around her.

Floating free of gravity, free from the confines of a spacesuit, Lisa watched as her planet bobbed and quivered as it streaked by the black, starry backdrop. She circled the world again, orbiting faster and faster. She was falling, dropping like a rocky meteor from some unknown region of space. As she spiraled closer and closer to the earth, she panicked, flailing and whipping her arms in a futile, frenetic motion.

Lisa screamed again, but this time no sound came from her mouth.

The dream changed as only dreams can do. Now she was in her car, her Lexus, plummeting to the ground. Dream or no dream, she was about to die. She knew that.

Light reflected off her rearview mirror, stabbing her sensitive eyes. Gazing into the bright beams, she struggled to make out the source of illumination. She saw two lights

— headlights — closing in on her at a frightening speed. The sound of a horn echoed through the car. It sounded again and again, bellowing like a rogue elephant.

Her heart pounded percussively, her head shrieked in pain. She was going to be rammed. She pressed the accelerator as if spinning wheels could propel her faster. She turned the wheel of the car. Nothing happened. And still the lights closed the distance between them. The lights. The horn. The spinning earth. The descent, the fall, the fear.

Then the sound of screeching metal erupted in her ears, and her head snapped back. Her car lurched forward and began to spin out of control. As she turned, she could see the headlights and the vehicle that had been pursuing her — a red Dodge Ram pickup truck. It spun out of her sight as she was rammed again. Now her car was flipping and spinning. Stars came into her view, the earth, the truck, then . . .

Lisa sat straight up in bed, sucking air. Perspiration trickled down her forehead. Her chest heaved as she gasped for sweet air.

"Oh, Lord," she prayed. The words seemed natural to her, normal to her speech. "Oh, Lord."

Looking around, she struggled to make sense of her location. She was sitting on a strange bed in a strange room in an unknown house. Swinging her legs over the edge of the mattress, Lisa sat, willing her thundering heart to calm and her shaking hands to still. Her mind raced. The dream was so real, so powerful, so dreadful.

Taking a deep breath, she held it for a few seconds, and then slowly released it. She repeated the act several times until her tripping heart settled into a normal beat. Her confusion began to clear up. The room was not strange. She remembered having walked into the room. She recalled lying down to nap. She remembered Nick and the motel room and the truck drive.

Glancing at the clock radio next to the bed she discovered that she had been asleep for only forty minutes. Something about the clock was familiar. It took only a moment for her to realize that she had seen one just like it at the Pretty Penny Motel. "How ironic," she said softly.

She paced the large bedroom. Turning to face the dresser, she saw her image cast back at her. She was a mess. Her black hair was tousled. Her white T-shirt was severely wrinkled. Only her jeans seemed unscathed by the long trip and the thrashing dream.

She felt dirty, soiled by the grimy motel room, worn by the long drive, sticky from terror-induced perspiration. Nick's offer of his sister's clothing came to mind. A shower and a change of clothing would make her feel better. In the closet she found a large selection of garments. *Nick's sister must be quite the clotheshorse,* Lisa thought. She selected a pair of striped Capri pants and checked the size by holding them up to her hips. It looked as if they would fit. She also found a white sleeveless cotton T-shirt. The size of the garment also seemed right. Nick had been correct; his sister and she were the same size. Seeing a terry cloth robe, she grabbed it. She found everything else she needed in the drawers of the dresser. She felt odd using another woman's clothing, but she was thankful that it was available.

Two minutes later she was in the hall bath, hot water streaming from the showerhead and caressing her body with its warm fingers. She washed her hair and scrubbed her body, focusing on every act as if she were performing surgery. Every act was meant to push away the raw emotions that lay beneath the surface. In her mind, she constructed a dam to hold back the pressure of fear and loss.

Tears began to pour from her eyes, and trying to ignore emotions that would not be denied attention, she scrubbed her bruised body hard. Sobs and ragged breathing joined her tears.

Setting the soap on the small shelf in the shower where she found it, Lisa leaned back against the cold tile, then slowly slipped down until she was sitting on the floor. As hot water rained on her head and shoulders, her eyes caught the motion of the water spiraling down the drain, disappearing from sight. It was a metaphor of her life: Everything she had known, everything she had been, was gone.

Lisa continued to weep, the sound of water pouring from the showerhead drowning out her deep sobs.

The painful throbbing in Carson McCullers's jaw prodded him back to consciousness. He rubbed his tongue mindlessly along the front row of his teeth. One tooth felt loose. He groaned aloud and raised a hand to rub his jaw. Blinking back the blurriness from his eyes, he took in his surroundings. He was in the front passenger seat of the rental car. Next to him was Massey, who was staring out the window and holding a device that reminded

McCullers of a policeman's radar gun. "What did you hit me with? It felt like a brick."

"You're an idiot." The anger in Massey's voice was unmistakable, his words rumbling like an earthquake. "I should have left you in the street for the police to deal with."

McCullers repositioned himself in the seat, stretching to relieve his stiff muscles. "It was a lucky punch. I didn't see it coming."

Massey, his face rock hard and his eyes like flint, redirected his attention to McCullers. "You do anything like that again, and I'll make sure that it's your last day on earth. Do you understand me?"

McCullers had been in more fights than he could remember and had never lost one, yet Massey had dropped him with one punch. Whoever he was, there would be a payback time. "They teach you to hit like that at Moyer Communications?"

"No," Massey said flatly. He turned his attention back out the window.

A part of McCullers, a very large part, wanted to reach over and strangle the man next to him, but he thought better of it. There was more to Massey than McCullers knew, and that made him cautious. Looking around, he saw that they were parked across the street from a line of upscale homes. Between the homes, he could catch glimpses of the ocean. He had no recollection of being driven there. "Where are we?" he asked.

"Fifteen minutes south of where you played your little game," Massey answered. "That house is the one we want. I found the truck half a block away."

"How do you know that's the house?"

Massey held up the device. "I've been listening."

"What's that?"

"It's a laser-based listening device. It lets me listen to what's going on in the house."

McCullers knew of such devices. The devices projected a laser beam on a windowpane and measured the vibrations made by sounds on the other side. They were extremely expensive. "What have you heard?"

"Not much of substance. The man started making calls, but I couldn't get much. He's a smart one. He turned on a radio and put it by the window. He may also be using a PNG — a portable noise generator. I could only make out a few words. He mentioned a woman."

"What man doesn't?" McCullers said. "What's this?" he asked, reaching for a small electronic instrument that looked like a walkie-talkie.

"It's a scanner," Massey answered. "It's set to pick up calls from cordless phones. I was hoping to listen in on any phone calls he made."

"Let me guess: He doesn't use a cordless phone."

"That's right."

"You must be very disappointed that your toy didn't work," McCullers said sarcastically. "Can we get this over with?"

"First things first," Massey replied. "I'm taking no chances. You see that unopened briefcase in the back?"

"Yeah, what about it?"

"Pull it up here. I want something out of it."

"Like what?"

"Just get it," Massey barked. "We don't have much time. The police could roll up any minute. That family is sure to file a report. I was able to convince the woman that her husband needed to be in a hospital and that the nearest one was back in Santa Barbara."

"Is that true?"

"I don't know. Maybe. I gave them a card."

"You gave them a business card?" McCullers was aghast. "And you said I was an idiot."

"It's a dummy card. Fake name and phone number. It will take them a little while to figure that out, but not long, so we have to move fast."

"You carry dummy business cards?"

"They have their advantages," he said. "Now open that case."

McCullers turned in the seat and brought the briefcase forward. Opening it, he saw two small, black plastic boxes. "What are these?" He reached for one.

"Don't touch them," Massey said loudly. "They're clean. I don't want your fingerprints on them. There are latex gloves in the other case."

"Okay, don't be so sensitive."

"Those are tracking devices. They work with the global positioning satellite system. We're going to put one on the big rig and one on the car in the garage if there is one, and I assume there is."

"What if he has two cars?"

"Then guess."

"Me. You want me to do this?"

"Yes. Place them underneath the vehicles. A magnet will hold them to the chassis. We'll be able to track them no matter where they go."

"Why don't we just whack them in the house and go home? Then we wouldn't have to play with all this James Bond stuff."

"It's a contingency plan, McCullers. Something isn't right here. Someone thwarted your attempts once, it could happen again."

"Not likely."

"Was it likely that I could knock you on your can?"

McCullers chose not to respond.

"You may be good at what you do, but you're overconfident. You assume nothing can go wrong. Well, things do go wrong. A smart man plans for those events."

"Okay, so I plant the tracking devices. Then what?"

"Then you come back to the car. Once I know that the traces have been planted, you can do what you were hired to do: kill the woman."

McCullers liked that. "What about the guy?"

"I don't care. Kill him, too, if you want, but don't underestimate him."

"I can handle him. He's probably just a good Samaritan or something."

Massey shot a hot glance at McCullers. "That's what I'm talking about, stupid. This guy is no good Samaritan. Do the math. He appears out of nowhere in an unmarked, untraceable truck. Just in time to rescue the damsel in distress. He brings her here. When he makes a phone call, he cranks up a noise generator. Who has a noise generator in their house? Not an accountant and certainly not a truck driver. This guy's a spook of some kind; I just don't know what kind."

"How many kinds are there?" McCullers asked, eager to get to work.

"The government kind, the foreign interest kind, the industrial spy kind, your kind. Get the picture?"

"Yeah, I get it. Can we go now?"

"Do the truck first, then break in through the side garage door. Here," he said handing him a small, soft plastic kit. McCullers recognized it as locksmith's pick set, used to open locks. "Be careful of alarms. If you're lucky he won't know you're there. If you're not lucky, you will have to earn your money the hard way."

"You make it sound like I'm going alone."

"You are. I'm going to pull down the street and wait for you to reappear."

"Why aren't you coming? You're not afraid, are you?"

Massey shook his head. "I am traceable to my boss; you're not. It's that simple. Here, take this." He pulled a pistol from beneath his suit coat. "In case you get caught."

"Well, now," McCullers said. "Isn't this a cutie? I prefer something with a little more weight —"

"And that is a little more obvious. This 'cutie' as you say is a nine-millimeter PT111 Millennium by Taurus. It's my personal weapon. It is unregistered so it can't be traced. Despite its size, it will get the job done." He reached in his pocket and removed a black oxide cylinder. "This is a noise suppressor that has been designed just for that gun. Use it. It's close to dinnertime around here, and the neighbor houses are sure to be filled with families. When you're done, come back to the car. Now get going. We've been here too long as it is."

After retrieving a pair of latex gloves and sticking them in his pocket, McCullers exited the car with the briefcase. First things first, he told himself. Position the tracking device. Kill the girl and the guy. Make his escape. Then he could plan how to get even with Massey for sucker-punching him. Massey was going to pay for that. For now, he would play along.

The clothing felt odd but good. Lisa was having trouble putting aside the thought that she was wearing another woman's clothes; a woman she had never met. Still she felt slightly refreshed. The nap had been helpful, at least until the unwanted dream had so frightened her. The long, private cry in the shower had been cathartic. Some of the emotional weight that had been pressing upon her had dissipated.

Standing at the top of the stairs, she took a deep breath and started down. She had been hearing familiar but indistinct sounds coming from the lower floor ever since she had left the shower. Nick was up to something, and it was time to find out what.

Each step down caused her some pain. Her body was stiff, and her injured foot throbbed. She would be glad to be on the flat surface of the first floor.

A sizzling sound radiated through the living room, as did a wonderful aroma. Lisa's stomach growled. Until then, she had not realized that she was hungry. She had eaten only a couple of bites of a breakfast sandwich at the McDonald's in Mojave and just a few more bites at lunch. She had no idea when she had last eaten before that. Judging by her stomach's reaction, it had been awhile.

Inhaling deeply, she sniffed the wonderful aroma. Eggs. Nick was cooking eggs. Passing through the spacious living room, she found the kitchen, a large room with oak cabinets and peach-colored tile. Standing before a six-burner stove was Nick. He was dressed in jeans and a T-shirt. It was clear from the adroitness of his movements that he was comfortable at a stove. *Rugged good looks and domestic,* Lisa thought. *Why isn't this guy married?*

"Good evening," Lisa said softly.

Nick jumped. "Whoa! You startled me."

"I'm sorry. I didn't mean to sneak up on you." She couldn't help smiling. "I thought you said you were out of food."

"I did," Nick said easily, "but then I got to thinking that I might be able to scrounge up a few things. I knew I had some eggs, but I also found some enchilada sauce, a few corn tortillas, and a can of refried beans. Voilà! Nick Blanchard's famous huevos rancheros. How do you like your eggs?"

Lisa paused.

"Oops," he said quickly. "That's probably not a good question."

"That's okay. Over easy, I think."

"Over easy it is." Nick turned back to the stove and spoke over his shoulder as he continued to cook. "I hope you don't mind eating here. If you'd rather go out, we can do that. I know a great little Italian place."

"Actually, this will be fine."

"I like to cook. It's different from anything else I do, and I don't get to do it enough. It's creative and productive. How was your nap?"

A shudder ran through Lisa, but she chose to keep the nightmare a secret. Talking about it would make no difference. "It was fine. I took a shower. I hope you don't mind."

"I don't mind at all. By the way, you look good in those clothes."

"Thanks. Lucky for me your sister and I are about the same size."

He turned to look at her. "Exactly the same size I would say."

"Can I help?" she offered.

"No. I've got a system going. But thanks for asking."

Lisa watched as Nick worked. Everything he needed was arranged neatly on the counter: plates, silverware, napkins, a large can of frijoles, a carton of eggs, a package of corn tortillas, and a can of enchilada sauce. It was well organized, everything in reach. He would have to look for nothing.

"It smells wonderful," she said.

"I think you'll like it. This is going to take a few more minutes, and then we can eat on the rear deck. Eggs by the ocean. Life doesn't get better than that. Feel free to look around."

"Okay. A little walk might be good for me. My muscles have stiffened up a little." The comment was an understatement.

"Well?" Massey asked impatiently.

"It was a cakewalk," McCullers answered as he situated himself in the front seat of the rental car. "The truck was the easiest. I put the device under the cab instead of the trailer, just in case they decide to take the rig and leave the rest behind."

Massey nodded his assent. "Good idea."

"I had a little trouble getting into the garage. The lock is a high-end Yale. It took me awhile to pick it."

"But you got in and put the tracer on the car?"

"Yeah, it's a Mitsubishi Gallant, silver. I put the device on the undercarriage."

"Good job."

"It's a waste of time," McCullers said, his enthusiasm waning as he sat with Massey a half-block away from the house. Massey had moved down the street, waited for McCullers to reemerge from the house, and then returned to pick him up. He then drove a quarter-mile down the boulevard, turned around, and parked on the side of the road. They could see the house, but Massey was sure they could not be seen by anyone inside

— not without coming out to the street.

"Be patient."

"You be patient. I was in striking distance when I was in the garage. I could have walked straight in, done the deed, and walked out."

"Too risky. It's important that we not be identified."

"You worry too much," McCullers said. "You should have just left this up to me."

"If I had, you'd still be trying to figure out how to get out of that Bakersfield hospital. We're here because of the work I've done. You didn't find them, I did."

"You know, Raymond, you have a big mouth. Someone ought to shut it for you."

Massey turned a steel-cold glance at him and watched as the arrogance washed from McCullers's face. "When this task is finished, I'll give you the opportunity to try. Until then, we'll do this the right way — which happens to be *my* way. You'll have your chance to finish the job as soon as it's dark enough."

"When will that be?"

"When I say it is and not a minute before. I figure an hour."

"Anything can happen in an hour."

"That's why we've taken precautions. Now sit back and relax. Your moment will be here soon enough."

Chapter 11

Tuesday, 5:15 P.M.

"It sure looks like our truck," Bill Hobbs said. He took a sip of 7UP from a can. His stomach was still unsettled from the helicopter flight from Mojave to Ventura. He and Tanner were in the small conference room of the Ventura office of the California Highway Patrol. Hobbs had already checked in with local law enforcement to identify himself and his mission. Since the CHP was a state organization and since Tanner was with him, Hobbs had set up shop in the CHP administrative center on Valentine Road.

"Best we can tell, anyway," Tanner said. They were studying a video taken by a highway patrol helicopter. "The pilot did another flyby, and the truck had been moved to the end of the block."

"Makes sense," Hobbs said. "The street isn't very wide, and I don't imagine the neighbors would like looking out their front window and seeing the broadside of a tractor-trailer rig. It's a good picture."

"It could have been better, but he didn't

want to fly too low. That might alert the people we're looking for."

"A wise decision," Hobbs agreed. Then, using the remote control he held in his hand, he rewound the tape and paused it on the street scene. The image came to a stop. Hobbs could see the truck parked along the curb. "I count fifteen houses."

"And all right on the beach. Must be nice."

"We're lucky he parked in front of the houses for a while. That limits our choices. I'd hate to have to go door to door trying to find someone."

"We still don't know which house," Tanner commented. "Assuming he parked in front of his own home, we're still looking at three possible houses. It's not like he pulled into the driveway."

"That would have been nice. You're right, of course. We're close, but not close enough. How do we pick the right house?"

"That's not our only problem," Tanner said. "The biggest crime we have is leaving the scene of an accident. I don't think we can get a search warrant on that, especially if we don't know the exact address."

Tanner was right. Leaving the scene of an accident was a serious matter, but hardly deserved a forced entrance. There was also the matter of the untraceable VIN and license plate numbers, but that too seemed a little thin to obtain a search warrant. "Can you get me the addresses of these five houses?" Hobbs pointed at the screen, making a circular motion with his index finger. "We can check ownership through the county. Maybe we'll see the name Nick Blanchard."

"Unless he's renting," Tanner said.

"You're starting to depress me with all this negative talk," Hobbs joked. "If we're lucky, we'll at least know which door to go knocking on. If that doesn't pan out, then we may have to stake out the area for a while. Maybe we'll catch a neighbor coming home. We could show the pictures we got from the motel video."

"I'll get on it," Tanner said. "It should only take a few minutes to make the call. My guess is that the name won't show up."

Hobbs knew that Tanner would be right.

Aside from its size and location on the beach, Nick's house was everything Lisa expected it to be. There was a hint of luxury, but in a modest way. Everything looked new, and that struck Lisa as odd. The furniture seemed unused, the art on the walls looked fresh from the studio, and the carpet bore no marks of wear or stains. It was as if he had bought the house last week and had everything delivered over the weekend.

That didn't make sense. If she understood correctly, Nick and his family had lived here for some years before his parents passed away and his sister had moved. Yet the house looked unlived in.

"Ready to eat?" Nick asked as she approached the kitchen again.

Her stomach growled. The food smelled delicious. "Yes, I'm actually hungry for the first time today."

"I hope you like it. There's something about huevos rancheros that hits the spot. If you'll open the back door, we'll eat outside. We can watch the tide come in."

"Sounds wonderful," Lisa said. A few minutes later they were seated on the redwood deck at the rear of the house. The sun, a disk of golden orange, was descending into the darkening sea and pulling the shadow of night behind it. Its waning light painted a ribbon of glittering ivory along the surface of the ocean. The air was heavily laced with the smell of brine. White and gray gulls flew lazily in the near-windless evening.

"I hope you don't mind water to drink," Nick said. "I really need to get to the store.

Living alone, I eat out all the time."

"At those fancy restaurants you took me to?" Lisa quipped.

He laughed. "If it weren't for bachelors like me, there would be no fast-food industry. We're a national treasure."

"I bet," she said, taking a bite of the dinner. The sauce was slightly sweet, the eggs hot, and the beans tangy. It tasted magnificent and she said so.

"Thanks. You should taste my peanut-butter-and-jelly sandwich. Julia Child has been pestering me for the recipe, but I won't give it up."

Lisa laughed lightly, then turned her attention back to the solacing scene before her. For the first time since awakening, she felt a measure of peace. "It's beautiful out here."

"I've never gotten used to it, and I hope I never do. After being on the road for several days I like to sit out here and read."

"You like to read?" Lisa said between bites. She was truly hungry, and her stomach was impatient for more food. "I didn't see any books lying around."

"I send them to my sister when I'm done. I'm not much of a collector. What about you? Do you think you like to read?"

She shrugged. "Perhaps. If I do, I'd probably keep them all."

"What makes you say that?"

"I don't know, just a gut feeling. That's all I have to go by — gut feelings."

"It's a start. Be patient with yourself."

"What's that?" Lisa asked, pointing behind Nick. A mark, like a giant, swelling scar, rose from the northern horizon and pushed its way up into the darkening sky. The trail, a long white stream, seemed to effervesce in the sky.

Nick turned and studied the streak. "Vandenberg," he said flatly. "Missile launch."

"Vandenberg?"

"Vandenberg Air Force Base," he explained. "It's north of Santa Barbara, just west of Lompoc. The air force runs missile tests there and also launches satellites into space."

Lisa's stomach knotted into a tight fist and her heart began to pound.

Nick was still staring at the unexpected light show and didn't notice. "The contrail will spread out pretty soon and make quite a display. The setting sun shines through the frozen fuel particles, making a rainbow effect. It's pretty. You'll like it."

When he pulled his chair around to better view the sight, he said, "What's the matter? You look sick."

She didn't speak.

"It's nothing to be afraid of," Nick said softly. "They send up a missile every now and then. People around here see them all the time."

His words were ringing like large brass bells warning of a pending crisis. *Missile. Rocket. Launch. Satellite. Vandenberg.* Undefined terror swirled in her like a hurricane. What was it about what she was seeing? About the words she had heard?

"Lisa?"

The matter was important, threatening, fearful, crucial, but none of the pieces fit together.

"Lisa, talk to me."

Something about the growing vapor trail, something about the launch, something about Vandenberg.

"Lisa, look at me. Look at me now." Nick grabbed her shoulders. "Come on, Lisa, look at me." She turned her gaze from the scar in the sky to his face. "That's a girl. It's all right. Do you hear me? It's all right. Nothing is going to hurt you."

"But —"

"It's going to be all right."

Hot tears flooded her eyes. Abysmal sorrow. Failure. "I've failed."

"What?" Nick asked with surprise. "What do you mean you failed?"

"I don't know. I just know that I failed."

"Failed at what?"

"I don't know!" she shouted. "I don't know!" She shot out of her seat.

"Okay, okay," he said, taking a step back. "Settle down. I'm just trying to help."

"I've failed," she repeated loudly. "I can feel it. I was supposed to do something, something important." Her tears were no longer tears of fear or apprehension but of anger.

"Lisa," he said in a low voice. "Whatever you should have done doesn't matter now. You're here and you're safe. We can figure the rest out later, but first you must be calm."

"I can't be calm," she shot back. "I can't."

Nick stepped forward and took her in his arms. At first she started to push away, but he pulled her back. "You're not alone, Lisa. I'm here." Despite the turbulence that raged within her, she felt herself soften in his arms. It felt good to be held, to know that she was not alone in whatever this was.

"I don't know what to think —"

"Don't think; just relax."

A small sob erupted from her lips.

"Let it go, Lisa. Get it out so that we can face this thing."

Another sob. Then another. As her tears grew hotter, her terror subsided. For the second time since entering Nick's home, Lisa poured out her pent-up emotions.

Lisa dissolved into the arms of a man she had known for less than a day, and he stood ramrod straight and as unmoving as a statue, letting her cry until she could cry no more. Then he said, "Let's go inside."

Gregory Moyer was too excited to sit in his plush office chair. Instead he stood before his desk watching on his computer monitor the rocket that carried his prize possession into outer space. A camera at Vandenberg followed the ascent of the rocket, keeping it in tight view. Moyer knew the optics that made such a detailed image were in themselves remarkable achievements and their details still top secret. But he didn't care about the camera work. He cared only for the payload that was on the front end of that rocket — a payload that would increase the already substantial flow of money into the coffers of Moyer Communications.

Strange times required innovative approaches to business. During the Cold War, defense-department dollars were as easy to garner as falling autumn leaves. But the steady cutbacks on military expenditures had made the once abundant dollars more difficult to get. The competition had grown more rigorous too. Several upstart companies piloted by young, aggressive techno-geniuses had threatened to supplant Moyer Communications's position in the defense community. New sources of income had to be found; new uses for technology created. That meant new partnerships had to be forged. Moyer now dealt with more than congressmen, senators, and the DOD; he had new clients, many of whom made their homes on foreign soil. It had not been part of his initial plan, but plans had to be changed — especially if money and power were involved.

"Go," he said, willing his might into the craft. "Go!"

The rocket continued its long climb, and each second of its ascent brought Moyer closer to success. Had anyone else been in the room, he would have seen a man completely composed, as if watching a simple news event. What the observer would not be able to see, however, was the churning apprehension that Moyer felt. At any instant a rubber ring could give way, a valve could open, or some other malfunction could force the rocket off its course, necessitating that some nondescript little man in a room at Vandenberg Air Force Base push a button to abort the mission. The rocket would then explode into a million useless pieces and Moyer's one-billion-dollar satellite would rain to the earth in fiery sparks. Such things happened more often than most people knew. There had been sufficient problems with the Titan 4 series of rockets for Moyer to insist that a Boeing Delta II be used to launch his prize. Still, there were no guarantees. Something could go wrong.

He feared that possibility — and he feared that woman on the run. That thought pulled his attention away from the launch. Three keystrokes later, he issued a command to the satellite that had so effectively located Blanchard's truck. Bernard Cox, the young engineer who had found the truck, had transferred basic control to Moyer's terminal. Moyer couldn't access the sophisticated recognition software, but he could direct the satellite's line of sight and its zoom. He could also lock its tracking computer on Raymond Massey's car, which now came into view. Moyer could now not only speak with Massey by cell phone, but he could also watch his every move.

To Moyer, directing the satellite was like

a video game he had seen some of the younger engineers play on their breaks. Except this was real. And the image of a man exiting the car was not the creation of a game designer. He was flesh and blood, McCullers, the killer Massey had hired. Moyer hoped that the man would work out — for his sake and for Massey's. Failure could not be tolerated.

Massey watched McCullers walk casually down the street and disappear between two houses. Even though the killer was now out of sight, Massey knew exactly what the man was doing: entering through the side garage door to gain entrance to the house. With any luck, and assuming that McCullers didn't mess up again, the two occupants would soon be dead with gunshot wounds to the head, and then the two men could be on their way — Massey to his job at Moyer Communications and McCullers to whatever rock he lived under.

McCullers was the variable in the formula. When Massey had hired him to find and to kill the woman, he had been led to believe that the man was the best in the country. He now had serious doubts about that assessment. Ideally, Massey knew, he should have gone with McCullers, helped in the killing, made sure that no mistakes were made. But that would be tempting fate. One oversight and a fingerprint or a track from his shoe could be left, or some piece of DNA evidence could be traced to him. And if it were traced to him, it would be traced to Moyer. He had to trust McCullers, even against his better judgment. At least the man had a taste for the work.

Massey took in a deep, impatient breath, drummed his fingers on the steering wheel of the car, and waited. This would be a long ten minutes.

Detective Hobbs studied the paper before him and frowned. It was a list of the homeowners in the area where they believed the runaway driver and trucker were staying. He had hoped to find the name of Nick Blanchard on the list, but he wasn't surprised at its absence. He had already encountered a bogus license-plate number, an unassigned vehicle identification number, and had found no information whatsoever on a man named Nick Blanchard. It was all starting to sound like some kind of a spy movie.

"A whole lot of nothing," Hobbs said to Tanner. Both men were back in the conference room, studying the results of the search. The county tax records had listed the owners of each house, but the information was useless.

"I guess the guy is renting," Tanner commented.

"I doubt it," Hobbs said. "Too many coincidences. Something is going on here, and I haven't the foggiest idea what."

"At least you're not alone," Tanner commiserated.

"My guess is that it's one of these three houses," Hobbs said, pointing at the image printed from the helicopter video. "I can't be sure, but my guess is that he parked in front of his own house, then moved the truck. But which house?"

"There's no way to know without knocking on the door."

"You're right. Let's go pay a visit. Maybe we'll get lucky."

"Have a seat," Nick said. "I'll get you a tissue."

Lisa let him lead her to the couch. He still had his arm around her. She was glad; the last thing she wanted was to be alone. Nick had let her weep until the poison of her fear had subsided. The gentle crashing of waves on the private beach and the sharp but pleasant cries of sea gulls overhead had eventually replaced the sounds of her sobs.

"Thank you," she said as she lowered herself to the sofa. "I'm such a bother."

"Nonsense," he answered quickly. "Let me run into the bedroom. I have some Kleenex in there. You just relax."

"Okay." Lisa leaned back and rested her head on the couch, closing her eyes. She took in a ragged breath, and a new anger rose within her, this time directed at herself for losing control. It seemed so wrong, so out of character for her.

The sound of the ocean seeped into the living room. Nick must have left the back door open. The tangy air smelled good. Life always goes on, no matter what. Hers would too. It might be different; it might be missing a few decades, but she was alive. She had survived a horrible auto accident, and now she was seated in a nice home, listening to the orchestra of creation.

She was not defeated. Not by a long shot. She would figure things out, make things right. And she was sure of one thing: She was not alone.

The last thought made her pause. Was she not alone because Nick was there to help? No . . . Her subconscious was sending a message. Someone else was there to help her? But who?

"Isn't this sweet?" a strange and heavy voice said.

Instantly Lisa sat straight up and snapped her eyes open. A man with a thick build stood before her. First she noticed his evil grin, then she noticed the handgun he held on her. The gun itself was small but made large by the silencer on the end of the barrel. *A PT111,* Lisa thought. *How did I know that?*

"Who are you?" she asked forcefully.

"I've been looking for you, lady," the man said. His voice was gruff but carried a measure of enjoyment. There was no nervousness, no fear, no anxiety, just pure pleasure. "You've caused me a lot of trouble and tarnished my image. I don't appreciate that." He approached her. Lisa started to stand, but he ordered her to sit, and as he did he pushed the gun forward.

"I don't know what you mean," Lisa objected. *Buy time. Make him talk.* She wondered where Nick was.

"You don't recall us meeting before?" the man asked with a wicked chuckle. "I thought I had left quite an impression."

"My memory isn't what it used to be." Her heart was pounding so hard she was sure the man could hear it.

"You might say we bumped into each other last night."

Him! "You're the one who tried to run me off the road!" Her fear was now laced with anger.

"If you had had the good sense to die then, I could have been spared all this trouble."

"But why? Why are you trying to kill me?"

"No stalling, lady. This ain't some movie where the bad guy explains everything. It's real life — or in your case, real death."

"That's it? You're just going to walk in and kill me?" *Where is Nick?*

"That's what I do. That's my job." He raised the gun higher, pointing it at her head. The little gun seemed to grow in size, becoming more ominous, more frightening.

Seconds stretched longer as the man stepped closer, his gun unwaveringly extended. He was within arm's distance. Lisa could see down the barrel of the gun. Her mind raced with possibilities for action, but none made sense. He could squeeze the trigger faster than she could duck. What she needed was —

Nick came flying out of the hall that led to his bedroom with a scream. The man spun on his heels, turning the gun on Nick. He squeezed off a shot, the bullet making a *ftzzz* sound. Lisa was on her feet a split second later. In a single fluid motion she hit the gunman's hand, knocking it up. She had hoped to knock the weapon free, but failed. The second round was fired into the ceiling.

The force of Nick's body slammed into the stranger, knocking him backward but not off his feet. The blow had been powerful enough to stun the attacker for a moment. Nick, who had hit the man headfirst, tumbled facedown to the floor.

Lisa didn't wait to see what would happen next. Without thought she charged the attacker.

"Lisa, no!" Nick shouted, but she was acting on instinct. No more than five steps separated her from the man with the gun. He brought his arm up and around to bear on her. Lisa dropped, letting her momentum carry her forward. She hit him just below the left knee as she heard the muffled *ftzzz* of another shot.

As she landed prone on the floor, the man twisted and fell, landing hard on her back. The pain was enormous. Her already battered body screamed in torment as the heavy gunman fell on her. He rolled off, and Lisa turned her head just in time to see the man on all fours, the gun still in his hand.

Nick was back on his feet and plowing forward. The gunman quickly raised the weapon and fired. A splatter of blood filled the air and Nick screamed, tumbling forward. Lisa rolled on her back as the assassin lumbered to his feet. He hopped on one leg while holding the other, the one she had hit, a few inches off the floor. Lisa struck again. This time she kicked at the man's good leg, striking him hard in the ankle. Her thick-soled Nike shoes dug into his flesh. She felt his foot slide to the side, and the man fell again.

He began screaming obscenities, but she took no time to notice. Despite the searing hot pain that ignited every nerve, she struggled to her feet. The man started to raise the gun, but Lisa was kicking again, using all her weight. Her fury was fueled by the knowledge that he had tried to kill her once and was now trying again. Raising her right foot as high as she felt she had time, she thrust her leg forward. The obscenities stopped when her shoe caught the man on the bridge of the nose. She heard a snap followed by a scream of pain. *Don't stop until you're sure you're safe,* a voice said in her mind. She didn't recognize the voice, but she recognized the truth of the statement. How many women had been harmed because they didn't seize the opportunity to strike?

She kicked again and again. One blow impacted the gunman's hand, sending the weapon bouncing across the carpeted floor. Another landed on the man's upheld arm. Still another caught him on the side of the head. The screams stopped. Lisa kept kicking. Tears of fury flowed from her eyes.

The man stopped moving.

"That's enough!" Nick said. "Help me, quick."

His words snapped her attention back to him. She turned to face Nick, who was seated on the floor. Blood oozed from his left arm. "You've been hit."

"I think it just grazed me, but it's bleeding pretty good. At least I'm not him. Remind me to never make you mad."

She looked back at the unconscious attacker. He groaned softly and rocked from side to side. Lisa had no idea how she had known what to do.

"Come on, Lisa," Nick said. "He's going to wake up and be very unhappy. Get the gun and let's get out of here."

"Let's just tie him up," she suggested.

"No," Nick responded forcibly. "He may not be alone. We can't wait around for any pals he may have to come looking for him. Now get the gun and help me up. I think I busted my knee when I fell."

Lisa raced to the weapon, then, despite

her own piercing pain, helped Nick to his feet. He hobbled, unable to put his full weight on his right leg.

"Let's go," he said. "Into the garage."

"But the truck is down the street and —"

"I have a car in the garage. We'll take it. You're going to have to drive."

Lisa nodded and moved to the door that joined the garage with the house. As she took hold of the doorknob it occurred to her that the attacker must have come in this way. Swinging the door open, she stepped through, the gun aimed before her. Her eyes swept the wide-open space of the garage, the gun in her hand aiming everywhere her eyes looked. She saw a silver Gallant parked in the middle of the floor.

"Get in the car," Nick said loudly.

"No," she replied. "You get in first. I have to open the garage door."

"You can open it from inside the car. There's a remote control on the visor."

Lisa heard a loud moan behind them. A hot stream of cursing followed the guttural groan. The attacker had come to. Lisa stepped aside to let Nick pass through the doorway and then turned to shut the door. Out of the corner of her eye she saw the assassin's bulk charging at her. Like Nick, he was limping badly, but he still came forward like a locomotive. "Move!" Lisa shouted. Nick hobbled out of the way, and Lisa slammed the door hard against the jamb. The house shook with the force of it. Then it shook again as the attacker hit the door. Lisa reached for the lock before she realized her mistake. The lock was on the other side of the door. He could lock her out, but she could not lock him in.

Leaning against the door with all her weight, she struggled to keep the man at bay. There was no way, she knew, that she would make it to the car, open the door, get inside, start the engine, and back out of the garage. Pain rifled through her once again as the large man threw his weight into the door. The jamb vibrated with the impact. She felt like she was holding back a charging buffalo.

"Hold on," Nick shouted as he staggered back to her.

"I can't hold him any longer," Lisa lamented.

"Give me the gun and hold him for a couple more seconds."

She released the weapon, and Nick limped back to the passenger side of the car, opened the door, got in and then leaned out, pointing the pistol at Lisa's position.

"Now!" he shouted.

Lisa scampered away from the door and into the car as fast as she could. "The keys!" she screamed frantically.

"In the ignition. I left them in the ignition."

The door to the garage exploded open, and the attacker bowled his way in. The doorjamb next to him exploded into splinters as Nick fired a round at the man's head. Instinctively, the man ducked back into the house. Nick fired another shot as Lisa started the car. The engine roared to life.

They were still trapped inside. "The visor. The door opener is on the visor. Left button." Lisa pressed it and the door behind her began its slow rise.

"Come on, come on," Lisa encouraged the door.

"I should have killed that guy when I had a chance," Nick said through clenched teeth.

Inch by agonizing inch the door rose in slow motion. Nick closed his door, resting the gun in his lap. A loud, fierce shriek pierced the darkening evening. Just as Lisa slammed the gearshift into reverse, the attacker reemerged from the house, careening toward the car. The tires of the car screeched as she mashed the accelerator to the floorboard.

There was a thud. The attacker landed on the hood of the car, digging his fingers into the gap between the windshield and the sheet metal hood. There was no doubt that this madman would hold on until he figured a way to get inside. It was irrational, but the expression on his face said that reason had left him a long time ago.

Nick rolled down his window and stuck the gun out, trying to bring the barrel to bear on the madman clinging to the hood.

"No, wait," Lisa said. As the car plunged into the street, she cranked the wheel hard to the left, sending the front of the car sliding to the right. The man's inertia caused him to slip along the hood, his fingers failing and his nails leaving long scratches in the paint. He flew sideways into the street. The jerk also caused Nick to lose his grip on the pistol.

"The gun!" Nick shouted as it slipped from his fingers.

Slamming the gearshift into drive, Lisa again pressed the accelerator to the floor. Looking in the rearview mirror, she saw the attacker rise to his feet and wave an angry fist at them. Then she saw something that caused her thundering heart to race all the more. A dark sedan pulled up as the would-be killer scrambled for the small pistol that had slipped from Nick's fingers and lay on the asphalt.

"You were right," Lisa said. "He wasn't alone."

"I hope you are as good behind the wheel as you were in the house. Where did you learn that stuff?"

"I have no idea."

Chapter 12

Tuesday, 6:30 P.M.

Massey pulled from the curb and quickly drove to where the agitated McCullers stood shaking his fist in the air and yelling obscenities. McCullers was in the middle of the street, forcing Massey to pull into the oncoming lane and stop so the passenger door was next to McCullers. He lowered the automatic window.

"Get in!" he shouted. "Get in, now!" McCullers complied, grimacing as he did. He was in pain.

"I'll kill those —"

"That's what you were supposed to do when you went in there," Massey said as he pulled off slowly down the street. "It was a three-minute job: in, kill, leave. That's it. But you screwed that up."

"Hey, you weren't there. You don't know what happened." McCullers shouted back. "They jumped me. But I'll get them, and I'll make them pay in the most painful way."

"You weren't hired to be a sadist. You were hired to kill a woman. That should have been done in the simplest, most direct way. But you can't do things that way. You have to have fun in the process. Well, your fun is driving away, and our work is not yet finished." The houses faded behind them and gave way to a short, isolated stretch of road. Massey remembered it from the drive in.

"Shut up and step on it, they're getting away."

Massey pulled to the side and stopped the car.

"Hey, what are you doing? Didn't you hear me? They're getting away."

Massey took a deep breath, then sighed loudly. He backhanded McCullers across the face, striking his already swollen nose. The man screamed in pain, then pulled his right hand back, ready to bury his fist in Massey's face. He stopped when he felt the cold barrel of a gun pressed hard into his cheek. "What . . . what are you doing?" he shouted.

"Give me the gun and get out."

"What? What do you mean?"

"Give me the gun and get out. Now!" Massey's voice had turned hard and cold. He cocked the hammer back on the nine millimeter.

"You gave me your gun," McCullers said with confusion.

"That's the difference between us, McCullers, aside from my being a rational man and your being a buffoon, I mean. You assume everything will go your way and that your plans will never fail. I assume just the opposite. Consequently, I'm prepared. Do you think I would give you my only gun and leave myself unarmed, especially after our little incident with the family in the van? I imagine you have a bone to pick with me over that."

"You sucker-punched me."

"Get out."

"Your boss ain't gonna like you letting the woman get away."

Massey pushed the gun another inch closer to McCullers's eye.

"Okay, okay, I'm getting out."

McCullers opened his door and slipped out. "We can talk about this."

The gun's report echoed down the street. Massey reholstered his weapon and then set the PT111 in the glove compartment. He sped away, the open door of the car slamming shut from the sudden acceleration. Glancing in the rearview mirror, he saw the still form of McCullers lying in a heap in the weeds that lined the road. For a brief moment, the image of the bullet impacting the center of the man's chest and yielding an ever-widening circle of blood flashed across his mind. It brought no remorse. It had been a long time since he had done anything like that. It almost felt good.

"Idiot," he said with disgust. A quarter-mile down the street, he pulled over again, reached into the backseat, and removed the yet unopened briefcase, the one in which the extra gun had been concealed. He removed a white plastic box with a four-inch-square screen in the middle. He switched on the electronic device. The green screen came to life. A series of buttons lined the left and right sides of the display. He entered some commands. A second later a map appeared on the monitor in yellow-green lines. A small triangle moved along one of the streets. The GPS tracking system was working perfectly. Because he'd had the foresight to order McCullers to plant the tracer on the car, he knew exactly where she was and what direction she was going.

"It's time we put an end to this nonsense," he said aloud as he pulled back onto the street and began his leisurely pursuit.

"Are they following?" Nick asked.

"No," Lisa answered softly. She looked in the mirror again. "You were right; he wasn't alone. A car pulled up to our friend right after we left. The man got in and started to follow. I thought they were going to chase us, but then he pulled off."

"Maybe the man is too injured to give chase." Nick leaned forward and rubbed his leg.

"Maybe." That couldn't be right. Something else was going on. Her subconscious screamed warnings, but she couldn't understand the message. She did, however, understand the intent. "How's the leg?"

"The pain has let up some, but it's swelling."

"And the arm?"

He opened his shirt and pulled it down to reveal a long gash just below the shoulder. Lisa suppressed a shudder.

"The bleeding has stopped. It just grazed me. I can't tell you how much it hurts."

"I'll take your word for it."

"How about you?" Nick asked

"I feel like I've been through the accident all over again. My side burns, my head hurts . . . everything hurts."

"I imagine we'll be feeling a lot more pain when the adrenaline stops."

"Let's talk about something else — like what do we do now?"

"Did you get a good look at the car or the driver?" Nick asked.

"It's too dark to see much. I didn't see the driver at all. All I saw of the car was that it was a dark sedan."

"That's not much help. That could describe several thousand cars in the area."

"Actually, I think we may be overlooking a bigger problem," Lisa said. Her mind was racing, analyzing. It was as if someone had thrown a switch in her brain, releasing a thousand watts of mental energy.

"I don't need any more bad news."

"It may be coming anyway," Lisa said. "How did they find us?"

Nick stared out the window. "I was wondering that myself. It's not like I hung a sign on the front door. And what did that guy want?"

"To kill me," Lisa said. She swallowed hard. Saying the words had been easy; hearing herself saying them was painful.

"But why?"

"Two attempts in less than twenty-four hours. I must have made someone mad. I'm so sorry to have gotten you involved."

"It was my own doing. We need to find a place to regroup. Maybe get some help."

"No police," Lisa said. "I don't know why, but my gut says that's a bad idea." Nick didn't object. "I need to get you to a hospital," she said.

"Not if you want to avoid the police," Nick replied. "All gunshot wounds have to be reported. One look at my arm, and some doctor or nurse will be picking up the phone."

"I could drop you off," she suggested. "That way —"

"I'm not leaving you alone," Nick stated flatly. "Not until this is over."

"I don't need a protector."

Nick laughed. "I think you do."

Lisa knew he was right. If it hadn't been for Nick's heroics, she would be dead on the floor of his living room. A thought struck her: "Your license-plate number. Could they have traced that? You left the number at the motel, didn't you?"

"Yes, but that wouldn't work," Nick explained. "I work out of my home, but the truck is registered to a different address. I'm a little paranoid about strangers knowing where I live."

"Then how did they find us?"

"Turn right up here," Nick said. "That will put us back on the 101. Let's go north. Stay in the right lane. We'll come to Highway 150 in a few miles. That will take us back into the San Ynez Mountains. There are a few small towns up there. If we're not being followed, we might find a place to hide out and get our thoughts together."

"Okay." Careful of her speed, Lisa drove the car north as Nick directed, glancing in the rearview mirror every few seconds. No one followed them. As she drove, she struggled to bring things into focus. Flapping in her overactive mind was her emotional response to the sight of the rocket launch at Vandenberg, the car crash, the enigmatic Nick, the assault she had just endured, her loss of memory, the ever-present sense of dread.

Highway 150 was an uneven, sinuous affair that demanded all her attention. Groves of oak trees stood sentinel along the road, and thick foliage covered the ground. Quaint houses dotted the hillsides. If she hadn't been running for her life, the scene would have been beautiful. Now it was foreboding. What lay behind the trees? Who was hidden in the bushes? What eyes watched as she drove along? What would happen next? Would she survive another encounter?

"Stop," Hobbs ordered suddenly. He and Tanner had signed out an unmarked highway patrol car and were driving down the frontage road that led to the short row of houses that lined the ocean. "I saw something. Back up."

"What did you see?"

"On the left, about ten yards back. I think it was a body." The evening had quickly metamorphosed into night, the sun finally dropping below the horizon. The only light available came from the car's headlights and the sparse street lamps that cast down an eerie, amber glow.

Tanner quickly pulled a tight U-turn and drove back. Hobbs lowered his window and stared at the passing road. A narrow, weed-filled planter strip separated the street from a chain-link fence. The fence in turn divided the road from the short slope that led up to the freeway.

"There," Hobbs said, pointing. "It's a body all right."

Tanner pulled the car to a stop. As Hobbs stepped from the vehicle, Tanner pulled a beacon from the car and set it on the roof. Pulsating splashes of red light filled the area. "I'll call for an ambulance."

"No need," Hobbs said. Using the car's spotlight, he had checked out the body. It was that of a middle-aged white male. The body was slumped against the weeds close to the fence. The man's eyes were open but no longer seeing. His shirt was stained a dark rust color. "He's dead. Place a call to dispatch and ask the locals to send out a homicide team."

After Tanner radioed in the report, he joined Hobbs, who stood staring down at the lifeless man. "You know . . ." he trailed off. "This is the guy. At least one of the guys who impersonated the cops back in Mojave." Hobbs stepped to the car and removed the folder he had been carrying throughout the investigation. Removing one of the photos that had been captured from the Pretty Penny Motel security video, he showed it to Tanner. "Does this look like the same guy to you?"

"Yes. He has the same build and same clothes. That's him, all right."

"With every step we take, this case gets all the more bizarre." Hobbs thought for a moment, then looked south down the street. They were a few hundred yards from the row of houses that had been their destination. "I need you to do something else for me."

"Name it."

"Get back on the radio and have the homicide boys come in from the north. Let's keep this quiet for now, keep the neighbors out of this. No sirens."

"You're thinking something happened at Blanchard's house?" Tanner stated.

"That's exactly what I'm thinking. Are there any latex gloves in the car?"

"We can look in the trunk. There's probably a first-aid kit in there. It would have gloves. What are you thinking?"

"The motel clerk said that one of the men who came to see him flashed a badge. I want to see if this guy has it on him."

"I'll pop the trunk," Tanner said and returned to the car. Hobbs followed.

It took only a few minutes for Hobbs to find and don the pale white gloves. Being careful not to move or destroy anything that might be considered evidence, he searched the fallen man's pockets. In the left rear pocket, he found and removed a wallet with a badge inside that read DETECTIVE, LOS ANGELES POLICE. There was also a number on the badge. Hobbs searched the wallet in more detail. "No police identification," he said. "Just a driver's license: Carson McCullers."

"McCullers?" Tanner said with surprise. "That's the same guy who was in the other accident. One of our men interviewed him in a Bakersfield hospital earlier today."

"Apparently, he gets around."

A Ventura County sheriff's patrol car rolled up on the scene. After Hobbs gave a quick explanation of who he was and what he was doing in Ventura County, he said, "I want to check something out down the street. I'm leaving the scene in your hands."

Hobbs and Tanner turned off the red police beacon and drove the last few hundred yards to the houses they had initially set out to see. "Drive by," Hobbs said. "I want to reconnoiter the area first."

Tanner complied, driving slowly, but not so slowly as to draw attention. "One house has its garage door open," Tanner said.

"Better than that," Hobbs said. "The garage light is on, and I can see the door that leads into the house. It's open too."

"You think they're in there?"

"Not anymore. Take us back. I'm going in."

"It's really not our jurisdiction," Tanner reminded the detective.

"I know that, but someone may be hurt. Something happened here. Something violent."

"Off," Moyer said coldly, and the automated phone went dead. Pacing around his office, he considered what he had just heard. Massey had reported in and, using cryptic phrases, brought him up to speed. Moyer replayed the brief conversation in his mind.

"I had to downsize the project," Massey had said easily, like any executive conversing about business over a cell phone. In previous conversations he had been freer in his discussions, knowing that the call was encrypted. The fact that he was now using euphemisms told Moyer a great deal. Massey was afraid that they had been compromised. By the stranger who was linked to the woman? "The on-site man just wasn't meeting expectations, so I had to let him go."

"I understand," Moyer said, knowing that McCullers was no longer involved. He had seen the whole thing through the unblinking eye of his spy satellite. "I saw the memo. It was picture perfect." Moyer was certain that Massey knew his every move was being watched electronically.

"I see," Massey answered, relaying his understanding.

"That's good," Moyer replied. McCullers was out of the way permanently, and Moyer felt no remorse. That had always been an option. Bringing in outsiders had inherent risks. Had McCullers shown any leanings toward blackmail, he would have been disposed of quickly. Even trained killers could be murdered. Massey had exercised that option.

"I'm still looking for a new staff person and believe that I have found the right woman for the job. I'm driving out to meet her right now. Maybe we can close the contract this evening. I think we can."

He had the woman in his sights. That made Moyer smile. It was all just a matter of time now, and Massey would put an end to the nightmare. There would be bonuses for him. Huge bonuses. "Good," Moyer said. "I'm sure you'll make all the right decisions on this. Do you expect any ramifications from the dismissal?"

"None, sir. None at all."

"Wonderful. Take care and hurry back. We need you at the office." Massey would understand the implication. Moyer wanted this done and done now.

"Yes sir. I'll keep you posted."

"You do that. I'm willing to commit whatever resources are necessary to secure the proper help."

"I understand, sir, but I think I have all that I need."

Moyer knew that Massey did indeed understand.

Chapter 13

Tuesday, 7:10 P.M.

Hobbs's heart pounded in his chest. His mouth was dry, and his tongue felt like burlap. He was frightened. With his weapon drawn and aimed in front of him, he made his way slowly into the open garage. A sudden inrush of adrenaline coursed through his veins. His senses were on fire, as if someone had turned up the volume on his hearing and had fine-tuned his eyesight.

Tanner was behind him, his weapon at the ready. His movement was slow and determined. He heard every sound from outside. He listened for voices or the sound of a television that might indicate someone's presence.

Breaking the rules. That was what he was doing. He was out of his jurisdiction and entering a house for which he had no search warrant, a house he couldn't even be sure was the one Nick Blanchard and the mystery woman had been in, and proceeding with insufficient backup. All he had to go on was the video from the helicopter and his guess that Blanchard had parked his truck in front of the house he had now entered. For all Hobbs knew, he was entering the house of some hard-working citizen who just happened to live on the same street as the man Hobbs wanted to talk to and who had simply left the door to his garage open.

But there was a compelling reason to make entry into the house. A dead man, one who had pretended to be a police officer and who had showed an unusual interest in Blanchard and the woman, lay a couple of hundred yards away. Hobbs should have waited for backup from the local boys. That was protocol.

Something caught Hobbs's eye in the garage: skid marks, the kind a car lays down when accelerating from a still position. Someone had left the garage in a hurry. Bending down, Hobbs touched the rubber marks. A fine black powder clung to his fingertips. The tracks were fresh. He held up his fingers to Tanner, who nodded.

Glancing over the rest of the floor, Hobbs saw something else: small dark splatters on the concrete. He stepped over to them, stooped down, and studied the blotches: blood, freshly dropped to the porous cement. Someone had been hurt. This had to be the right house.

Moving stealthily forward, he paused at

the door that connected the garage with the home. With an expert's eye for detail, he immediately noticed that the doorknob was loose and that long, thin cracks ran vertically up the edge of the door. The door had been rammed or kicked — from the inside. Hobbs didn't have to look to know the doorjamb would bear the same stress fractures. The most convincing proof was found farther up the jamb: a bullet hole.

Not wanting to leave his own fingerprints on the doorknob, Hobbs reached down with his left hand and placed two fingers on the door's damaged edge while still holding his gun in his right. He nodded to Tanner, who returned the gesture, pointing his .357 at the door. If someone was waiting on the other side, Tanner was ready.

Hobbs stood motionless, listening. Nothing. He pulled the door back, thankful that it swung silently on its hinges.

His advance changed from slow and tentative to fast and forceful. He led the way, bursting into the empty living room, Tanner on his heels. They pushed through the hall, examining every room and opening every closet.

They found nothing. No gunman, no bodies.

Then, "Blood."

Tanner was crouching over several dark spots on the thick carpet. There were blood splatters and a dark smear. "It looks like a gunshot wound. Whoever was shot probably fell here."

"How can you tell?"

"Experience. I can't be sure without the proper lab work. The smear tells me that the victim fell to the ground and that his wound marked the rug. I wonder which one of them took the bullet?"

"No way of knowing," Tanner admitted.

"At least we have some evidence. Forensics may come up with more. We might be able to get a match with the blood found in the wrecked Lexus. If we do, then we'll know that it was the woman who was shot."

"What about the dead man? Could it be his blood?"

Hobbs shook his head. "I don't see how. He was shot square in the chest and wouldn't have been able to move more than a few feet, if that."

"This raises everything up a few notches. We have gunplay in the house and a dead man on the street. This is no longer a missing person–accident investigation. It just became murder."

"Swell," Tanner said sardonically.

"You had better let the locals know what we've found."

"Okay," Tanner said. "What are you going to do?"

"Talk to the neighbors. Maybe one of them can give us a description of the car that was parked in the garage. Surely someone has seen the car used. I doubt Blanchard drives his truck down to the local store to pick up milk."

"Someone needs to take a look at the truck, too. I'll do that just as soon as the other officers arrive."

"Good idea."

As the men left the house, Hobbs reminded himself that every minute lost was more time for his quarry to put distance between him and them.

"Do you have any money?" Lisa asked as she made yet another turn on 150.

"Some. Why?" Nick asked.

"There's a drugstore up ahead. I want to pick up something for your arm."

"It's okay. The bleeding has stopped."

"It needs to be cleaned," she said firmly. "You're going to need some pain relievers, too, both for the arm and the leg."

"I don't think we should stop," he said. His voice had weakened.

"I haven't seen anyone behind us since we left the house. I think we shook them."

"Maybe, but you don't know that," Nick protested.

"I know if that wound gets infected that we're going to have bigger problems than we have now. There would be no way to keep you out of the hospital. We'll be okay. It's a public place. I'll be fast."

Nick fell silent. He didn't like the plan, but he knew it was necessary. He shifted in his seat and pulled out his wallet with his uninjured arm. "Do you think a twenty will do?"

"It should."

Nick sighed. "Okay. But please be quick."

"I will. You figure out what our next move should be."

The shopping center was situated at the junction of Highways 150 and 33. Finding an open spot near the front door of the drugstore, Lisa parked the car. "It looks like a mom-and-pop shop," Nick said.

"Just as long as they have what we need." Without hesitation, she exited the car and walked quickly through an automated glass door.

The inside of the drugstore seemed unusually bright. The overhead fluorescent lights beamed their brilliance onto several rows of product shelves and off the highly polished linoleum floor. Coming from the early dark of evening, Lisa had to blink several times while her eyes adjusted to the glare.

"Good evening," a voice said, startling Lisa. A young woman with blond hair was standing behind a counter at the far end of the small store. "Can I help you find something?"

"No," Lisa said, watching the woman's response. The young lady stared at her for a moment as if she recognized her. *The bruises,* Lisa thought, remembering the bump on her head and the bluish cast of the skin on the side of her face. "Well, actually yes. I'm looking for disinfectant and pain relievers."

"Aisle two for the disinfectant; aisle three for the other. We have aspirin, ibuprofen in various names, and —"

"Ibuprofen will be fine," Lisa said, remembering that that was what Nick had offered her. He must prefer it. Moving as quickly as she could without being obvious, she walked down the aisles. She picked up a large bottle of pain relievers, some antiseptic spray, then as an afterthought a small first-aid kit. The gauze and bandages would be useful.

"That will be nineteen fifty-five," the woman behind the counter said when Lisa brought her purchases to the register. "Will there be anything else?"

"No, that will be —" Lisa stopped short as she looked up from the counter and past the young woman. Looking back at her was the single eye of a video camera. Her heart tripped, and her stomach plummeted.

"Ma'am? Are you all right?"

"Um, yes. I'm fine."

"You look like you've just seen a ghost."

There was no ghost, but the video camera terrified her. What was there about it? Maybe that someone could be watching her right now? Or could be recording her face and purchase, or tracking her through the store —

"Tracking," she whispered.

"Excuse me?" the woman said, bagging the items.

"Nothing," Lisa said quickly. "I was just thinking out loud."

"Oh, I do that all the time. My husband teases me about it."

"Thank you," Lisa said and quickly exited the shop.

She returned to the car, but before opening the driver's side door, she circled the auto twice.

"What was that all about?" Nick said. "Some sort of good-luck dance?"

"Have you seen anything? Any strange people? Strange cars?"

"No, and you had better believe that I've been looking."

"Why didn't they follow us?" Lisa blurted as she started the car.

"Maybe we hurt our attacker more than we realize. Maybe they were slow to get off the dime."

"I doubt it," Lisa said. She drove slowly, purposefully. "I need a dark spot, or at least a place that's out of view."

"Why?"

"They may not have chased us because they didn't have to. They may know where we are."

"What do you mean?" Nick asked.

"The attacker came into the house through the garage, past the car."

"So?"

"So, they wouldn't have to chase us if they knew where we were all the time."

Nick looked out the side window, digesting what Lisa had said. "A tracker? Of course! The best place to mount a tracking device would be in the trunk. But I doubt they had time for that. It would be too risky to install in the garage. That means something was attached to the outside of the car. Did you see anything?"

"No, but that means nothing. Could they have put it on the undercarriage?"

"How would you know that?"

"I don't *know* it. I *suspect* it. Now let's find a place off the road where I can check."

Lisa started the car and pulled away from the lot, directing the vehicle north through the heart of the small community of Ojai. As she reached the end of town she saw a sign that read SOULE GOLF COURSE. She pulled off the road and onto a long macadam driveway that was sheltered on both sides by tall, full oak trees. The spot seemed ideal. The driveway gave way to a small parking lot that fronted several buildings and a breakfast-lunch-only restaurant. After circling the near-empty lot once to see if she had been followed, she parked under a street lamp.

"I'll be right back," she said as she opened her door. To her surprise, Nick's door opened a moment later. Slowly he lowered himself to the ground on his side of the car. She wondered what any passersby might think if they saw two people painfully exit a car and lie down on the parking lot. It had to be a strange sight.

"It's too dark to see," Nick said, talking to Lisa as he lay on his back. Even at the unusual angle at which she was seeing him, she could tell that the effort had paled him. "Hang on a second." He sat up, stood, did something in the car, and then returned to his supine position. He had a flashlight in his hand. Flicking on the switch, Nick directed the light beam along the underbelly of the car. "I don't see anything."

"Let's try farther back," Lisa suggested. "He would want to place it as quickly as possible and in a position where it could be retrieved later."

Lisa crawled to the rear of the car. Every muscle she had protested painfully. She ignored the pain. God willing, there would be time to feel pain later. God willing? An odd sensation — pleasant warmth — swept through her. *Frightened beyond reason one moment,* Lisa thought, *comfy and peaceful the next. I need professional help.*

Meeting at the rear of the car, Lisa and Nick lay on their backs again, the flashlight illuminating the underside of the trunk. They could see the fuel tank, the springs, the struts, and a long, narrow black plastic box that hung to the metal straps that held the gas tank in place. Protruding from the box was a thin wire.

"Gotcha!" Lisa said. With no hesitation she reached up and tugged at the device. At first it resisted her efforts, but on the third tug the strong magnets yielded and the instrument came free in Lisa's hand. "It's a transmitter," Lisa said. "The wire is its antenna." They stood.

"So it transmits some kind of signal?"

"Maybe more. It may transmit our location through the GPS system."

"Global positioning satellite," Nick said. "So whoever planted this thing doesn't have to follow behind us, he just has to wait until we stop, read the coordinates on his end, and drive to the spot."

"Exactly."

"Give it to me," Nick said reaching forward. "I'll destroy the bugger."

"I have a better idea," Lisa said. She turned and faced the buildings. Parked curbside was a UPS truck. "Looks like someone is making late deliveries." Walking as fast as her stiff muscles would allow, Lisa made her way to the large brown truck, knelt down, and attached the device to the underside of the rear bumper. The magnets snapped the transmitter in place. Then she returned to the car. "Shall we?" she said, motioning to the vehicle.

"You are a devious woman," Nick said. "I think I may love you."

"Is that all it takes to win your heart?"

"Right now it is," Nick said with a smile and then eased back into the car. Lisa took her place behind the wheel. "The UPS station is in Ventura, about a half-hour from here. That should put some distance between the bad guys and us."

"I hope so," Lisa said. "Now let's find a place to get you cleaned up."

Massey watched unflinchingly as the Mitsubishi Gallant pulled from the driveway of the golf course. The woman was behind the wheel. That was a good sign. That meant that Blanchard was injured. He was, after all, a professional driver. At least McCullers, incompetent as he was, had achieved that much. Glancing down at the GPS tracker on the front seat, he noticed something was wrong. The indicator, which should have matched the movement of the Gallant, was fixed in the same position. It took less than a second for him to figure out the problem. They had found the tracking device and discarded it.

"Clever girl," he said softly as he restarted his car and pulled back onto the street. *I guess we have to do this the old-fashioned, low-tech way,* he said to himself. As he drove, keeping several car lengths back, he congratulated himself on his foresight. It was the very thing he had told the thick-headed McCullers before he killed him: "You assume everything will go your way, that your plans will never fail. I assume just the opposite. Consequently, I'm prepared."

Massey had never been more thankful for that philosophy than he was right then. Had he relied on the GPS device alone, he would have lost his prey, but by following as closely as he could without being seen, by being as stealthy as possible, he would not now be lost.

He was forced to acknowledge that luck had played a part in it too. He didn't like luck because it was subject to whimsy, there one moment, gone the next. He had learned to accept it when it came along, but never to rely upon it. Fortune smiled on the prepared and the disciplined.

Their finding of his device was a setback, but one with some positive spin to it. They now knew someone was on their trail, but they would have learned that in their confrontation with McCullers. Hopefully, he had not carried on a conversation with them revealing important details about Massey. Surely the woman knew who was after her, but she couldn't know him. The positive side was that they would relax a little, maybe even become careless, assuming that they had shaken whoever it was that was tailing them.

Chapter 14

Tuesday, 8:15 P.M.

"Not much in the truck," Tanner said. "One thing was odd though."

"Just one thing?" Hobbs asked. The two men were standing in front of Blanchard's house. A small crowd of onlookers stood a discreet distance away. This was an upscale area where gawking was considered undignified. A concerned interest was, however, allowed.

"I found a cell phone in the sleeper cab."

"That's not strange. A lot of people —"

"This one was dismantled. Someone had pulled the battery pack out of it. And before you ask, I plugged the battery back in place. It had almost a full charge on it, so they weren't just changing out the power source."

"You're thinking of the wrecked car, aren't you?"

"Exactly," Tanner said.

Hobbs was thinking about it too. The crumpled Lexus they had found on the roadside had had the hands-free cell phone torn out of its mountings. The onboard GPS system had also been deactivated. The phone in the truck had to be more than mere coincidence.

"So she tore the battery out of the cell phone," Hobbs said, speaking more to himself than to Tanner.

"Or he did," Tanner suggested.

Hobbs shook his head. "It has to be her. I imagine the phone is his."

"It is. I had the number traced. It's registered to a Nick Blanchard."

Hobbs rubbed his temples in confusion. "The more we learn, the deeper in darkness we plunge. We can find no record for a Nick Blanchard, but the cellular phone company has an account on him. How does that happen? I don't suppose you asked for his billing address, did you?"

"Sure did. Once I gave my badge number to the cell phone operator, I was able to get all kinds of information. Unfortunately none of it is worthwhile. The address is a post office box."

"Let's get a list of the calls he's made on the device. Let's also get one on the home phone. Maybe we can learn something useful that way."

"My gut tells me that we're going to run into a dead end with that."

"I think your gut is right, but we have to look. You never know what you're going to find. Besides, even dead-ends can teach us something."

"Like what?"

"Do you know what a doctor does when he can't find out what's wrong with his patient? He starts determining what the problem isn't. Bit by bit, he eliminates possibilities."

"Did you get anything from the neighbors?" Tanner asked.

"Yeah, but not much. Only one had seen the car that had been in the garage and recognized it as a gray or silver Mitsubishi Gallant. Lucky for us, the guy's daughter drives the same model."

"But no license number."

Hobbs shook his head. "I didn't expect one. I don't know the license number of my neighbor's car, and I'm a cop. Why should he? I asked for an APB. The sheriff's department has helicopters up, but finding a sedan after dark is going to be hard. I'm hoping that they're holed up somewhere and not running on the freeway."

"I assume you made calls to the local hospitals," Tanner said.

"Yes. They've been alerted to be on the lookout for a gunshot wound. That's the greatest possibility. I've also asked that the local pharmacies be polled. It's possible that they may try to pick up something to treat the wound themselves."

"Step by painfully slow step," Tanner opined.

"I hate to ask this again," Lisa began, "but how much money do you have?"

"I don't know," Nick said. "Seventy-five, maybe a hundred dollars. Thinking of doing a little shopping?" His voice was softer, breathier. Lisa was afraid that he was weakening.

"We need to find a safe place for you to rest," she said. "How's the arm?"

"It hurts. I think it may be bleeding again."

"I was afraid of that. You should have stayed in the car while I looked for the tracking device. I'm going to find a place to stop." They were driving up the winding Dennison grade that led to the expansive ranch area of Upper Ojai. "Maybe I should turn around."

"No," Nick said. "I think there's a small motel once we get to the top of the grade. It's a few miles farther down. At least there used to be one. I haven't been up here in a long time."

"Hang in there," Lisa said, her voice thick with concern.

"I'm not going anywhere," Nick said. "It's funny in a way. I rescue you from a highway in Mojave and take you to a motel to rest, and now you're returning the favor. People are going to start talking."

"Just as long as they don't start shooting."

Nick had been right. A small motel that looked as if it had been built in the fifties lay on the south side of the road three miles from the crest of the grade. Lisa pulled into the parking lot. Nick reached for the door.

"You stay put," Lisa commanded. "You don't need to be moving around any more than you have to, and that bloody shirt is sure to arouse suspicion."

"Okay, but take one of my credit cards. They'll want it for a deposit."

"No credit cards," Lisa said. "They're traceable." She exited the car and walked into the lobby.

The establishment was better than the Pretty Penny Motel she had stayed in the night before. Although the buildings were old, they were well maintained, the walls freshly painted, and the grounds well manicured. The parking lot was free of weeds and lit by several light standards. "At least

I'm moving up in the world," Lisa said to herself.

The lobby was filled with art deco furnishings and painted a pale flamingo pink. In contrast to the walls the ceiling was a startling white and the carpet an orange-brown. Lisa shuddered. Behind the counter was a woman she judged to be in her early fifties trying to look like she was in her late twenties. Her hair was teased and her eyes caked with blue eye shadow.

"May I help you?" the woman asked. Her voice was hoarse and scratchy, like an old phonograph record. She smiled briefly.

"I would like a room for the night, please," Lisa said.

The woman studied her, staring at her bruised face. Looking down, Lisa noticed her white cotton shirt was dirty from where she had lain on the golf course parking lot. "What happened to you?" the woman asked unabashedly.

"I had to crawl under my car. Not much fun." It was all Lisa planned to offer. If the woman asked any more questions, she would just leave.

"I hate that. Had my share of car trouble this year myself. No joy in that for a woman. Now my husband, well, he can fix anything. You want him to look at your car?"

"No. But thanks. I just need to clean up and rest. Do you have a room?"

"Yup," the woman said. "You got a credit card?"

"I've got cash," Lisa said.

"Good enough for me," the woman said. "One or two beds?"

"Two please."

The woman eyed Lisa again but said nothing. She pulled a piece of paper from under the counter and pushed it toward her. "Fill this out. I need a license number for your car and a ten-dollar deposit for the phone. The room is thirty-two bucks."

"That will be fine." Lisa counted out the money then looked at the form. It asked for a name. Lisa couldn't decide if the irony was funny or tragic. She wrote *Nick Blanchard* on the name line and then walked to the lobby window to read the license plate number of the car.

"I can't remember my plate number either," the woman said.

Lisa handed the registration back, leaving the other information blank. The woman picked up the money and the form without comment. Lisa tried not to show her relief. Things were working out and she prayed that they would continue to do so.

"Room 102," the woman said. "You can

park right in front of the door. Checkout time is noon tomorrow. Any calls, including local calls, are extra. The best restaurants are down in Ojai. I recommend the restaurant at the golf course for breakfast." The woman pushed a brass-colored key across the counter.

Lisa had had all of the golf course she wanted. "Thank you." She took the key and left the lobby.

Lisa moved the car to a space in front of the room and unlocked the door. She held the door as Nick hobbled in. Just before entering the room herself, she cast a glance back at the lobby. The clerk was staring back at her. "Just what we need, a busybody."

"What?" Nick asked. He had already made his way to the first bed and was sitting slump-shouldered on the edge.

"Nothing." Lisa stepped in, carrying the bag of items she had purchased at the drugstore. "Take your shirt off," she said as she locked the door behind her.

"But we've only just met," he joked. His face was pale in the incandescent light, and his voice lacked some of the vigor she had come to expect.

"Cute. Do you need help?"

"No," Nick replied. "I can get it. Just give

me a minute." He began to unbutton his shirt. The left sleeve was dark with blood but looked drier than the last time she had seen it. She was relieved to see no wetness that would indicate new bleeding. That relief changed when he removed the shirt. The skin just below the shoulder lay open in a wide gap. A wave of nausea washed over Lisa, but she willed it back. Rising, Nick walked the short distance to the sink and vanity that separated the bathroom from the closet. He studied the wound in the mirror. His face paled all the more.

"I think you had better sit down," Lisa said.

"Odd," Nick said. "I would think a wound like this would hurt more. It hurts plenty, but it looks like it should hurt much worse."

"You may be a little shocky," Lisa said. "Go back and sit on the bed."

"I need to clean this first. This thing is begging for an infection." He turned on the water and reached for a white washcloth that, along with a face towel, rested on a wire shelf mounted to the wall.

"Let me do that," Lisa said.

"Are you sure? This isn't pretty."

"I'll manage." The nausea returned. "We should rethink the hospital option again. I think I saw a sign for one back near the drugstore."

"In Ojai. I saw it too." Nick shook his head. "We can't do that. The bad guys are still out there. Hospitals would be the first place they would look."

"I don't think they would try anything in public."

"These days people shoot each other over parking spaces. I don't think a hospital will stop these guys."

"We can't run forever," Lisa said.

"So you're ready to go to the police now?"

The thought chilled Lisa. "No. But you can. I don't need to go with you." Lisa felt the water. It ran lukewarm, just as she wanted. Too cold or too hot would only heighten the pain that Nick was about to feel.

"I can be as stubborn as you. I'll go to the police if you do."

"That's not fair, Nick." Lisa dipped the washcloth in the warm flow until it was wet through and then gently placed it on Nick's wound. Nick didn't flinch, but he closed his eyes tight and inhaled deeply. "Painful?"

"I'll live." His voice was breathy and uncertain.

"It needs stitches and proper medical care."

"I've told you: Doctors are required to report all gunshot wounds. The bullet may have just grazed me —"

"It's more than a graze," Lisa interjected.

"Nonetheless, a doctor would recognize it for what it is."

The cloth turned pink then red as it absorbed blood from the wound. As gently as possible, Lisa cleaned the open gash, repeatedly rinsing the washcloth. "I could call for an ambulance and then just disappear into the night."

"No way, Lisa," Nick objected through clenched teeth. The cleansing was becoming more excruciating. "I'm not leaving you to the wolves. Fate has thrown us together. I intend to see it through."

"So you really are a white knight? Some would tell you that you need psychoanalysis."

"I'd be a case study, all right." He turned his shoulder to the mirror. "It's deeper than I thought, but not too bad."

Lisa shook her head. "Yeah, right. Not too bad." There was sarcasm in her voice. "I suppose you've seen worse."

"Actually, I have."

"Yeah? Where?" She stepped away for a moment to retrieve the first-aid kit and other items she had purchased.

"Vietnam. I was there for a few months before the troops were pulled out. Not a very fun party. In fact, it was no party at all."

"I don't imagine that it was." She pulled the plastic top from the spray antiseptic bottle. "This may sting a little, but it should ward off infection." She sprayed a fine mist on his arm. He jerked and drew in a noisy breath but said nothing. "Are you okay?"

He took another ragged breath. Tears of pain welled up in his eyes.

"I'm sorry," Lisa said softly. "I wish there was a better way."

"Antiseptics sting. That's not your fault, Lisa."

"That's not what I mean. If you hadn't stopped to help me, you wouldn't be here with a gaping wound in your arm. Instead, you'd be safe at home."

Nick turned and placed his hands on Lisa's shoulders. He pulled her a step closer. "Now you listen to me," he said softly, but firmly. "The word *if* is the most useless word in the English language. People think that by putting the word *if* in front of a sentence, then whatever *could* have been *would* have been. That's nonsense. If I hadn't stopped to pick you up, I might have driven five miles farther and been killed in an auto accident. How likely is that? I don't know. No one knows what might have been. Helping you may prove to be the best thing that has ever happened to me. I have no way of knowing. So no more *ifs*, okay?"

"Still, I feel that —"

"No," Nick said shaking his head. "Feelings get you into trouble. You saved my life today in the way that you handled that attacker. You didn't fight back because you felt like it; you fought back because you had to. You did what needed to be done. That's it, that's the bottom line. Feelings are blind, they have no intellect, and they just pop up to make us feel good or bad. It's our brains that will get us through this, not our emotions. Do you understand that?"

Lisa nodded. Nick's words were making sense.

"Things happen, Lisa. They just happen. The universe grinds its gears at its own speed, and we have to move with it. Fate has its own plan. We just do the best we are able."

That seemed wrong to Lisa. It was too mechanistic, too . . . she couldn't find the right word . . .

Nick released her and turned back to the mirror. "It all pans out in the end, Lisa. Everything balances in the end; the yin and the yang, the black and the white, the good and the bad. The universe is a pan balance, and we are just grains of sand in one of its pans."

"That's kind of New Age, isn't it?" Lisa said. She had turned back to the first-aid kit, removing a large gauze pad. She placed the dressing on the wound. "Here, hold this."

"Call it what you like, I believe it. Sooner or later, everything works out for the good."

The words struck Lisa hard, as if they had dislodged a piece of memory, a nugget of recollection from the rubble of her mind. "Everything works out for the good," she mumbled.

"That's my philosophy," Nick said.

Everything works out for the good. Lisa let the words swim around in her mind. Something familiar. Not quite right, but close. *Everything works out for the good. All good things* . . . No, that wasn't it. She closed her eyes, trying to pick through the remains of her memory. *All work is good?* No. *All good is work?* Still wrong. *All things work . . . All things together work . . . All things work together for the good of . . . the good of* . . . She was close. She knew it, could feel it. *All things work together for the good of those . . .* But the words were gone, replaced by churning frustration.

Opening her eyes, she found herself staring into the tiny medical kit. She picked up a roll of gauze and wrapped it around Nick's arm, securing the dressing in place. "That should do for now." She popped the top of the ibuprofen, removed the protective seal and the cotton, and poured out three tablets. "Here. You're a big guy; you can handle three tablets. They should take the edge off the pain. How's the leg?"

"Swollen a little, but better. I smacked it pretty hard. I won't be running any races soon."

"Let's pray you don't have to." Lisa took a plastic cup she found on the vanity, removed its sanitary wrapper, filled it with water, and offered it to Nick. He downed the pills in a single gulp. As an afterthought, Lisa took two of the pain relievers herself. "You go lie down. I'll clean up this mess. Leave your shirt off; I'll soak it in some water and see if I can't get the bloodstains out."

"Okay, doctor. I suppose I'll be getting a bill for this."

Lisa smiled at the small humor. "No, I owe you for three meals and two motel stays. Let's just call it even."

Nick walked to the bed closest to the door

and reclined on the covers. Lisa closed up the first-aid kit and replaced it and the other items in the pharmacy bag. Then she rinsed out the blood-impregnated washcloth, filled the sink with cold water, and submerged the cloth. Taking Nick's shirt, she placed it in the sink of water too. After an hour, she planned to remove the shirt and hang it in the bathroom to air dry. Poking her head in the lavatory, she saw a heat lamp mounted in the ceiling. That could be used to help dry the shirt, she decided.

By the time she had finished cleaning up, Nick was asleep, snoring softly. Lisa was exhausted too, but she refused to lie down. Her mind was cluttered with images of all that had happened that day, but especially the attack.

For the first time since stepping into the room, Lisa took in her surroundings. The room was old but quaint. An inexpensive dresser stood next to the wall opposite the beds. A television rested on its surface. There was no artwork on the cream-colored walls. The carpet was tan and of thin pile. A round table and two chairs were situated next to the window. Brown drapes hung over the opening. Lisa sat in one of the chairs and rested her head in her hands.

Her sadness was returning, but she was

tired of crying. She needed to think, to reason, to summon up her intellect.

Standing again, she began to pace in the small space between the beds and the opposite wall. She could take no more than five steps before turning around, but she paced anyway — back and forth, back and forth. The swell of emotion faded slightly with each step.

What next? she asked herself. *I can't stay here forever. I must do something, but what?*

Perspective. She decided that she needed perspective, a frame of reference. When she had awakened that morning, she had no idea where she was. She could recall neither the Pretty Penny Motel nor the town of Mojave in which it was located. Nor did she recall knowing the community of Fillmore where they had stopped for lunch and where she forced her way into the ramshackle church.

The church. The memory of it, dusty, broken down, long abandoned, brought warmth to her. It was a balm to her troubled spirit, a palliative to her mind. She had been alone in the building, yet she had felt welcome, as if she had belonged. It made no sense.

The familiar phrase she had struggled with a few moments ago came again to the forefront of her mind: "All things work together for the good . . ." She was no closer to completing it. It still lay just beyond the reach of her memory.

Perspective, she reminded herself. *I need a frame of reference. I don't know where I've been or even where I am.* The city and town names meant nothing to her. Santa Barbara, Fillmore, Ventura, Ojai, and the others she and Nick had passed through were just meaningless titles. Lisa began to feel that if she could gain the bigger picture of her surroundings, the details of her life might come back.

Turning her attention to the table, she saw an aged vinyl folder. She sat down again and opened it. Inside were a few sheets of letter-size paper, a small brochure about the motel, and a pamphlet about the history of the Ojai Valley. The pamphlet called Ojai "The Shangri-la of California." Another brochure, a map, was in the folder. With her finger, Lisa traced backward the path she and Nick had followed until she had found Highway 101. She remembered that and followed the red line that represented the highway until it ran off the page. Turning the paper over, Lisa found another map, one that covered all of southern California. She began the reverse trace again: The 101 to the 126 to Interstate 5 for a brief jog, then to the 14 back to Mojave. North of Mojave was a city named Bakersfield. Nick said he had been coming from Bakersfield when he found her.

Lisa stopped. Something seemed wrong. She studied the area where Nick's house was and compared it to Bakersfield. Nick had taken the long way around. If he had wanted to drive directly home from Bakersfield, he would have taken Interstate 5 to Highway 126 and skipped Mojave all together. Why didn't he do that? Maybe he didn't know about the more direct path, but she dismissed that thought as soon as it arose. He was a truck driver; it was his job to know the shortest and fastest routes.

"This is silly," she whispered to herself. *He must have had some reason to come through Mojave.* She studied the map some more, feeling a little better about knowing where she was. Still, it was small knowledge compared to all the other things about which she was ignorant.

Leaning back in the chair, Lisa tried to muster her thoughts. She let her eyes fall on Nick, watching his bare chest rise and fall in even rhythm. He had done so much for her, sacrificed for her; now he was wounded for her. And during the entire time, he had always been gentlemanly, direct, humorous, and encouraging. He deserved the rest he was receiving, she decided. Next to his bed was an end table with a radio alarm. The clock read 8:30. It seemed later — much later. But the clock revealed that it was only early evening and not —

Something about the clock seized her attention. She studied it for a moment and was sure she had seen the brand before. Then it hit her. There had been a radio alarm in Nick's sister's room, the room where she had napped and changed. That in itself was not unusual, but she now recalled that it was an identical match to the one in her room at the Pretty Penny Motel. That clock had been the only new thing in the room. It had struck her as odd that the clock would be new when everything else looked as if it been rescued from a swap meet.

Coincidence? That is what she had assumed when she first made the connection in Nick's sister's room. What else could it be? Lisa wondered. How many different brands of radio alarm clocks were there? It was not unreasonable to assume that Nick had purchased one like the one in the motel.

She was getting nowhere. All she wanted were some answers, and all she was getting were more questions. She paced again, letting her thoughts bounce around like billiard balls. A moment later she turned her attention to the dresser.

The dresser had six drawers; five were empty, and one held a Gideon Bible. Lisa stared at the book. There was something about the Bible, something attractive. Picking it up, she quietly closed the drawer and returned to the table.

The Bible felt good in her hand. It felt comfortable in her grip, like a hammer might feel good in the palm of a carpenter. There was a familiarity about it. Pulling open the cover, she read the title page. It was a New Testament, not a complete Bible. A sense of comfort seemed to migrate from the book to her heart. Just touching it brought back the sensation of memory, of good memories.

In the dim light of the room, she began to read.

Chapter 15

Tuesday, 8:15 P.M.

A warm breeze wafted through the open window of the Mercury and caressed Raymond Massey's moist skin. A large man, he was prone to perspiring. Sitting in a parked car with the engine off and no air conditioning made him all the more uncomfortable. It had been a long day, and he'd had no time to change clothes. The three-piece suit he wore was appropriate attire for the office and boardroom, but not for the field. Already he had flown from San Francisco to Bakersfield, driven to Lancaster, flown a helicopter to Santa Barbara, fought with McCullers, staked out Blanchard's home, and followed him and the woman to an isolated motel in Upper Ojai. To add insult to injury, he hadn't eaten since breakfast. His mood was souring fast.

Despite his discomfort, Massey listened as the laser microphone picked up the conversation through the motel window. The sensitive device picked up most of their conversation, dropping only the occasional word or phrase. He had learned several interesting things. First, Blanchard was injured. He had been wounded in the arm by McCullers's weapon, and he had also sustained some kind of injury to the knee. Second, Blanchard was reluctant to involve the police or to go to the hospital. That was odd. Fleeing to the arms of the police would be the normal thing to do — and the safest. And not only did Blanchard refuse, but *she* also refused. When Blanchard asked her if she was ready to go to the authorities, her response had been quick and resolute. Massey wondered which one feared the police the most.

And there was something odd about her conversation. She seemed uncertain, at times confused. This was different from the attitude he had known her to have. Yet while the woman had moments of uncertainty, Blanchard seemed firm about everything. For a man whose house had been invaded by an armed gunman, he was too calm.

Then there was his comment that he had been in Vietnam. That could mean nothing or everything. Many Vietnam veterans had returned to civilian life to work, rear their families, play with their children. Various government agencies recruited others to carry on an intelligence war. Large corporations hired some to handle certain difficult situations. Massey understood that; he himself had recruited such men into Moyer Communications.

Nick Blanchard had no past and had appeared at just the right time, in just the right place. He had to be the one who had run McCullers off the road. Why was he here? What did he want? Who had hired him?

Massey could kill Blanchard easily enough, but it would be better to know whom Blanchard worked for first. There might be a greater threat to Moyer Communications and its plans than they presently knew.

Massey needed to pass the information on to his boss, but talking on a cell phone was risky. Any communication that was broadcast through the air was subject to interception, and he had no way to encrypt the conversation from his end. Most Americans would be shocked to learn of the UKUSA network, a shadow system of listening posts and tracking stations that intercepted and filtered all communications broadcast through the air. Since most telephone calls, faxes, telexes and e-mails were relayed through satellites that hovered above the earth, almost any conversation could be tapped. Using a sophisticated filtering software, UKUSA and other programs like it listened for key phrases or addresses that might be a threat to the government.

But it wasn't UKUSA or Echelon or any other government system that concerned him — it was whoever Blanchard worked for.

That meant he had to use a land line. Phone lines could be tapped, but the interceptor would have to know where the call was to be made from and then make a physical connection. But to use a land line meant leaving the street in front of the motel. His prey would be out of his sight while he made the call.

It was a chance he would have to take. Moyer needed this information. He would be interested in these new revelations; these and the one new fact Massey had learned: The woman was using the name Lisa. Why had she changed her name?

Massey's frustration was growing geometrically. The whole mission had been an avalanche of setbacks and hindrances, not the least of which was McCullers, who lay dead on the side of a frontage road. It wouldn't be long before he was discovered and the police would be involved. Police investigators were not stupid, and they had many resources at hand. The investigation would take some time to get started, but things would snowball from there.

Massey had no fear that he would be captured and linked to the murder. That would require a witness or, at the very least, luck on the part of the police. If he were sufficiently suspect and somehow detained, they could prove that his gun had killed McCullers. And gunpowder traces on his hands and clothing would show that he was the one who had fired the weapon. But first they would have to have reason to link him to the crime, and no such reason existed. He had been too careful.

Massey's real concern, then, was that the police would be looking for Blanchard. If they entered Blanchard's house, they would discover evidence of a struggle. Massey had not been in the house, and he had no idea of all that had taken place, but McCullers had said something about a fight.

He had not heard any conversation for the last ten minutes. Perhaps they were asleep. *At least one of them,* Massey thought. A light still shone through the thinly draped window.

He made his decision. He would find a pay phone and make his call to Moyer. Most likely he would be asked to finish the job and return home. That would be the easiest and most forthright approach. But that would leave an unresolved mystery: Who was Nick Blanchard?

Bill Hobbs bent forward and touched his toes. His back was beginning to hurt. The day had been long and unrelenting, but most of all it had been confusing.

"I think we've got something," Tanner said, walking toward Hobbs. He had been standing by one of the patrol units that had cordoned off the street.

"Oh?" Hobbs's interest was piqued.

"You were right about the drugstores. A sheriff's unit in Ojai found a clerk who said someone fitting the description of our woman had been in and bought some first-aid stuff."

"Where's Ojai?"

"It's a small town up the valley, maybe thirty or forty minutes from here."

"Let's go," Hobbs said.

"I've got more good news," Tanner said. "The store has a video camera."

"Outstanding." Hobbs wasted no time marching to the car. Tanner was close behind. "I don't suppose you know how to get to this Ojai?"

"As a matter of fact, I do," Tanner said.

"Good, then you drive," Hobbs said, getting in the passenger's seat.

The drive to the quaint valley town took just over thirty minutes. "I've heard of this place," Hobbs said as they passed the city limits sign.

"It has several claims to fame," Tanner said. "Amateur tennis matches, annual jazz festival . . . a few movie and television stars live here."

Hobbs cast a curious glance at Tanner. "You work for the chamber of commerce or something?"

"Nah," Tanner replied. "My parents used to drag me down here when I was a kid. It's a popular tourist spot. If you're into New Age philosophy, this is the place to be."

"I'm not," Hobbs said.

"There it is," Tanner said, pointing. "In that shopping center, next to the grocery store."

"I see it."

After parking the car, Hobbs and Tanner entered the small pharmacy and showed their badges to the sheriff's deputy, who was standing next to the counter talking to a young woman. The officer introduced the woman as Marie Kimble. She was thin, with straight brown hair. She looked to be in her midtwenties. Standing next to her was a tall, gangly man with gray-speckled black hair. He was in his late forties or early fifties and wore a white smock. *The pharmacist,* Hobbs surmised. The officer introduced him as Mark Redding.

After exchanging pleasantries, Hobbs got down to business. Pulling from a folder the picture he had taken from the Pretty Penny Motel security tape, he pushed it across the counter to the two employees. "Is this the woman who was in your store earlier tonight?"

"Yes," Marie said confidently. "That's her, all right. Except she was wearing different clothes."

"Can you describe what she was wearing?" Hobbs said.

"Sure," the woman replied quickly. "White, sleeveless T-shirt and striped Capri pants."

A smile crossed Hobbs's face. He was always amazed how one woman took notice of what another woman was wearing. In the course of his work, he had asked many men the same kind of question and almost always received a vague description: "Um, I don't know, jeans and some kind of shirt."

"Capri pants?" Hobbs said.

"Yeah, you know, Capri pants."

Hobbs shook his head, indicating his ignorance of women's apparel.

"They're narrow-legged pants, and the legs are short, about to the midcalf. You're not married are you, Detective?"

"No, I'm not," Hobbs said defensively. He pushed another picture from the folder across the counter. "Was this man with her?"

"No," Marie said quickly. "She came in alone."

"How can you be sure that it's the same woman?" Hobbs asked.

"She's pretty," Marie answered. "And of course . . ." she trailed off.

"Of course what?"

"The bruise on her face. It's hard to miss."

The picture Hobbs had presented had been computer enhanced. It clearly showed a dark area on the side of the woman's head.

"I see." Hobbs turned to the man. "You're the pharmacist here, Mr. Redding?"

"It's Dr. Redding and, yes, I am."

"Do you agree that this is the woman who was in your pharmacy earlier this evening?"

"I didn't see her. I was in the back filling prescriptions." He motioned behind him to an area marked off by a glass partition and filled with long white shelves of bottles and boxes.

"So you didn't see the woman at all?"

"No. As I said, I was in the back."

"I understand you have a video surveillance system." Hobbs looked up and saw a camera mounted to the ceiling.

"Yes," Redding answered. "It's a must these days, especially in the drug business."

"I would like to see the tape for this evening."

"It's back here," Redding said as he turned and disappeared into the work area. Hobbs led Tanner past the counter and into the shelf-filled space. At the rear of the room was a small desk with a color monitor and player on it. Next to the desk was a set of metal shelves upon which rested a video recorder. Redding removed the tape from the recorder, inserted a new one, meticulously labeled the one he had just removed, and then placed it in the player. He pushed REWIND and a moment later pushed PLAY.

The monitor filled with a wide-angle view of the shop. Unlike the tape from the motel in Mojave, this one was in full color. Hobbs could see people come and go, each moving in a stiff, robotic fashion. Like most video surveillance systems, this one recorded images every second or so, not continually, allowing more time to be placed on each tape.

The store emptied and for a full minute Hobbs, Tanner, the officer, and Redding hovered over the monitor. Redding pointed to the white numbers emblazoned in the bottom right corner of the screen that indicated the time of day the picture had been taken. "Marie said the woman came in a little after eight. We should see her soon."

As he spoke a pair of bright headlights could be seen shining through the glass wall at the front of the store. "I can't make out the model of the car," Hobbs said. "How about you, Tanner?"

He shook his head. "All I see are headlights."

The door to the store opened and a woman entered. She was wearing the clothes described by the clerk.

"That's her," Hobbs said, excitement tingeing his voice. She walked with a slight limp. "She doesn't look very comfortable."

"With good reason," Tanner said, but offered nothing more.

Hobbs watched intently as the woman looked around the store, picked up a few items, paid for them, and then left. "Thank you, Dr. Redding. You and Ms. Kimble have been very helpful. I'll need to take that tape into evidence. Can you take care of that for me, Officer?" he asked the deputy. The man indicated that he could.

Before leaving the pharmacy, Hobbs thanked Redding and Kimble again. Outside the store, he congratulated the deputy on his discovery. Returning to the car, Hobbs and Tanner discussed the next step.

"Okay, what do we have?" Hobbs asked as he closed the door to the sedan.

"Well," Tanner answered, "we now know that your suspicion was right. Someone, most likely Blanchard, was injured in whatever happened in his house. Otherwise, he would have been the one to have gone in the store."

"Probably," Hobbs agreed. "It didn't look like she had any wounds that would account for the blood we found in the house. The question now is, Where did they go next?"

"I bet they're close by," Tanner said. "If they went through the trouble to buy the things the clerk said they did, then she must be planning to do a little doctoring."

"Roadside or someplace else?" Hobbs scratched his chin, noting that stubble had erupted on his face, a testimony to the length of his day. By morning he would look like a derelict in a suit.

"There is no way to know," Tanner said.

"We have the neighbor's description of the car," Hobbs said. "How many silver Mitsubishi Gallants can there be in the area?"

"A few maybe, but not many."

"If they're on the road, there's nothing we can do but wait for them to show up somewhere else or be stopped by the APB. These two seem pretty smart. They'll take action to hide."

"What would you do if you were in their place?" Tanner asked.

Hobbs thought for a moment. "Assuming the wound is serious but not life threatening, I would find a place to fix up my partner and plan my next step." He thought some more. "I'd find a motel off the beaten path. I would want to be off the road for a while and travel when there are more vehicles on the highway. Get lost in the crowd. I would also attempt to rent a car, getting rid of the Gallant."

"Makes sense to me. So we start searching motel parking lots?"

"Yeah. We need a list of motels," Hobbs said, opening the door to the car. "I'll be right back. In the meantime, get on the radio and see if we can't get the sheriff's department and CHP to start searching motels and parking lots. We can use all the help we can get."

"Will do."

Hobbs returned two minutes later with a phone book. "Dr. Redding said we could have this," he said, shuffling through the pages. "I think we should start outside the community and work our way back in." Reading addresses from the book and comparing them to a map in the front of the directory, Hobbs quickly made his first choice. "I'm assuming they would go in the opposite direction of the crime scene."

"We don't know that these are criminals," Tanner said. "They may be victims."

"I understand that, but they're still human, and human nature says they would move away from the trouble. Here," he said, pointing to the small map. "There's a place not too far from here in . . ." He squinted in the dim illumination offered by the dome light. "In Upper Ojai. There are others in Miner Oaks, Mira Monte, and Ojai proper, but I want to start there."

"Tallyho then," Tanner said and buckled his seat belt.

Gregory Moyer was seated behind his desk watching a steady stream of information play across his computer screen. He liked what he saw. The MC2-SDS satellite had deployed perfectly. Its solar panels had extended without a hitch, and its positioning rockets had nudged it into its designated orbit. So many things could go wrong in a satellite launch that it was pure pleasure to see a perfect deployment.

A soft tone filled the room, informing Moyer that someone was calling on his private line. Only half a dozen people had that number, and only one could be calling now. "Answer," he said to the automated phone.

Massey's voice sounded from the speaker. "I'm on a pay phone," he said without preamble. The message was clear: The line was not secure, and Massey had reason not to use the cell phone.

"It's good to hear from you," Moyer said. "I hope your trip goes well."

"A little better now," Massey remarked carefully. Moyer knew that the message he received would be just as cryptic as last time. Most such messages would have been done through encrypted e-mail. Sophisticated 128-bit encryption systems made it impossible for anyone to read such messages. He chastised himself for not having included a laptop computer equipped with such a program in with the other equipment he had provided for Massey. That would have made things much easier. But then hindsight was always 20-20.

"I'm sure you're eager to return home," Moyer said.

"I am. I was wondering if I shouldn't bring some company."

"Company?" Moyer hated the sound of that. Massey had concerns about following the plan. That meant he had learned something new.

"Yes, there's a nice couple with some interesting ideas. I'd hate for us to miss out on a good story. The gentleman tells a good tale."

"I see," Moyer said. So the man may know something important, something damaging. He had to make a decision quickly. "He likes to tell stories then?"

"I think so. I'm not sure whom he has shared his talent with."

"I see. My schedule won't allow for any more visits. You know how intense it is around here. Perhaps you should just learn as many tales as you can, then say good-bye. You can share them with me when you return."

"I understand fully." Massey hung up.

Moyer leaned back in his chair and wondered if he hadn't just made a big mistake. Killing the two was the most efficient course of action. Still, Massey was right. It was important to know whom they had spoken to and what they had said. But since Nick Blanchard was untraceable, an amazing feat in the present age of technology, he had to be more than just an average guy. Bringing him back to Moyer Communications was too big a risk. No, Massey would have to learn what he could and then finish the job. If some new problem arose, they would have to deal with it then.

Knowing. It was all about knowing everything that went on. That was what Moyer Communications was about: knowing everything. He returned his attention to the screen before him. The new satellite was working perfectly. On the monitor was the mansion of the African politician. He zoomed in on a window. The optics were incredible, beyond even his educated belief.

A broad smile crossed his face, and he placed a call to a phone in Khartoum, Sudan. The country had been at war with itself for nearly two decades. Nearly two million of its inhabitants had been killed. Racked by political strife, abrogated constitutional rights, and famine, it was not a nice place to visit. It was a dark place in the bright sun that no longer understood the meaning of tolerance.

"Greetings, my friend," Moyer said. "The system is up. Go to the window and wave."

"I can find them with this?" the heavily accented voice asked. "It is as you said? I will see them with this?"

"It is what you have paid for," Moyer said. "No one will be able to hide. But hurry. Your time is limited, and others need my help too."

Moyer hung up unceremoniously.

Chapter 16

Tuesday, 9:10 P.M.

The Bible lay on the table before Lisa. She was spot reading, flipping pages and taking in the odd verse here and there. Each passage she read felt like a long-lost friend. She sampled Matthew, Mark, and the other Gospels, glanced at the letters of Paul and Peter, never settling on one particular book in the New Testament. She scanned portions of Romans, then the Corinthian letters, and then returned to Romans. Something there touched her, so she began to read from the beginning. Her eyes skimmed across the page, drinking in each word. Each chapter brought new recollection of its truth, a truth she felt she had accepted sometime in the past.

She paused at chapter 8. Selected verses seemed to radiate with the warmth of recognition. Her stomach turned again, but not from fear or uncertainty as it had done so many other times that day, but from excitement. Something rang true.

She read, "There is therefore now no condemnation to them which are in Christ Jesus," and that brought a smile to her face. In verse 9, a phrase made her stop: "But ye are not in the flesh, but in the Spirit, if so be that the Spirit of God dwell in you." Lisa blinked several times as if trying to clear her blurry mind's eye. *If the Spirit dwells in me, then surely He must know who I am,* Lisa thought. There was peace and thrilling excitement in that realization. God knew who she was, even if her memory failed her. She was not alone — not alone at all. More important, she had never been alone.

Reading with more earnestness than before, Lisa devoured the next few verses, then stopped on: "For I reckon that the sufferings of this present time are not worthy to be compared with the glory which shall be revealed in us." *Sufferings of the present time,* she thought. The phrase carried a sense of the temporary with it. "There will be glory later," Lisa said under her breath.

Again she let her eyes travel down the page, her mind absorbing each word as a sponge capturing water. Her heart skipped a beat, and then pounded in her chest. The words that had seemed so familiar when Nick uttered them were right before her eyes. Not his words. His were merely similar enough to fan an ember of memory. Before her now was the concrete reality of the vague recollection. "And we know that all things work together for good to them that love God, to them who are the called according to his purpose."

The piercing icy chill of fear had several times that day permeated every cell of her body. But now, reading those words, she felt an opposite effect. Warmth, like golden spring sunlight, covered her. No . . . The warmth came from *within,* not from without. A tear of joy dropped from her eye, and she took a deep breath. The air seemed sweeter.

Of all that had happened in the last twenty-four hours, this was the only truly positive, comforting, encouraging event. Nick had been wonderful in his support, but he had been unable to ease her fears or to quell her storm of confusion. The Bible's words came as a balm to her wounded soul. She was not alone. She had never been alone. God was with her, and the verse promised that the last page of her life had yet to be written. Things, good things, could come out of her trials. It was a truth she desperately needed to know.

Lisa read the words repeatedly, and each time she felt a little stronger, a little surer, and a little more confident about the future.

The incident at the church in Fillmore now made sense. She had been attracted to it, because church was a familiar place. Although she had never laid eyes on that dilapidated, run-down structure before, it still represented something dear and precious to her. She was a Christian, and relearning that truth bolstered her spirits dramatically. Fear was giving way to courage; anxiety was surrendering to peace.

Lisa knew full well that her problems were not over. Her memory was still gone, and she was in a motel room with a wounded man she had known for less than a day. Her car had been pushed off the road with her in it, and someone had tried to kill her less than an hour before.

But her problems had now been bathed in a holy perspective.

Massey was unhappy. He had sworn off such things years ago, but here he was skulking around an old motel on a warm summer evening. A decade ago, he would have found this exhilarating. The spy game was custom-made for a man like him. His mannerisms, speech, and portly appearance made him seem the least likely person to be involved in skulduggery. The truth was, he had thrived on it. With a degree in political science and a gift for languages, the CIA had recruited him right out of Yale. Massey had accepted the offer and soon learned all the subtleties of the profession. During the heyday of the Cold War, he had worked in Germany, turning spies for the other side into spies for the United States.

But the Cold War had died, and with it Massey's cloak-and-dagger career. His connections, however, were desired, and through a friendly superior officer, he found himself talking to the wealthy and powerful Gregory Moyer, who offered him an executive position with an obscenely large salary with benefits to rival that received by the presidents and CEOs of most major corporations. Massey was no fool. He knew the money and rewards were meant to buy his loyalty, and he was glad to give it. He was, above all, loyal.

Moyer made good use of his acquisition. Massey understood the world political scene as well as the U.S. secretary of state. He was a man gifted in many areas, but he had grown older and less enthusiastic for the hands-on work. He was now an executive in a powerful firm; his days were filled with paperwork and meetings. He had proven himself invaluable to Moyer, and no one wielded more power.

Then why was he here, slinking in the shadows? He was here because Moyer had told him to be, and one did not trifle with Moyer.

Massey cursed McCullers, and then he cursed himself for hiring the man. He made few mistakes, but McCullers had been a big one. Massey cursed the ego that made McCullers fail in his mission. Now he had to do the job himself. Allowing another second to pass, he wished he could kill McCullers again — just on principle.

But he had a job to do, and only a few moments in which to do it. In some ways, he had been lucky. The woman feared the police. Had she run to them, she would be out of his reach.

The motel was similar to many of those built in the fifties: L-shaped with a corridor separating one wing of the building from the other. In the corridor was an ice machine, a snack dispenser, and a door with a brown plastic sign marked EMPLOYEES ONLY. It was the door that Massey had been looking for. He studied the lock for a moment. It looked like the original, which would make it over forty years old. He tapped a finger on the door, and it yielded a hollow tone. He could easily kick it in, but that would make too much noise and draw unwanted attention. He pulled a small knife from his pocket, exposed the blade, and slipped it between the doorstop and the jamb. The thin wood strip parted easily from the jamb. Massey worked the blade farther into the door until he felt it scratch against the tongue of the lock. A contemporary lock would have been more difficult, but the ancient device was easy to defeat. The door swung open easily. He stepped in, closed the door, and switched on the light.

The room was what he expected. A three-shelf metal cart was situated in the middle. Piled on top were folded white towels and washcloths. A plastic bucket held tiny bottles of shampoo, bar soap, and hand lotion. Bottles of cleaning fluid rested on the second shelf. Massey was interested in none of those things. He was after only two items.

He found the first hanging near the door: a key on a long string — the passkey. He searched the room for the second item. A series of metal shelves filled with items used by the maid were mounted to the far wall. A red metal toolbox was resting on the bottom shelf. Massey opened it and found what he was looking for: duct tape.

Careful to turn off the storage-room light before opening the door, he exited and pulled the door shut. He took a moment to press the doorstop back to its original position. A close examination would show that it had been tampered with, but at least for now it couldn't be noticed by a passerby.

Now came the hard part.

Since the motel was small, the walk to the room took only a minute or so. Massey walked slowly but naturally. If seen, he wanted to be mistaken for a sleepy traveler. He paused at the door and listened intently. There was no sound, no television, and no conversation. He desperately wanted to peer in the window to see where Blanchard was, but the curtains were drawn shut. Blanchard concerned him. He had been able to handle McCullers, and he seemed to be a smooth operator. Massey was confident in himself and his abilities; still, a lucky punch, an unseen weapon, or some other unplanned contingency might give Blanchard the edge. The key would be the woman. Control the woman and control the situation.

Holding the roll of duct tape under his arm, Massey took hold of the doorknob and held it still, slowly inserting the key into the lock. It slipped in easily and noiselessly. He turned the key and felt the lock surrender its hold, but he held the door shut. He had one more thing to do before entering. Reaching his right hand behind him, under his coat, he extracted his gun. He took a breath and walked casually into the room.

Lisa had her back to the door when she felt the sudden rush of warm night air. She cranked her head around just in time to see a thickly built man dressed in a three-piece suit step into the room. He held a gun, its barrel pointed at her forehead.

"Nick!" Lisa shouted.

"Shut up," the man said loudly.

Nick stirred on the bed and then opened his eyes. "What the —" He fell silent as the man swung the gun from Lisa to Nick. She watched as the man calmly closed the door behind him, locking it.

"Take this." He tossed the roll of duct tape to Lisa. She let it fall to the floor. "Pick it up."

Lisa bent forward and picked up the roll.

"I'm getting a little tired of this," Nick said as he started to sit up. "This is the second time I've been attacked in the last —"

"I told you to shut up," the man said. "Lie back down."

"I'm done with my nap," Nick said belligerently.

"Lie on your back or I'll make your nap

permanent." The man held the gun rock steady.

"What do you want?" Lisa asked.

"In a nutshell, I want you, Ms. Keller."

"Keller?" Lisa said, shocked at hearing the name.

"Yes, Keller. Robin Lisa Keller, and I don't have time for your games. Please be kind enough to tape Mr. Blanchard's wrists together."

"I still don't understand," she said. Her head was spinning with fear and confusion. *Robin Lisa Keller*. Lisa was a name that Nick had chosen for her at the fast-food restaurant in Fillmore. Was it coincidence that Lisa was her middle name? *If* Robin Lisa Keller was really her name.

"You know," Nick said calmly, "if you fire that thing in here everyone in the motel will hear it. Then what will you do?"

"I'd fire it once more into Ms. Keller and then drive off into the dark. It's not very complex, really."

Lisa pulled a long strip of the silver tape from the roll and struggled to tear it off.

"Use your teeth," the man said.

She did, biting at the edge of the tape. It tore away easily. Nick, who lay on his back on the bed, held his hands up and Lisa applied the tape, being careful not to cut off the circulation. Knowing that the gunman would inspect the job she did, she secured the tape well.

"Now his feet."

"Why his feet?" she asked. Her fear was giving way to anger.

"Because I don't trust Mr. Blanchard. He has secrets, and people with secrets make me nervous."

"What makes you think I have secrets?"

"You're an enigma, Mr. Blanchard, if that's really your name. You seem to be untraceable, as does your truck. Untraceable people usually have something to hide."

"Maybe I just like my privacy," Nick responded as Lisa taped his feet.

"Yeah, right," the gunman said sarcastically. "Just who are you, Mr. Blanchard?"

"Maybe we should be asking *you* that question," Lisa said.

"No need," Nick said. "Our uninvited guest is Raymond Massey; he works for Moyer Communications."

Lisa's stomach seized into a tight fist. *Moyer Communications? Why would Nick know?*

Nick continued, oblivious to Lisa's response. "He fancies himself a highly placed executive, but he's really a tool of Greg Moyer. In point of fact, he's just a middle-aged former spy. He does the work that no one else would do — those with any principles, that is."

Taking a few faltering steps back, Lisa sat on the edge of the second bed. Her mind was reeling with unchecked emotions and sensations of fragmented memory. She had had something to do with Moyer Communications.

"I fear you have me at a disadvantage, Blanchard. It appears you know all about me, but I know nothing about you."

"That's the plan," Nick said with a twisted smile. If he was frightened, Lisa couldn't see it. "That's the way it is supposed to work."

"My compliments," Massey said. "You've been successful in your charade . . . until now." He turned to Lisa. "Tape your feet," he demanded.

Lisa sat unmoving, paralyzed by confusion, fear, and anger.

"I said, tape your feet!"

His harsh tone jarred her back to the frightening reality of the moment, and she turned to face Massey. *All things work together for good to them that love God.* The words washed cool over her feverish terror. Alive or dead, God would work all things out for her good. That was a fact to her, not a mere wish. "No." Lisa said softly.

"What?" Her resistance caught Massey off guard.

"I said no."

"Who holds the gun here, lady?"

Lisa shrugged. "You do. And if I tape my feet together, you'll still hold the gun, won't you?"

"I could kill you, Ms. Keller," Massey said, his voice heavy with threat.

"That's your plan anyway, isn't it? If I'm going to be shot, I think I prefer to be unbound."

Massey fell silent for a moment, clearly astonished by Lisa's sudden resistance. "I don't have time for this —"

"Then leave. I wouldn't want to hold you up."

Nick laughed, and Massey turned his attention back to him. "How about if I shoot your boyfriend."

"Do you think that will be less terrifying if I'm bound hand and foot with duct tape? I'm not stupid, mister. I don't believe for a moment that you're going to let Nick or me live. I may have lost my memory, but I haven't lost my mind."

"Lost your memory?" Massey said. "What . . . Oh, now I see. That would explain a few things."

"Ironic, isn't it, Raymond," Nick said. "You and your buddies are afraid of what she knows, so you try to have her killed. But she can't remember a thing about her life before you ran her off the road."

"I didn't run her off the road. That buffoon we hired did. He was a mistake. I, however, don't make mistakes."

"Is that a fact?" Nick said mordantly.

"Yes, it's a fact."

"So what is it you want?" Lisa asked. "Why stand here and talk to us?"

"Because I need some information," Massey said. "Mr. Blanchard is a bit of a puzzle. Whom do you work for?" he asked Nick.

"I'm a truck driver."

"I don't buy that for a moment. Your truck was untraceable, your behavior goes beyond what an average citizen would do, and you were able to defeat a trained killer. You also seem to know a great deal about me and my employer, so come clean, Blanchard."

"I've told you all I'm going to."

Massey pulled back the hammer on the gun and pointed the weapon at Lisa. "Maybe Ms. Keller is willing to watch you die, but I'm betting that you feel differently about watching her brains scatter all over the wall. Or maybe I should just beat her until you talk. You know, break a few fingers and knock out a few teeth."

Dread rippled through Lisa, but she refused to let it show. The last twenty-four hours had taken their toll. She was tired to the point of apathy.

Nick said nothing.

In a startling display of speed, Massey shot forward and brought a crashing backhand across Lisa's face. The blow knocked her from her perch on the edge of the bed. She tumbled to the floor in a heap, her hands raised to her face.

Curses filled the room, and she removed her hands in time to see Nick struggle to his feet between the beds, his shoulder lowered to ram the gunman, but Massey had anticipated the attack and brought a brutal elbow to Nick's nose. With his feet bound by the duct tape, Nick was unable to steady himself. He fell back on the bed. Blood gushed from his nostrils.

Massey took two steps back. "Well, how much longer would you like to do this? I have a little time, and I could use the exercise."

"Leave her alone," Nick said, the force of his words blowing drops of blood that ran from his mouth and nose. "You coward.

Cut me loose and I'll give you all the exercise you can handle."

"Really?" Massey replied with a sardonic smile. "Another day, another time, I would welcome it, but I have a job to do. Now tell me who you are and what your interest is in all this."

Nick hesitated, and Massey started for Lisa.

"All right, all right," he shouted. "But you have to promise to leave her alone."

"I make no promises, and you're in no position to demand them."

Lisa made eye contact with Nick, whose eyes conveyed profound sorrow and deep apology. "I'm okay," she said, rubbing her jaw.

"I'm a federal agent," Nick said flatly.

"Which agency?"

"Does it matter?"

"Which agency?" Massey repeated hotly.

"NSA," Nick said.

"National Security. So you deal with intelligence work done in communications," Massey said.

"What? I don't —" Lisa retook her seat on the bed. She fought back hot tears.

"The NSA," Massey said, sounding like a schoolteacher lecturing a high school class, "and its companion, the CSS — the Central

Security Service — work to keep secret transmissions secret and to collect foreign intelligence. There's more to it, but you get the idea." Then, turning back to Nick, "What's your interest in Ms. Keller?" Massey demanded.

"Oh, please," Nick said mockingly. "You know that as well as I do. That's what started all of this."

"She contacted you and said she had information about Moyer Communications? Whom have you talked to?"

"No one," Nick answered. "The accident — or something else — caused her to have amnesia. I've been protecting her."

"Hoping that her memory would come back, is that it? In fact, that's why you took her to your home, isn't it?"

"I still don't understand," Lisa said. "Nick, you offered to take me to the police or to a hospital more times than I can count."

"I'll answer that, Ms. Keller," Massey said. "Had you accepted the offer, he would have led you along for a while and then begun to drop hints about all sorts of bad things that might happen at the police station. You would have changed your mind."

Lisa felt sick. The one man she was starting to trust turned out to be lying to her. "You've been watching me the whole time." Pieces were starting to fall into place. "You've been spying on me."

"No, Lisa, it's not like that at all," Nick protested.

"Yes, it is," Massey said. "It's probably worse, Ms. Keller. I find it interesting that he calls you Lisa, your middle name. I'll bet that he was hoping the name would jog your memory."

"The call you made from McDonald's," Lisa said, feeling her anger rise. "It was part of the setup. You had your friends fix the house, filling it with clothing just my size."

"Lisa, listen," Nick began. "You were in danger. When you contacted us, you were enmeshed in Moyer's organization. That's why you ran. Whatever you learned put your life in danger. You came to us for help. They blew your cover."

"My cover?" The churning in Lisa continued. Everyone around her was untrustworthy. Each presented a threat.

"That is a good question, Ms. Keller," Massey said. "Are you a Good Samaritan or a professional player?"

"I don't know what you mean," Lisa countered.

Massey turned to Nick. "I bet you know. How about it, Mr. Blanchard? Is she a teammate or just some do-gooder?" When Nick hesitated, Massey took a step toward Lisa.

"Agent," Nick blurted. Massey stepped back. "She's one of ours."

"What!" Lisa was numb with shock.

"What is an NSA agent doing driving a truck?" Massey asked.

Nick frowned. Lisa focused on Nick, wanting to hear the answer too.

"It was my cover," Nick finally said. "I drove a truck in college. The NSA uses unmarked, unregistered trucks to transport their equipment."

"And the house?" Lisa asked. "Is that really yours?"

"Yes," Nick said. "Everything I told you about my family is true."

"Including your sister?" Lisa asked.

"Yes. I really have a sister on the East Coast. You're wearing her clothes."

"This is too much to take in," Lisa said. She turned to Massey. "What was I doing in Moyer Communications?"

"Systems security," Massey said, "and that's all you're getting out of me. It's time to adjourn this meeting."

"There has to be another way," Lisa said, refusing to surrender hope.

"There's not. Now who dies first?" Massey raised the gun and pointed it at

Lisa. "I think you should be first, Ms. Keller. After all, you're at the center of all of this."

There was a loud knock at the door.

Chapter 17

Tuesday, 9:45 P.M.

Detective Bill Hobbs stood to the side of the motel room door, as did Officer Jay Tanner. Hobbs knocked on the door again and waited, listening intently. He was sure that he had heard voices prior to his first knock.

Hobbs and Tanner had arrived at the motel just ten minutes before and had driven through the parking lot looking for the Mitsubishi Gallant.

"There must be twenty ways to leave the area," Tanner had said to Hobbs, "and a hundred motels and hotels in Ventura and Santa Barbara Counties. Yet you ferret it out on instinct."

Hobbs and Tanner had parked in front of the lobby and questioned the desk clerk. She recognized the woman in the picture that Hobbs showed her as the same woman who had checked in a short time before.

"Is she a dangerous criminal?" the clerk had asked. "She must be or you wouldn't be here. I knew it the moment I laid eyes on her. You can tell these things when you've been in this business as long as I have. Do you want me to show you the room?"

"No ma'am," Hobbs had said, wondering why the woman hadn't called the police if she was so sure she was renting a room to a fugitive. "Please stay here. We'll find the room just fine. Do the rooms have a back window or door?"

"No, they're just like every other motel you've stayed in. One door, one window, both on the front wall."

"Okay, thank you." Hobbs turned to leave.

"You're not going to have a bunch of cops racing in here with sirens on, are you? I got a business to run, and I don't want you scaring all my guests away. We got a reputation, you know."

"I don't think that will be necessary," Hobbs replied. "Do you have a master key?"

"Yes," the woman said. "Do you want it?"

Hobbs thought that was obvious but politely said, "Yes, please." She handed the key to him. "Are there additional locks on the doors?"

"You mean like a chain lock?" the woman asked. "No. I've been meaning to have them installed."

"How many guests do you have tonight?" Hobbs asked.

"Not many. The people you're looking for are at the end of the wing. The room next to them is unoccupied. The rest of the lower rooms are filled. There's no one on the second floor."

Outside the lobby, Tanner asked, "Should we call for backup?"

He looked across the lot at the end room of the motel wing. "I don't want to wait for them to get here. We know someone is wounded, probably Blanchard, since the woman did the actual check-in with the clerk."

"They may also have been the ones who killed the man we found in the street."

"My gut tells me different. Call for backup, then let's see if anyone is home," Hobbs said.

"You know that we are out of our jurisdiction," Tanner said seriously.

"As you've mentioned before," Hobbs answered without emotion. "I know. But time is important on this."

Now Hobbs was wondering what to do next. He had hoped that he would knock on the door and the woman and Blanchard would answer, invite them in, and explain everything. That, of course, was a fantasy. He raised his fist and pounded on the door loudly. "Police," he said. "Open the door!"

Two doors down, an elderly man poked his head out. "What's going on?"

Tanner spoke up. "Go back in your room, sir, and lock the door."

"But what's going on?"

"Do as I say, sir." Tanner's voice carried the solid ring of authority. The man ducked back into his room.

Hobbs inserted the master key into the lock and looked at Tanner, who stood ready with his gun drawn. Tanner nodded.

Hobbs jumped as he heard a loud bang from inside the room. The dim light that had been shining through the thin drapes suddenly went out. In a single fluid motion, Hobbs turned the key and pushed open the door hard. The room was black inside.

Tanner charged it, his gun leading the way. "Police! On the ground — everyone on the ground!"

There was a shot.

When Lisa had first heard the knock on the door and someone shout "police," she had felt a moment's hope. But Massey's commands had been quiet, succinct, and filled with dark threat, and now she sensed only horror. Massey held her by the hair, his gun, the barrel still warm from the spent shot, pressed to her head.

"No words, no screams," he had said. His professional, gentlemanly manner had dissolved into something visceral and primitive. "You will not resist, or I'll put a bullet in your brain. I can move faster without you."

Lisa wondered why he hadn't done so. Then she realized, she was his hostage, his security in case things failed to go as planned. She held no hopes that she would live one moment past the end of her usefulness.

As they moved through the empty motel room, Lisa wondered if she was fortunate that he had not been cornered, or unlucky because he might actually make his escape.

Massey was quick on his feet. Within a second after the first knock and the word "police," he had taken in the situation. She had watched his eyes settle on the thin door that connected their room to the adjoining room.

By the second knock, Massey had already opened the door to the other room. He paused for a moment, and Lisa saw him clench his jaw. There was another door on the other side, and it was locked. Of course there would be two doors, Lisa realized. It was the only way to maintain privacy. Each room could lock the other room out.

Just as she was thinking that Massey was trapped, he kicked the narrow panel and the door flung open. In a brutal lunge of unbelievable speed, he yanked Lisa by the hair, dragging her to his side, then pushed her ahead of him as if she were a human shield, pausing only long enough to fire one round at the entrance door.

"This way," he whispered harshly and shoved her toward the window. He stopped, pulled the curtain back slightly, and peered out. "Good," he said. His affirmation made Lisa feel even more anxious.

He shoved her toward the door. "Open it," he commanded.

"But —"

With cruel force he rammed the gun into the small of her back, sending fiery bolts ripping up her spine. Lisa nearly fainted from the pain, but she held on to consciousness by a strength that originated beyond her. Groping for the handle, she found it and turned the knob sharply. The door opened, and she and Massey exchanged the dark of a lightless room for the gloom of night.

Tanner fell to the floor with a cry of pain. Hobbs, knowing that any hesitation could mean his death, kept moving. "On the ground! Everyone on the ground!" He caught movement to his left. The dim light that poured in from the parking lot lamps was enough for Hobbs to see only the two beds and the other furnishings in the room.

Backing up, he reached behind him, feeling for the light switch. The room was suddenly bathed in effulgence.

"Bed!" Tanner said hoarsely. "Behind the bed."

Hobbs was on the move, stepping over his fallen friend, pointing his gun between the two beds. A man lay facedown on the floor. "The other room," the man said. He rolled over on his back and then sat up. He was struggling with something. Tape. His hands and feet had been taped.

"Shut up and sit still!" Hobbs commanded. Slowly he moved to his right, checking to see if anyone was hiding behind the other bed. There was a closet and a bathroom in which an attacker could hide. And the door to the next room was standing open.

"They went out the other room!" the man between the beds shouted. "He has her!"

"I got him," Tanner said weakly. Tanner had managed to sit up and was pointing his gun at the man sitting on the floor. The man continued to struggle with the duct tape that bound him, biting at it with his teeth like a dog chewing through a leather leash.

Hobbs checked the bathroom and the small closet. Both were empty. "Clear," he said to Tanner.

"The other room, you idiot!" the man bellowed. "Look at the access door."

Hobbs approached the passageway between the two rooms with caution. Pushing through, Hobbs found the room empty and the front door open. He made it to the door just in time to see a dark Mercury race from the parking lot, its tires squealing loudly.

A gunshot sounded from the other room. Hobbs spun and raced back through the access door. He was greeted with the barrel of a gun — Tanner's gun.

"Hand it to me slowly." Hobbs recognized the man holding the weapon. He had been searching for him all day. Now it appeared that Blanchard had found him instead. A ragged length of gray duct tape hung from Blanchard's left wrist. On the floor near the bed rested the wad of the tape that had secured Nick's feet.

"Listen buddy," Hobbs began. "I don't know what —"

"Give me the gun!" Nick yelled. "We have only seconds; let's not waste them."

Reluctantly Hobbs complied. Nick stepped aside, and Hobbs saw Tanner lying on the floor, a small reddish-brown circle spreading out from beneath his thigh.

"I'm sorry," Tanner said, his voice quavering with pain. "He's quick, and I'm . . . I'm not real sharp right now. I . . . I missed."

Blanchard had somehow taken the gun from Tanner.

"Not by much," Blanchard said. "You almost blew my head off. It's a good thing you missed; you need me right now."

"I don't need a gun in my face," Hobbs spat harshly.

"Believe me, I know the feeling. I've looked down the barrel of too many guns today. Now let's go."

"I'm not going anywhere," Hobbs said. "I need to help my partner."

"He took a shot in the leg," Blanchard said hurriedly. "The bleeding is pretty slow, so he's not in any danger."

"That's easy for you to say."

Nick stepped to the bed, picked up a pillow, and threw it at Hobbs. "Remove the case, fold it tightly, and then hand it to your friend."

Hobbs did. "Press this on the wound, help will be here soon," he said to Tanner.

"Did you call for backup before you decided to waltz in here?" Nick's voice betrayed his anger.

"Maybe."

"Good. That means they'll be here in just a couple of minutes. Let's go."

"Go where?"

"I'm going after them, and you're going with me," Nick said forcefully. "Every second we wait is a second closer to her death. Now move it."

"I'm staying with him," Hobbs replied, nodding at Tanner.

"Go," Tanner said. "He's right. Someone has to pursue. I'll be okay."

"Your backup will be here soon. They'll take care of him. Out the door!"

Hobbs turned and exited the room, Nick following close behind.

"Your car," Nick said. "You have a service radio. We're going to need help."

"How do I know you aren't going to shoot me as soon as we're away from the motel?"

"You don't, but if I wanted you dead, you wouldn't be talking to me now. We're on the same side here, buddy. I'll explain everything in the car. I must find the woman before he has a chance to kill her."

"And if I refuse?"

Blanchard frowned and then turned the gun on Tanner. He pulled back the hammer. "I won't kill him," he said, "but I'll put a hole in his hip. That should ruin a promising career."

Hobbs could not remember a time when he had felt more furious or more helpless. He couldn't let Blanchard shoot the already wounded Tanner. Hobbs had to comply.

Chapter 18

Tuesday, 9:55 P.M.

The interior handle of the car pressed against Lisa's tender ribs, but she refused to move. If she did, she would have to sit a few inches closer to the man who had abducted her, and the very thought of that was repugnant. Her eyes darted from the rapidly moving road in front of her to the man Nick had called Raymond Massey.

She had an impulse to open the door and jump. It was a crazy thought, but for an instant it seemed reasonable. Better to tumble to death along the dark, rough pavement than to be murdered by the monster behind the wheel. But when she let her gaze slip out the side window, she knew she could never toss herself to that kind of death.

This was not over. Massey had not won. Moyer Communications had not won. *All things . . .* she reminded herself. *All things . . .*

What now? Sitting scrunched in silence against the passenger door of the car made little sense. It achieved nothing. She had to act on her own behalf and trust God for the rest.

"What's the next step, Mr. Massey?" Lisa asked in a formal tone. "Pull over and shoot me?"

"It crossed my mind," he said, his eyes fixed forward. He was driving at a fast rate of speed.

"Driving this fast will draw attention to you, you know," she said, forcing her voice to remain calm, detached, as if she were a director talking over a few script changes with a writer.

"I must have initial distance," he said. "I need a few miles between me and them. That will give me time to make my next move."

"Which is?"

He offered no answer.

"What makes you think you can gain any distance? The police might be right behind you."

"Not possible," Massey said sharply. "There were only two officers and no backup. The other officer will have to take care of the wounded one. That's why I didn't kill the man. A wounded man requires more care than a dead one."

A small wave of relief rolled through Lisa. She had heard the shot but hadn't known the result of it. Her biggest fear was that Nick had been killed. "You purposely avoided killing the policeman?"

"Everything I do is on purpose," he said matter-of-factly.

"So you don't think they're pursuing you?"

"Of course they are. And at the very least, Nick Blanchard is. He's not the kind who gives up easily."

"You don't think it would be better if you just pulled over and let me out? It would be much easier to make a getaway."

"And how many getaways have you made?" Massey asked harshly. "I think I'll just keep you. I have a mission to complete."

"Your mission is to kill me?"

"That's what it's finally come down to."

Lisa was amazed at how dispassionately he could talk about murder. Aside from the anger and tension he obviously felt, he seemed controlled and calculating.

"What did I do to you or Moyer Communications to earn a death sentence?"

"You know very well what you did or were threatening to do."

"No, I don't. I don't even know who I am. I remember nothing past this morning."

He slowed the car and glanced at her. His

face was dimly lit from the glowing instrument panel, giving him an eerie, demonic countenance. "That changes nothing."

"There must be something I can say to convince you that this is all wrong. There must be some words —"

"There aren't, so you can save your breath," Massey snapped. "Now shut up and let me think."

Reaching up to the ceiling of the car, he pushed a button that opened the sunroof. The warm August night flowed in, bringing with it the intensely sweet aroma of orange blossoms from nearby orchards. He took several quick glances through the opening, alternating his eyes from the road before him to the sky above.

"Expecting someone?" Lisa asked, surprised at the cynicism in her own words. Her emotions were mixing and merging into an amalgam of something entirely different. She was tired of being afraid and uncertain. If she was going to die tonight, she was going to do so not as a terror-stricken woman but as a thinking human being.

"As a matter of fact, I am," Massey said. "An APB has certainly gone out on this car, and a helicopter has been dispatched. That's the quickest way to track us. It's hard to hide from an eye in the sky, but then you know that, don't you?"

"What's that mean?"

"Just what it sounds like."

In the distance, Lisa could hear a faint thrumming. Massey swore. He heard it too.

The road was changing from an easy two-lane ribbon into a sinuous, twisting affair. He slowed the car even more. His eyes moved constantly from the road in front of them to the sky to the rearview mirror. Lisa reasoned that he was looking for a turnoff, a place to hide. But hiding would not be enough, she realized. He wanted escape, and hiding would not bring that.

Lisa forced herself to think. What did she know about this man? Nothing. No, that wasn't right. She knew a few things. She knew his name and that he worked for Moyer Communications, an organization with which she apparently had had some dealings, although she didn't know what. What else did she know? He was intelligent and seemed committed to his mission. Could his intelligence overpower his loyalty?

"Mr. Massey?"

"What?" he said sharply.

"How much do you know about Nick Blanchard?"

"Not enough. Just what he said in the motel room."

"I see," Lisa said. "He seemed to know you."

"That is his job. Moyer Communications has provided the NSA with a great deal of its equipment. They probably know every employee, their families, and their pets. So what?"

"I was just wondering why you were running."

"That's a stupid question."

"Is it? Nick is with the police right now. He knows your name and where you work. So let's say you do escape the police tonight; where are you going to go? Back to work? Back home? They'll be there waiting for you. How's your boss going to feel about that? Federal agents, local police knocking on his door, asking questions about you."

"Didn't I tell you to shut up?" Massey shouted.

Lisa ignored him and continued. "Your life has just changed permanently. You can never go back."

"Moyer Communications is a global company. There are many places for me to start over. A new name, a new history, a new city. I'll be fine."

That had not occurred to Lisa. Still, she kept up the pressure. "Moyer will drop you in a second. You're baggage now. You can do nothing for him but hold him back. He'll divest himself of you like a snake sheds its skin. And then it gets worse."

Lisa waited for a reaction but got none. She pressed on. "He might even have you killed."

"That's not going to happen. He needs me. I'm vital. I'm crucial on several projects . . ."

"And you know too much," Lisa said. "Face it, Mr. Massey, everyone is expendable. He sent you and whoever that guy was in the house to get me. What makes you think he won't try to destroy you?"

"You were a threat."

"And now so are you."

"You were going to divulge everything. I would never do that. Moyer knows that." He paused then repeated, "He knows that."

"Someone once told me that people who repeat statements don't believe their own words." Lisa had no idea where she had heard that, but she felt a small sense of joy at remembering something from her past.

"Pop psychology," Massey said dismissively.

"Maybe."

"So what do you think I should do?" he asked sarcastically. "Give myself up?"

"Why not?" Lisa knew why not, but she

wanted to keep the conversation going. She needed time to think, and the more time that passed, the more likely she was to live.

"Let's see," Massey said, feigning thoughtfulness. "I've followed you, participated in an assault, shot a police officer, resisted arrest. Oh, I almost forgot. I killed a man today. Those sound like pretty good reasons not to turn myself in."

"Killed a man? Whom did you kill?"

"The *gentleman* who attacked you in Blanchard's house." He acerbically stressed the word *gentleman*. "He was supposed to kill you. It was his job, not mine, but he was a screwup from day one."

This wasn't working the way Lisa had hoped. Massey was a desperate man in a situation that was becoming more desperate with each passing minute.

The drone of a distant helicopter became louder.

Massey swore again.

A small bead of perspiration formed on Gregory Moyer's forehead. He was watching the action unfold on his monitor. The spy satellite he had used to find Blanchard's truck was working perfectly. It was locked on Massey's car and was following it as it sped down a dark road. Something had gone very wrong. Why was his man racing at such a high rate of speed? Such action begged for attention from the police.

For a few minutes, Moyer had switched his attention to the new MC2-SDS while he contacted his Sudanese client. He had then placed a few calls to other foreign clients who were eager to hear of the successful launch. That hadn't taken more than thirty or forty minutes. What had he missed?

Hobbs shook his head in profound disbelief as he guided the unmarked CHP car down the street. "You're a federal agent?" he asked. "Why couldn't we find any information on you or your truck?"

"I bet you tried to trace Lisa's car and failed at that too." Nick was seated in the passenger seat. He had returned Hobbs's gun to him only after he had explained everything to the detective. He had placed Tanner's gun in the glove compartment.

"That's right. Why is that?"

"With all due respect, Detective, the measures used by the police today are good, but they fall short of being state of the art. Identities can be stolen, switched, concealed, altered if you know what to do, and the NSA knows what to do."

"So the truck, Lisa Keller's car —"

"All owned by the NSA and used for its purposes."

"That would mean that Keller is an NSA agent." Hobbs's mind was twisting and turning around the facts.

"Right. I was her contact. We were supposed to meet in Mojave and then take the next step."

"Which is?" Hobbs prompted.

"Which is secret," Nick answered bluntly.

Hobbs thought for a moment. The story made sense, and it answered a boatload of questions. Still, there were missing parts.

"Why didn't you take her to a doctor, especially after you discovered her amnesia?"

"I tried, but every time I brought it up, she went ballistic. I was afraid that her agitation would make her condition worse. You have to understand, Detective, that what she knows is extremely important. It's not an exaggeration to say that the future of the country is locked up in her brain."

"The future of our country? That sounds a little melodramatic."

"Perhaps, but it is nonetheless true."

"Are you saying that our country could fall because of what she knows?"

"No, not fall, but change substantially.

The country would go on, but our freedom — well, that's a different matter."

"You'd better explain that."

"Sorry, that's all you're getting," Nick said resolutely.

"How well do you know this area?" Hobbs asked after a brief silence.

"Fairly well," Nick said. "I've lived here for a while, but we're in the backwoods of the county here. There are several small communities ahead, each with a long road that leads to them. Massey could take any one of them, and we would never find him from the road. If we don't see him soon, we may lose him forever."

"We have a helicopter up," Hobbs said. "That's our best hope right now."

"He's smart, Detective. Real smart. Dangerous, too."

"Can Ms. Keller handle herself?"

"In most cases, yes, but her memory has been thrashed. Who knows what she recalls about self-defense. Although she gave a pretty good show earlier this evening."

The frustration that Hobbs had been experiencing grew exponentially. Everything was as bad as it could get. He had called in his intentions and actions on the car radio using the phrase that would activate every police unit in the vicinity: "Officer down;

officer needs assistance." Even as he and Blanchard had sped off in pursuit of Lisa and her abductor, he could hear the sirens of approaching units. Tanner would be fine. He wasn't so certain about Lisa Keller.

"Put that on your lap," Massey ordered, pointing down to the floorboard where a briefcase lay upended. The case had been pushed there when he had forced Lisa into the car, leaving just enough room for her legs.

"Why?" she asked. He reached inside his suit coat. Lisa knew he was reaching for a gun. "Okay, okay," she said.

She hauled up the case and opened it. Inside was a set of electronics and a small green monitor.

"Turn it on," Massey commanded.

Lisa studied the open case for a moment, then found a button marked POWER. The monitor came to life in an eerie green haze. A second later a grid of streets appeared and a small triangle that moved along one of the lines.

"GPS," she said perfunctorily.

"It seems you haven't lost all your memory," he said. "Hold on."

The car suddenly yanked left off the pavement and down a dirt road. The road led a short distance into a mature orange grove. The trees were in full foliage and formed a canopy over the car. Massey braked hard enough to cause Lisa to throw up a hand to prevent her from careening into the dashboard. The car slid to a stop. She wished she were wearing a seat belt.

"You want oranges?" Lisa asked.

"For a woman who is in as much danger as you are, you sure have a smart mouth." Massey's voice was edgy. Clearly, he didn't like to be in a situation he couldn't control, yet he was far from panicked. In fact, he seemed more annoyed than frightened. Perhaps, she thought, he could be agitated enough to make mistakes.

"It was just a question."

He twisted the GPS tracker on her lap so that he could see it. Lisa had to lean to her left to see the full screen. In addition to the various streets on the screen were the names of towns and a small icon of an airplane. Massey punched a button and then said, "That's what I want — an airport."

"Where?"

"In Santa Paula. It's less than five miles from here." With his left hand, he reached inside his coat pocket. Instinctively, Lisa pulled back, expecting a gun. Instead, she saw a cell phone. She recalled that the gun was on his other side. She watched as he pushed a single button. The phone number must have been stored in the phone's memory.

As he waited for his call to go through, Lisa looked at the orchard that surrounded her. The trees were spaced in even rows like a battalion of soldiers standing at rigid attention. Between the trees were irrigation furrows. The car's headlights reflected off the tiny streams of water that nurtured the trees. Shrouded in the darkness of night, the stacked rows of orange trees looked like a deep, forbidding forest, the kind in which elves and trolls and monsters hid.

Hid. To hide.

It would be madness, foolishness, and could only result in her death. It was a crazy idea, but it might work. She was going to die anyway. Her abductor would surely kill her as soon as she was no longer useful as a hostage.

"Yes . . . yes, Mr. Moyer." Massey seemed surprised. Although she could not make out the words, she could hear Moyer's voice, despite the fact that her abductor had the cell phone pressed into his ear. "Things went differently than planned, sir. I'm sorry. Yes sir, I did pull off the road. I've made some changes too. They were necessary. She has made no revelations . . ." He paused for a moment to listen, then continued, "Blanchard is a Boy Scout."

Revelations? Boy Scout? The realization came to Lisa: Massey was afraid that someone might be listening in on the conversation. He was as paranoid as she was. Then another thought occurred to her: How did Moyer know they had pulled off the road?

Massey listened for a few moments. "Yes sir. I understand. I'm eager to get back to the office. Perhaps a helicopter would be best, sir." More listening. "I'm sure it will all work out, sir, but time is crucial. If you could arrange —" He had been interrupted by Moyer. "Very well, sir. I'll take care of it."

Lisa closed the case that contained the GPS electronics and latched it shut. Massey did not seem to notice. Then, as if gazing out at the orchard, she checked to see if her door was unlocked. It was. She also judged the line of trees closest to her to be only two feet away. There was, however, sufficient room to open the door between two trees in the row that was closest to the car. Had her abductor stopped a few feet farther, a tree would certainly have blocked her way.

She would have to be fast. Most likely, if

she tried this, she would be dead. But was that so bad? If God caused all things to work out for good, then death might not be all that bad.

From the corner of her eye, Lisa saw Massey switch the phone off and place it on the dashboard. "This is where you're going to kill me, isn't it?" she asked without emotion.

"It's your own fault, Ms. Keller. You poked your nose in where it didn't belong. You should have minded your own business."

"It's sad, really," she said. "You're going to kill me before I have a chance to remember why you hate me so much."

"Just like a woman," he said cynically. "It has nothing to do with hate or love or any other emotion. You stole secrets from us, and now we must protect ourselves. That is the extent of it."

"It's all business then? Nothing personal, is that it?"

"That's it."

"Then what? Do you go back to Moyer Communications and pretend that nothing has happened?"

"Not directly," he answered. "I can never go back there without a new identity. That's another thing you have cost me."

"I don't suppose an apology will suffice." She turned to face her executioner.

"Not even close, lady." Massey reached under his coat for the gun. "You'll need to step outside —"

His words were cut off when she rammed the edge of the briefcase in his face. She heard something snap: his nose, a tooth. She didn't know. Pulling back the case, she prepared to thrust it at him again, but he raised his hand quickly. She had anticipated this and brought the case down on his leg as hard as she could, digging one of its corners into the flesh of his thigh. He roared in pain and clasped his hands on the heavy case.

"Why you —"

She struck again, this time with her bare hand, aiming the nail of her right thumb at his eye. Something inside her took over. Each move she made was choreographed from the locked area of her brain. She had no time to analyze the source of her actions; she was too busy fighting for her life.

Massey's head snapped and hit the window with a resounding crack. Her thumb missed his eye but dug deep into his cheek. A bellow of indignant pain filled the car.

Lisa reached for the door handle and pulled. The door opened easily, and she tumbled out headfirst, landing on her shoulder in the soft dirt, her feet still in the car. A ragged pain ran up her leg, and she could feel the viselike grip of Massey's hand. He had grabbed her left leg, pressing his fingers into her calf. "No you don't."

Rolling on her back, she could see him lying across the passenger seat, his arm extended and pulling her back. Lisa kicked with all her might. The heel of her sneaker caught him between the eyes. His grip slipped, and she pulled herself free, her finger grasping at the moist earth of the irrigation ditch. Just as she thought she was out of reach, she felt his hand clamp down on her ankle. He jerked the leg, sending ripping bolts of agony through her body. She screamed at the flood of scorching, scalding pain.

Flailing, she sought a handhold, but the ground was too soft. Stretching, reaching, clutching, she made contact with the narrow trunk of an orange tree. With a grunt she caught it with one hand. Then, twisting her body so that she lay on her stomach again, she took hold of the tree with her other hand.

"You stupid . . ." Massey was shouting, but Lisa wasn't listening. All of her thoughts, all of her energies were devoted to getting away. Looking over her shoulder, she saw his dilemma: He had her with his right hand, and he was stretched even farther over the passenger seat. Like her, he was on his belly. He couldn't reach his gun. To do so he would have to let her go. It was a physical stalemate. He had the superior strength, but he lacked the purchase to reel her in. His body position was awkward. She had all the leverage; he had most of the muscle.

Lisa's eyes shifted from Massey to the ground around her. She desperately needed a weapon, anything to give her an advantage, even the odds. There was nothing. No rocks, no stakes, nothing but a thin limb of a tree that had been broken off. The limb was less than two inches in diameter and covered with thick green leaves at one end. At the other end, the end that had been attached to the trunk, was a ragged edge.

Feeling her grip loosen as Massey continued his inexorable tug, Lisa decided if the limb was the only weapon she was going to find, it would have to do. As hard as she could, she tried once more to pull away. The effort brought her one inch closer to the broken limb that lay just within her reach. Releasing the tree trunk, she grasped for the limb. She caught it with two fingers and quickly pulled it into her two hands.

The limb was far too light to use as a club, and the leaves and smaller branches made it unwieldy. Rolling on her back, she felt herself slip through the loose earth as Massey, now with two hands on her left leg, pulled her closer. "Nice try, woman, but not good enough."

As quickly as she could, Lisa sat up, raised the branch over her head and brought it down, not as a club, but as a dagger, driving the ragged end through his coat sleeve and into the flesh of his forearm. The skin gave way to the broken stalk, and blood ran freely down the man's arm.

Scrambling to her feet, Lisa seized the open car door and swung it closed, putting all her weight behind it. She slammed the door so hard that her feet slipped, and she fell back to the ground. She landed hard, hitting her head, but she saw the heavy car door close on Massey's arms and head. The door, unable because of Massey's interposed body to latch, sprang back open.

Lisa began to run.

Every step was agony. Her body protested with hot, piercing pain. Her stomach boiled with nauseating acid. She wanted to stop, to catch her breath, to calm the pain, to settle her stomach, but she ran. In a near-blind terror she raced through the trees in zigzag fashion, stumbling in the small, wet trenches with bone-jarring intensity. With each fall, she forced herself to rise again and to run.

When she fled, she first ran deep into the grove, hoping the trees would hide her, but she needed more than a hiding place, she needed help. If Massey found her again, there would be no way to fight back. He would put a bullet in her head with no second thoughts, no remorse.

"The street," she said to herself in an exhausted whisper. "Find the street."

Turning to her right, she headed back the short distance to the two-lane highway. The 150. Behind her, Massey shouted her name. His voice was different. It was the most horrible thing she had ever heard.

Her breathing was ragged, her lungs burned for air. She was no longer running. Her body was too drained of energy to move any faster. Whatever reserves she'd had before had been used up over the last twenty-four hours.

Massey was behind her. She didn't have to see him, didn't have to hear his voice. He was chasing her, stalking her, hunting her like she was some rabbit. She had to reach the road, had to find someone to help. But what if she couldn't? What if no one saw her? Or nobody was there, or they were afraid to help? Her life would end on the gravel shoulder of a strange road, next to an orange orchard. She would die not remembering her parents, not knowing anything. To her that was the most tragic thing of all.

The orchard gave way to the open expanse of gravel shoulder and the two-lane road. A car whizzed by just as Lisa emerged. She arrived too late, and now she was in the open. Making her way to the edge of the road she looked for headlights, she prayed for headlights. In the distance she saw a single pair of beams approaching.

Chapter 19

Tuesday, 10:25 P.M.

"What the —" Hobbs slowed the car as he caught sight of a woman frantically waving her arms and staggering along the roadside.

"That's her!" Nick shouted.

"Are you sure?"

"Of course, I'm sure. I've spent the whole day with the woman. Hurry up."

She was thirty yards ahead and on the right. Hobbs gunned the engine and steered directly for her. Seconds later, he brought the car to an abrupt stop, tires crunching on the gravel shoulder. Nick, despite his injuries, was out of the vehicle before Hobbs could bring the car to a full stop. "Lisa!"

Hobbs bolted from the car and raced around the front. Lisa had collapsed on the ground. Nick was helping her up. Cakes of moist dirt clung to her white shirt, face, and hands.

"Behind . . . behind . . . me," she said in a voice barely above a whisper. She was gulping for air, her eyes wide with fright.

"Massey? Massey is behind you?" Nick asked.

"He . . . has a . . . gun."

A loud bang echoed through the air a fraction of a second after a hole appeared in the front fender of the car.

"Down!" Hobbs yelled as he yanked his gun from its shoulder holster. His eyes darted along the first row of trees that marked the beginning of the orchard. In the dim light of the night he saw a man, his hand raised and pointed at the trio. Hobbs took aim and squeezed the trigger. There was another bang, and a second round ricocheted off the hood of the car. Hobbs flinched just as his gun fired, causing him to miss his target. The gunman recoiled and ducked back into the trees, out of Hobbs's sight.

"Get her in the car," the detective shouted, but Nick was ahead of him. Hobbs caught sight of the NSA man pushing Lisa into the backseat and climbing in after her. From his position near the driver's door, he could see Nick cover Lisa with his own body.

Another shot from the orchard shattered the windshield into a million weblike pieces held in place by the safety laminate. Hobbs ducked behind the car and popped up a moment later to fire in the direction from which he thought the shot had originated. He then ducked into the driver's seat, lying across it and the passenger seat.

"Get us out of here," Nick said.

Instead, Hobbs grabbed the microphone of his radio, keyed it, identified himself and his location, and spoke the words that would bring in the cavalry. "Shots fired. Repeat, shots fired."

The passenger window exploded into a thousand tempered-glass pieces, showering them like hail from the sky. The dispatcher responded and Hobbs heard her send out the call. Like Nick, Hobbs wanted to flee the scene. The attacker had better coverage and the advantage of position.

Wriggling back out of the seat, Hobbs moved forward, using the car as a shield. He would have preferred moving back, but that was too close to Lisa and Nick. A shot might pierce the door and hit one of them. By moving to the front of the car, he hoped to draw the line of fire away. It worked; another bullet hit the front of the car. Hobbs returned two shots.

"Lisa," Hobbs said as low as he could and still expect her to hear in the backseat. "Do you know what kind of gun he has?"

Hobbs had to strain to hear her. "A nine-millimeter, I think."

That meant the gunman could have fifteen or so rounds at his disposal. Hobbs shuddered. By his count, only four rounds had been fired unless . . . "Did he shoot at you earlier?"

"No," Lisa said.

"Sit tight," Hobbs said. "We're stuck here until help arrives."

"Can't you drive us out of here?" Nick asked.

"Not without getting my brains splattered," Hobbs replied.

Another shot bounced off the hood, missing Hobbs by inches. If he could only see the man, he might be able to put an end to this.

The street-side rear door opened, and Lisa crawled out with Nick behind her. "Keep your head down," Nick said to her. Lisa crouched down by the rear wheel. Nick, his face a mask of pain from being forced to bend his tender and swollen knee, shuffled over to Hobbs. "Do you carry a spare?"

Hobbs knew what he was referring to. Many officers carried concealed guns, usually around the ankle. They were backup guns for situations in which an officer might be deprived of his service weapon. When he was a patrolman, Hobbs had done that very thing but not since making detective. "I'm afraid not. Tanner's gun is in the glove compartment where you put it." Another shot sounded, and the men flinched.

"What about the trunk? Any weapons in there?"

"A shotgun." Hobbs remembered seeing it when he was looking for the gloves earlier that day.

"A handgun or a shotgun," Nick said. "Shotgun it is." While still crouched, Nick opened the driver's door and looked under the dash. He found what he was looking for: A black plastic lever with the word TRUNK on it. Reaching in, he gave it a tug. The trunk lid swung open. Closing the car door, Nick made his way to the rear of the vehicle. He stopped by Lisa. Hobbs heard him ask, "How are you doing?"

"I've been better," she replied.

"Hang in there. Help is on its way."

For Hobbs, help couldn't arrive soon enough.

Lisa could do nothing but wait and force herself to be calm. Closing her eyes, she tried to will her heart to slow and her breathing to settle, but just as she achieved a measure of success, the firing startled her again. She was out of Massey's hands, and for that she was thankful. She barely noticed her injuries. She was turning numb. *Shock,* she reasoned. *No,* she told herself, *I have to fight it. Use my brain. Emotions won't help. Think. Reason. Think.*

"Give it up, Massey," Nick shouted across the back of the car. "Don't make things worse than they are."

The response came in the form of a shot.

"Why doesn't he run?" Hobbs asked Nick.

"Who knows," Nick answered. "Maybe he's crazy."

"He's not crazy," Lisa said breathlessly. "He's driven. He blames me for his predicament. He wants me dead."

"Well, that's not going to happen," Nick said, pumping the handle on the shotgun and then firing into the orchard.

A car whizzed past them just as another shot was fired their way.

"Some passerby is going to get killed," Lisa said.

"The sheriff and his deputies will set up a roadblock as soon as they can," Hobbs said.

"Let's hope it's soon enough."

In the distance, Lisa could hear the ululations of police sirens. Then she heard another sound, that of a helicopter. She had forgotten about the craft. Massey had pulled off the road abruptly and driven into the stand of orange trees. The helicopter, which had not found them, must have continued searching Highway 150. Now it was back.

A blinding light shone down from the black sky. Lisa turned in time to see Hobbs motioning toward the orchard. The pilot redirected the light toward the trees. The orchard lit up under the artificial sun. The warm summer air was filled with the smell of orange blossoms and laced with the acrid odor of gunpowder.

Police units began to arrive with sirens wailing. Over the radio, Lisa could hear the pilot talking to the ground units. He had spotted the gunman, who was now running deeper into the orchard. Knowing that Massey was fleeing, Lisa peeked over the car. She could see the beam from the chopper move as it followed the man.

"I've lost him," the pilot said. He then began to circle the orchard. A second later, the pilot said, "I've got him again. He's southbound about two hundred yards from your location —"

Another shot rang out, and everyone ducked. Lisa waited for a moment and then peeked over the car again. She could hear the helicopter but could not see its light.

The radio crackled again. "This guy is crazy. He shot out my light. I don't believe it. He shot out my light."

Sheriff's deputies and CHP officers moved slowly into the orchard.

"It's just a matter of time now," Hobbs said. "He can run, but he can't hide."

"Don't underestimate him," Lisa said as she struggled to her feet. "Your pilot was wrong. He's not crazy. He's devious."

"Well, whatever he is," Hobbs said, "he's not your problem anymore."

"I hope you're right," she offered.

Hobbs leaned into the car and said something into the radio; a few seconds later an ambulance appeared.

Since the ambulance was in an area still considered dangerous, Lisa was loaded unceremoniously into the back and driven away. The routine field exam was waived in light of the menace. Nick had insisted on going along. At first Hobbs resisted, wanting Nick to describe Massey to the sheriff's sergeant who took control of the scene. After a brief argument, both men rode in the ambulance — Hobbs in front, Nick in the back with the attendant. Lisa was just glad to be away from the area and wished that the ambulance would continue on out of the state. Instead she was told that she was being taken to Ojai Valley Hospital.

Lisa gazed up first into the eyes of the attendant who looked like he had just graduated from high school, then into Nick's drawn and haggard face. He looked worn, thin, and on edge. His hair was mussed, and his still bare chest was soaked with perspiration. His arm was bleeding again; a rust-red patch had saturated the bandage she had put on in the motel room.

"Your arm," she said wearily.

"Don't you worry about my arm," Nick said.

The attendant said, "Let me see that, sir."

"I'll be fine," Nick said.

"It's my job, sir," the attendant replied firmly. Removing a pair of medical scissors from one of the many compartments that lined the inside of the ambulance, he cut away the bandage and removed the dressing. "That's going to need stitches," he said flatly. "How did you get that?"

"An unhappy houseguest," Nick said cryptically. "How much longer before we reach the hospital?"

"Another fifteen minutes or so," the attendant replied.

Lisa wondered what would happen next. It wasn't the hospital that concerned her, but the detective sitting in the front. He was sure to have many questions, few of which she could answer. Still, that seemed a small thing with all that she had been through. At least for the moment she was out of danger.

The ambulance rocked as it drove down the road, exacerbating the exhaustion Lisa felt. The relief of having escaped Massey numbed the pain that had been so acute minutes before.

Closing her eyes, she let her mind drift, searching for some pleasant memory, some captivating vision in which to project herself. She longed to be somewhere away, somewhere peaceful.

The image of the rolling surf as seen from Nick's rear deck painted the canvas of her mind. She smiled.

Chapter 20

Tuesday, 11:35 P.M.

Lisa had been given a mild pain reliever that was just beginning to take the edge off the soreness she felt. The ambulance had brought her, Nick, and Hobbs to the single-story hospital at the edge of town. Although the facility was small, it didn't lack for equipment or personnel. For the last ninety minutes, two doctors had poked, prodded, x-rayed, and examined Lisa. Her blood pressure had been recorded and temperature taken. Her cuts had been cleaned and dressed, the dirt removed from her hands and face.

Of all the procedures she had endured since arriving at the emergency room, the verbal exam hurt the most. Question after question was asked, and she had answers for none of them. All she could offer was the name she had learned earlier that evening, Robin Lisa Keller, and a few fragments of recollection.

Hobbs insisted on interrogating her, but the doctors made him wait in the lobby.

Nick was escorted to an ER bed and examined. He was waiting for the results of the x-rays on his knee when a technician moved Lisa to a small private room. In the pale glow of the single fluorescent light over her bed, she studied the shadows on the ceiling. They looked ghostly to her, specters of gloom that hovered above her, waiting for their opportunity to swoop down the moment she slipped off to sleep. Fear, irrational and reasonable, valid and imagined, descended on her like a fog.

"All things work together for good to them that love God." God. Had He been involved in her life? Had it been He who had kept her alive and free of serious, life-threatening injury? Was there something more here, something she had yet to see? The peace she had felt when she read the Gideon Bible in the hotel began to return, dispelling hours of anxiety. The ghostly shadows seemed to retreat from before her eyes.

Closing her eyes, Lisa thought of God. The passages she had read about Jesus were calming, and she called them back to mind. She began to pray. It was a simple prayer, like a child speaking to her father, and it was comfortable as only an action that had been repeated many times before could be. There was no pretense in her unspoken words, no formality, just a sharing of very real needs. She found God a willing and patient listener.

"Lisa?"

Lisa opened her eyes, her peace disturbed and her heart suddenly thundering again. Nick stood in the door, a crutch under one arm. He wore a green surgical shirt and his knee was wrapped in an elastic bandage. His pant leg had been cut away. Behind Nick stood a stern looking Detective Hobbs.

"I'm sorry to wake you," Nick said.

"I wasn't asleep," Lisa said. "Just . . . praying."

"Well, feel free to include me in those prayers," he commented with a broad smile. He ambled in, struggling with the crutch. He grunted slightly as he moved. Hobbs was close behind. Once inside, Hobbs pulled a red plastic chair over for Nick to sit in.

"I know it's late, Ms. Keller," Hobbs said, "but I have a few questions."

Lisa offered a wan smile. "I imagine you have a great many questions."

"Yes ma'am. I certainly do."

"How is your partner?" Lisa asked.

"He's doing well," Hobbs said. "The shot went straight through his thigh, but it missed the bone. He is resting a few rooms down."

"Will he be in long?" Lisa inquired.

"They're cutting him loose tomorrow. His wife is coming down to get him."

"It must have been horrible for her to get that call." Lisa realized that she had no one to call. If she had been killed, she would have died in obscurity, unknown, perhaps even unmissed. "Maybe I'll have time to thank him before he goes. You and he saved my life."

"Mine, too, Hobbs," Nick added.

Hobbs just nodded, and then said, "I have a lot of holes to fill about you two. I think it's time you brought me up to speed."

"I know very little," Lisa said. "I know I was in an accident and that Nick came to my aid." She went on to explain the day's events from her awakening in the Pretty Penny Motel to the moment she was loaded into the ambulance.

"You know, Ms. Keller," Hobbs began, "I'm normally a very trusting person, even for a cop, but I'm having trouble buying this amnesia thing. It sounds too Hollywood to be real."

"It's not Hollywood," a firm voice said from the doorway. A thin, bleary-eyed, bald man stood in the doorway. He wore a pale blue polo shirt, white slacks, and slip-on loafers. He held a file folder in his hand.

"Who are you?" Hobbs asked.

"I'm Dr. Brice. I'm the consulting neurologist, and you couldn't be more wrong." Brice stepped into the room, walking directly to Lisa's bedside. "How are you feeling, Ms. Keller?"

"Beat."

"From what I hear, you have good reason to feel that way," Brice said. He was a humorless man who spoke in quick clips. "I have reviewed your file and want to give you a once-over."

"Not another exam," Lisa complained wearily.

"It won't be bad," Brice stated. "A neurological exam is 80 percent questions and 20 percent physical exam."

"Maybe we should leave," Nick said.

"No need," Brice said. "Not unless Ms. Keller wishes you to."

Lisa looked at Nick and then said, "After all we've been through, I think you can stay."

The exam was quick. Brice peered into Lisa's eyes and ears, studied her bruised head, checked her reflexes, and asked what seemed to Lisa to be a thousand questions.

"What do you remember of your accident, Ms. Keller?"

"Please call me Lisa." The name Keller still seemed foreign to her. "Just snippets. I remember headlights coming up from behind. I remember being rammed and losing control. Everything else is dim."

"Is there a way to prove that the amnesia is real?" Hobbs asked, not unkindly.

Brice looked at Hobbs as if studying him. "Who are you?"

"Detective Bill Hobbs." He flashed his badge.

"Well, Detective, the short answer is no, if by proof you mean a physical test that yields an amnesia/no-amnesia result. However, amnesia is not that uncommon."

"Really?" Lisa said with surprise. Hearing Brice's words gave her some comfort. Her experience was not unique.

"There are many types of amnesia and many causes," Brice said. "For example, there is childhood amnesia where the patient has little or no memory of events in their lives from when they were ages five to seven. There is visual amnesia, which is a loss of memory of things seen; verbal amnesia, which is the inability to recall words. The most confusing is Broca's amnesia, in which the subject cannot understand language in its written or spoken form. Words just no longer make sense."

"Amazing," Nick said.

Lisa felt a rush of gratitude. Things could have been worse. "You said there were many things that could cause people to lose their memory."

"That's right," Brice responded. "For example, there is hysterical amnesia. A person sees something so horrible, so traumatic, that the brain simply shuts out the event. The patient disassociates from the incident. Disease can also cause memory loss: cerebral malaria, collagen diseases, diabetes, amyloidosis, sarcoidosis, and so on. Toxic agents like alcohol, barbiturate abuse, and carbon monoxide poisoning can short-circuit memory. And then, of course, there is TBI."

"TBI?" Lisa said.

"Traumatic brain injury," Brice answered. "That is most likely the cause of your amnesia. The x-rays show no serious damage to the brain and no lesions or edema, which is good, but you did take a nasty knock to the head. The amnesia that comes from an event such as yours is called posttraumatic retrograde amnesia."

"What I don't understand, Doctor," Lisa began, "is how I can forget my past but still remember how to talk and walk and speak."

"Let me explain," Brice said. "If you imagine the human brain as an orange, then the outer layer, the peel, would be the cerebral cortex. Injury to the cerebral cortex results in bruising, which in turn inhibits memory retrieval. Less personal memories, like language skills, are stored in a different part of the brain. Do you have any memories of your past at all?"

Lisa thought for a moment. "Some very nebulous ones. They're more like sensations than memories."

"Those are known as island memories. There are parts of the cortex that have not been affected by the accident."

Lisa took a deep breath and asked the question that had been haunting her. "Will I ever get my memory back?"

For the first time since entering the room, Brice smiled. "Your trauma is not too severe. Most cases like yours clear up within seventy-two hours. As the brain recovers from the trauma, those islands of memory get bigger. I think you'll be fine in a few days. Just take it easy, avoid exertion, and rest as much as possible."

Avoid exertion? Lisa almost laughed. The last twenty-four hours had been as stressful as she could imagine. She had endured three murder attempts. It was a wonder that she hadn't lost her mind as well as her memory.

"Thank you, Doctor."

Brice started to leave, but Hobbs stopped him with a question. "Is it all right if I ask Ms. Keller a few more questions?"

"Just don't upset her," Brice said sharply and then left.

Moyer swore at his computer monitor. He swore at the dead Carson McCullers, and he cursed Raymond Massey. The image on his screen had not changed in nearly an hour. He was still looking at the dark orchard. On the street that ran by the orchard, he could see the red-and-blue lights of the police. Occasionally a helicopter would fly across the screen. The satellite had not moved because it was locked onto Massey's car, which it had lost when he turned into the dense orchard. It no longer had anything to acquire.

Moyer had watched the shootout, the arrival of the police, and the coming and going of the ambulance. Now with time to second-guess himself, Moyer wished he had followed the ambulance. Then he could have directed Massey to whatever hospital they had taken the woman — assuming that

Massey was still in commission. If he wasn't . . .

Massey's fastidiousness had been harmed, and it ate at him. The last ninety minutes had been grueling. Most men would have been happy simply to escape capture, but it had never occurred to Massey that his arrest was even possible. He was too smart, too clever. He had never failed at anything that he had attempted.

Sitting in the dim light of the electronics room, Massey cleaned the mud from his shoes with a screwdriver he had found in a tool kit. The motion caused him pain, but the pain made him all the more determined. The woman was scrappy, fighting back in a manner he would never have expected. He paused, looked down at his arms again, and glowered. When he had first arrived at the radio shack, he had removed his suit coat and examined himself. There was a gash and a bruise the size of a lemon covering the forearm where she had stabbed him with the tree branch. When she had slammed the car door on him, the door had hit his head and arms. He was amazed that nothing had been broken. The egg-size knot on the side of his head and his swollen nose reminded him that he may have been fortunate not to have received more severe injuries, but he had not got off scot-free.

The police would never find him. Not even the sheriff's helicopter could peer through these walls. The satellite relay station on Sulphur Mountain was owned and operated by Moyer Communications. Massey had immediately thought of it when it was clear that the woman had made her escape. *Luck,* he thought. *She is the luckiest person alive. She should have been dead several times over.* But she wasn't dead. Instead she was once again out of danger, probably under police protection in some hospital. And here he was sitting in the stale air of a windowless room, surrounded by sophisticated electronics that received signals from satellites high above and relayed them to other satellites.

The journey had been one of determination and trial. Fleeing deeper into the orchard, Massey had used the trees as cover from the sheriff who would soon be hot on his trail. Not being able to see him, they would burn precious minutes wondering if he was playing the role of sniper, ready to kill anyone who approached the orchard. He knew that they would cordon off the street to protect passing motorists and then wait for additional officers. Only then would they attempt entry into the orchard. One man, hidden from view, could hold off an army. But he had no intention of fighting the police. He was a man of singular purpose, and his purpose was to finish his mission. First, however, he had to escape and to survive.

Running in zigzag fashion, Massey had sprinted between the rows of orange trees. Overhead the helicopter's rotor beat an unending thrum. A second helicopter had joined the pursuit since Massey had successfully shot out the searchlight of the first craft. The second chopper's artificial sun beamed a high intensity ray into the trees, filtering through the leaves to give the orchard an eerie, surrealistic glow, but the overhead canopy of leaves kept Massey hidden.

Treading through the loose earth and splashing in the irrigation ditches, Massey plowed ahead. He had run, by his estimation, a half-mile before he saw what he was hoping to find: a rancher's home. An outcropping of buildings sat in a small clearing. One was a large, sprawling, stucco house. Warm white light shone from the windows. Another building was a tall and wide wood structure that could only be a barn. Massey made his way to that structure.

He was in luck. A nearly new Ford pickup was parked by the barn's large doors. Inside Massey saw the keys dangling from the ignition. At first he thought the owner stupid and careless, but then he realized that there was no pressing reason not to leave the keys. The ranch was far from the city and a good distance from the road. Not many car thieves would travel this far out of the way to steal a truck.

Slipping into the driver's seat, Massey quietly closed the door and waited to see if he had been discovered. He heard and saw nothing. *The family is probably seated around the television watching a late-night sitcom,* Massey reasoned. He eyed his surroundings. He needed to know which way to drive out. Starting the truck could draw attention. If he was heard, the rancher would call the police and give a description of the missing truck. That would be counterproductive. It was a risk he had to take.

A dirt road stretched past the barn and into a grove of trees. That had to be the exit. The engine turned over the moment Massey turned the key. The truck purred, and Massey was thankful that he hadn't stumbled across an old noisy clunker. He eyed the house again, but nothing had changed. But Massey wasn't clear yet. He still had to drop the truck into drive and pull away. Being careful not to step on the brake pedal, which would cause the rear lights to glow bright red, Massey shifted the automatic transmission into drive and let the idling engine push the truck forward.

An eternity of seconds passed as he directed the slow-moving truck along the dirt road. The tires made a soft grinding noise on the gravel bed. Only after the truck had crept several hundred yards did he put his foot to the accelerator.

The dirt road led to a paved one that connected with the two-lane highway he had left sometime earlier. The intersection was a quarter-mile past where the police had set up their station. From there, Massey had driven along as if nothing had happened. The tracking station in which he now sat was four and a half miles up a winding road. Massey knew its location because he had overseen the project that placed six such stations in California. Once there, he had parked the truck under a nearby oak tree, walked to the building, forced the door open, and entered the room of automated equipment.

Massey continued to clean his shoes, scraping off the drying mud with the screwdriver, but his mind was elsewhere. Things were more difficult now. Driving back the way he had come from the Ojai motel would be too risky. He couldn't endanger his mission. To do so would mean the doom of Moyer Communications. Massey would not let that happen. Not as long as he had breath in his lungs.

What to do now? Massey tossed down the screwdriver, returned to the truck, rummaged through the glove compartment, and found a road map. Returning to the room, he unfolded the large paper and studied the colored lines. He found good news.

Highway 150 turned south, not far from where he had pulled from the road. It traveled to Santa Paula. From there, he could follow a loop of highways that would bring him back to Ojai without having to pass by the police cordon to the west. He figured it was a thirty-five-mile trip. Counting the time it would take to drive back down the mountain and then make his way to Ojai, the long way around would take him close to an hour. *Not ideal, but not bad,* he said to himself.

His biggest concern was not time, but place. Although he had moved deeper into the orchard when the helicopter arrived overhead, he had paused just long enough to see the ambulance arrive, load Blanchard and Keller in the back, pull a U-turn, and head west. Studying the map again, he saw that the closest hospital west of the shooting was in Ojai. The next closest would be in Ventura. Massey made Ojai his first choice. He could always backtrack from there.

He reached for his phone and found it missing. Puzzlement was replaced by anger when he realized that he had set it on the dashboard of the car a moment or two before Lisa Keller attacked him. He was now out of touch with Moyer. "No matter," he said to himself. "My next call will be to tell Moyer that his problems are all over."

Lisa watched as a uniformed Ventura County sheriff's deputy looked into her room and motioned for Hobbs to join him in the corridor. Hobbs complied and returned a few minutes later. He looked grim.

"Not good news, I take it," Lisa said.

"He escaped," Hobbs said sourly.

Nick looked up at Hobbs with astonishment. "Escaped? How does a man escape from an orchard?"

"It was because he was in the orchard that he got away. There was no way to surround the place."

"So he's still on the loose," Lisa said. The words seemed to catch in her throat.

"I'm afraid that's right," Hobbs said. "But you'll be safe here. He'd have to be out of his mind to attack you in a hospital."

"As I said before, he's not crazy. Dangerous, yes, but crazy, no."

"I shouldn't be surprised," Nick said angrily. "That guy is as slippery as an eel, just like his boss."

"How do you know all this?" Hobbs asked.

"I told you in the car, Detective."

"Actually you didn't. As I recall, you told me about the truck and Ms. Keller's car and next to nothing about yourself."

"There's not much more that I'm allowed to tell you," Nick said.

"National security, is that it?" Hobbs said. He sounded unconvinced.

"That's correct." Nick shifted in his chair.

"You can tell him what you told me in the motel room when the man broke in," Lisa said.

"I suppose so," Nick said reluctantly. "As I said earlier, this man's name is Raymond Massey. At least that is his present name."

"Present name?" Hobbs said.

"He has a false identity. He's former CIA, black ops. He did the stuff so secret that only a handful of people know about it. And before you ask, I don't know any details."

"Go on," Hobbs prompted.

"Now he works for Moyer Communications. He's Gregory Moyer's right-hand man. The NSA has been watching him for a long time. You won't catch him now, Detective."

"I'm not that quick to give up," Hobbs said.

"Why won't he catch him?" Lisa asked. "How far could he get?"

"His resources are nearly unlimited. He's no crook. Not a typical crook, that is. This guy has an IQ a third higher than anyone you've ever met. He's also as dedicated and loyal as they come."

"Anyone can make mistakes," Hobbs said.

"True, but don't expect that in this case." Nick looked nervous to Lisa. He shifted in his chair again. "If I were you, I'd put some guards around this place."

"We found a dead man near your house, Mr. Blanchard."

"I know," Lisa said. "Massey told me. A man attacked us in Nick's house. We saw him run from the house, and someone in a car picked him up."

"Massey," Nick said. "That would be just like him. Hire a man to do the job and kill him when he fails."

"Do you have a gun, Ms. Keller?" Hobbs asked. His eyes were fixed firmly on her.

"No, not that I know of."

"What about you, Mr. Blanchard?"

"No."

Hobbs shook his head slowly. "This has been the most bizarre case I've ever seen. I don't know what to believe."

"I know the feeling," Lisa said.

Greg Moyer looked out his office window into the dark night. The blackness on the other side of the window seemed to creep in through the glass and into the marrow of his bones. He had no doubts that things had gone all wrong. Massey should have called by now. The problem should have been resolved. But it wasn't, and there was nothing he could do but wait to hear from his man.

The seconds slipped by sluggishly. Each minute took on a weight, and with every passing minute, another weight was added to the load on his shoulders. He was not a man who believed in premonitions. He was a businessman and an engineer, not a psychic. Yet he knew deep within him that something was terribly wrong. It was time for him to act.

Chapter 21

Wednesday, 12:50 A.M.

The sleepy town of Ojai was sleepier still. The streets were nearly deserted. Only the occasional car plied the streets, followed by late-night trucks delivering dairy products, bread, and other commodities to the local food stores. Massey drove his stolen truck past the hospital, carefully eyeing the parking lot. Only one police car was visible, but he knew that there could be a back lot or that the local detectives might be using unmarked vehicles. He had to assume that there was a police presence.

The logistics of entering the hospital were formidable. After turning the truck around in the local high school parking lot a short distance down the street from the medical center, Massey returned to the area of the hospital. Across the boulevard from the facility was a strip mall. Massey pulled in and parked the truck facing the hospital.

His mind was sharp, unaffected by the lateness of the hour. Focus was the key to genius. Focus and experience, and he had both. If there was any weakness in him now, it was impatience. This job should have been finished long ago. Even now, he should be headed back to San Francisco, to his well-appointed condominium on the bay. In the morning he would report to his boss, receive his praise and a substantial bonus, and maybe even take a few days off. The Bahamas would be nice. That, however, was secondary. What mattered now, *all* that mattered now, was finding and killing Robin Lisa Keller before her memory could return. He would not fail now.

The ideal had given way to reality, and that reality rested in the hospital across the street. At least he thought so. There was still the possibility that they had taken the woman to a different hospital, but that was unlikely. This was the closest facility, and her injuries were not so serious as to require the specialties of a larger medical center. Still, he would have to confirm her presence. That would be step one.

As if the cosmos were lending its aid, Massey saw two men appear from the glass front doors of the building. One moved slowly and wore a green surgeon's shirt. Even from across the street, Massey recognized Nick Blanchard. He moved with one crutch placed firmly under his right arm.

That made sense. Massey remembered that the man had had a large bandage on his left shoulder. Apparently, he also had an injured leg. Massey filed that bit of information away.

With Blanchard was a man dressed in a suit. Massey couldn't be sure, but he thought that it might be the man who fired back at him at the orchard. It was too dark then to make a clear identification, but the man seemed to have the same build and height. Massey now had his confirmation. The woman must be there. But that knowledge was just the beginning. It was now time to form a plan. Seconds counted. Massey knew nothing of amnesia, so he had to assume the worst, that her memory might even now be returning. If so, Moyer Communications was doomed.

He would have liked the luxury of a few hours to formulate a stratagem that included undetected entry, the execution, and a stealthy retreat, but he understood that luxury was not his tonight. Finesse was good, but at times brute force was more efficient. Perhaps he could do a little of both.

He watched the two men talk. If body language was a trustworthy communicator, the man in the suit was put out with Blanchard. He stabbed at the air with his index finger, pointing it at Blanchard like it was a knife. Massey agreed. If the opportunity presented itself, he would kill Blanchard on principle alone.

"I find all this trench-coat stuff infuriating," Hobbs said to Nick. He and the NSA man were standing at the front of the hospital. Hobbs wanted to press Nick for more information, even though he doubted that he would get any.

"I can't help that, Detective," Nick replied easily. "I don't make the rules; I just live by them."

"How do I know what you're telling me is true? The only ID you have is a driver's license, and that's not real either."

"I bet you have people trying to confirm my identity at the NSA."

"Calls have been made," Hobbs said.

"Washington, D.C., is three hours ahead of us. It may be hard to find someone who could confirm my story at 3:00 A.M."

"We'll wake up whomever we need to," Hobbs said.

"If you doubt my story, why don't you arrest me?"

"If you try to leave, I will," Hobbs answered.

"I'm not leaving Lisa," Nick said.

Hobbs turned to the man next to him. He had been through a great deal — attacked in his own home, held at gunpoint in a motel, been involved in two shootings — yet he was as cool as ice, unflappable. Hobbs had been pushing him, trying to mine even the smallest nugget of information that might help him tie all this together. Nothing was working, and his frustration was growing. He had a mystery he couldn't solve, a mystery man from the government next to him, a killer on the loose, and he was out of his jurisdiction. Already he had bent the rules of police procedure and cooperation more than he should, but he had come too far to back off now.

"What does she know?" Hobbs asked bluntly. "What is so important that powerful people want her dead?"

"That, Detective Hobbs, is the sixty-four-thousand-dollar question." Nick limped over to one of the stucco columns that held up the front portico and leaned against it. Earlier he had told Hobbs that he had given up on trying to use both crutches since his left arm, the one ripped open by a bullet, hurt too much to support any weight. "Lisa works for us and had been undercover. She discovered something that frightened her deeply. That's why she bailed out on Moyer

Communications. We never found out what she learned."

"Would you tell me if you had?"

"No."

"All I get from you is the same tidy little story," Hobbs lamented. "I can't do anything with it."

"I understand your aggravation, Hobbs, but it's out of my hands. What you have is all that you're going to get."

"Why haven't you contacted your superiors?"

"What makes you think I haven't?"

This was going nowhere. "All right, Blanchard, I believe you. If you're not NSA, then you're the cleverest crook I've ever seen. No one could have his or her background erased as clean as yours. Not even people in the witness-protection program. You would need the help of a government agency."

"That's the way it works," Nick said.

"So what now?"

"We continue to protect Lisa until I can arrange to have her taken someplace else."

"Do you know her past?"

Nick shook his head. "No. Until yesterday, I had never met her. I was ordered to pick her up in Mojave, just as I told you earlier. The truck was my cover story. From there, I was supposed to protect her. Once she was with me, I would receive instructions about the next few steps. That call came in on my cell phone, but I never got to hear it. Lisa went ballistic and tore my phone apart."

Hobbs nodded. "Yeah, we found it in your truck with the battery yanked. Why would she do that?"

"Because the night has ears, Detective. It has ears and eyes. If her memory were working correctly, she would have remembered that the call would have been encrypted. We had taken precautions so that the phone couldn't be traced. That was just one more memory that was lost."

"The accidents in Mojave. One was Lisa's; the other — a Dodge Ram pickup — was the dead man's. Lisa remembers that she was rammed. Are you responsible for the second accident?"

Nick was slow to respond. Hobbs knew that he was weighing his answer, wondering if this was a trick question. "Yes," he finally said. "Lisa had made better time than expected. As luck would have it, she passed me around Tehachapi. I had trouble keeping up with her. It was a good thing the truck was empty, or I would have lost sight of her."

"So you recognized her car, but she didn't recognize your truck?"

"That's right, and when I saw her rammed, I took action. I wasn't able to stop her from going off the road, but I could keep the attacker from returning to finish the job."

"You then stopped and went to her aid."

"She was woozy, uncertain of where she was. I took her to the Pretty Penny Motel in Mojave, got her a room, and stayed with her until she was asleep. The next morning, I discovered that she had amnesia. I've been playing it by ear ever since."

"I thought you said Moyer Communications was in San Francisco. Why plan a meeting in Mojave? That's a long way from the Bay Area."

"True," Nick said. "I'll say one thing for you, Detective, you don't miss much. The answer is simple. She felt that her life was in grave danger in San Francisco, so when she stepped out for lunch, as she did every day, she took off and started driving south. She contacted us an hour or so later."

"From a pay phone I assume."

"I'm impressed, Detective. How did you know that?"

"Someone, we assume Ms. Keller, had dismantled and removed the built-in cell phone and the GPS system in her car."

"She was afraid of being tracked," Nick said thoughtfully.

Hobbs noticed that Nick looked puzzled. Apparently he was unaware of the dismantling. "Can a person really be tracked that way?"

"It depends on a number of factors. Some GPS systems are more than read-only. You've seen commercials on television where someone is lost or in need of a gas station and gets live advice over the GPS unit. That means someone must be able to determine the car's position. There are also security systems that people can buy and have installed in their cars. Should their car be stolen, the police can activate a transmitter and locate the vehicle. It's quite an achievement and has many safety advantages, and it's risk-free as long as the person on the other end is friendly."

"Moyer Communications wouldn't be the friendly type in this case."

"That's right, and they specialize in satellite systems for telephone, data, and military communications. They're pioneers."

"But the car was a blank too. The VIN and license plate numbers were untraceable. I assume NSA provided the car. Why wouldn't she trust those devices?"

"Systems can be altered or even tapped,

Detective. The GPS system came with the car. If anyone could intercept a GPS signal, Moyer Communications could. The cell phone unit could give away her location whether she was using it or not."

"So why does NSA plant a spy in the midst of Moyer Communications?"

Again Nick hesitated, weighing his answer. "There are some who think that Moyer may have more than his country's interest at heart."

"You mean he might sell out?"

"There are laws about selling certain technology to other countries. But there are ways around those laws. There's reason to believe that national security is at stake."

"Then why not arrest the guilty parties?"

"Because we only have suspicions. Lisa was to provide the evidence." Nick paused for a moment then said, "As you can see, there's much more here than a simple auto accident."

Hobbs frowned. "Nothing about this has been simple."

Massey watched as the two men at the front of the hospital turned and entered the building again. He started the engine and pulled away from the shopping center lot. It was time to get to work.

* * *

Lisa was exhausted; still she could not sleep. She closed her eyes, longing for the blissful nothingness of slumber, but it eluded her. Too much had gone on, and her mind continued to race with the events of the day. When she had been a child, she had overheard her mother tell her father that she had been too tired to sleep. It made no sense to her young mind. How could someone be too tired to sleep — ?

Lisa's heart skipped a beat. She had had a memory — an actual, valid memory. In her mind she could see her mother, a short woman with light brown hair and a thin frame. She could see her father, too. He was tall with a prominent nose, kind gray eyes, and a face that was accustomed to smiling.

As if a floodgate had been opened, additional memories poured in. She could see the living room of the house where she grew up. Jade green drapes hung over the windows, the carpet was brown, the walls white. A painting — a barefoot boy in a straw hat with a homemade fishing pole slung over his shoulder, walking toward a covered bridge, kept company by a golden retriever — hung over the sofa.

The smell of food came with the memory. Pancakes. Mom in the kitchen, pouring batter into a skillet. Lisa could hear the sizzle as the moist mixture hit the hot pan. On the counter rested a plate of flapjacks and a platter of bacon. Between the bacon and the platter were several sheets of paper towels. It was something her mother always did to remove the excess grease. It was her idea of making breakfast healthier.

She saw her father snitching a piece of bacon.

"What do you think you're doing?" her mother asked with pretend anger. "Can't you wait until it's on the table?"

"You know the house rule. It isn't Saturday unless the papa steals a piece of bacon."

"I know the rule," Mom said. "I also know who made it up."

"Truth is truth," Dad countered with a broad smile.

"Unless you plan to do the dishes, get out of my kitchen."

"I'm going. I'm going. Don't have a fit."

The loving banter was a joy to relive, and Lisa wished with all her heart she could step into that memory, to really smell the aroma of frying bacon, to see, to touch her parents one more time.

It was a real memory, and a joyful one at that. Tears of unexpected delight welled in her eyes. A single drop rolled down her cheek. What had Dr. Brice said? There were "islands of memories," and as time passed those islands would begin to connect. The image had been wonderful. Of all the possible memories that could have surfaced, this one brought her great joy.

Lisa tried to push the recollection a little further. Could she remember her parents' names? No. She tried to visualize her front yard, but nothing came to her. *Patience,* she told herself. *It will all come back.*

The domestic scene continued.

"So when do we eat?" her dad asked.

"Okay," her mom said, picking up the platter of bacon and the plate of flapjacks. "Let's pray and then we can eat."

Pray? Of course. Pray. It was what they did before every meal. Every day. Prayer. Sweet prayer.

Again, Lisa was reminded that although she had no recollection of attending a church, hearing a sermon, or participating in a Bible study, she was a spiritual person. The Scripture verse that had triggered something in her thinking, her Bible study in the motel room, and the attraction to the abandoned church in Fillmore were all bits of evidence that showed her faith. She might not remember her spiritual past, but

God had not forgotten her.

Prayer.

All that she had been through, all the terror she had experienced, she had survived because God's hand was upon her. She was as certain of this as she was of her very existence.

Another tear was followed by another wave of warmth.

"And we know that all things work together for good to them that love God, to them who are the called according to his purpose." The words were spoken only in her head, but they rang with a clarion quality. There was a purpose in all that had happened, a reason for the madness she had endured.

Her lips moved in silence, the words of her prayer being heard only in her mind and in heaven. The words were those of thanksgiving and praise. She asked for nothing, pleaded for nothing, attempted no bargains.

There in the hospital room, sore, battered, and confused, Lisa took a stroll with the Almighty, communed with the Savior, bathed in the Spirit. Anxiety was washed away and replaced by peace. Sweetness filled the air and electricity coursed through her soul. Calmness, like a warm familiar afghan, settled upon her.

"Lisa? Are you all right?"

The familiar voice seemed distant and out of place, like a radio in the midst of a deep forest. She continued her prayer, wanting to be no place other than in the throne room of God.

"Lisa," the voice said more forcefully. "Are you hurting?"

Opening her eyes, she saw Nick by her bedside. He was leaning on the crutch. "What . . . what?"

"I asked if you were hurting?"

"No. No more than an hour ago. Why?"

"You're crying," Nick said. His face was chiseled with concern.

"Oh. I was praying," Lisa said, shifting in her bed.

"Again? Praying makes you cry?"

She smiled. "Just like a man," she said. "Tears can be for good things, too."

"I suppose," Nick said without conviction.

"Actually I'm praying because of you."

"Oh? How so?"

"Back in the motel room, when I was doctoring your arm, you said that it all works out for the good. That sounded familiar. It's similar to a Bible verse."

"I don't know anything about the Bible," Nick confessed.

"I'm not saying you do. I'm saying that your words reminded me of something. It took me awhile to realize what it was, but it's like a verse in Romans, chapter 8." She recited the verse.

"Boy, your memory is returning."

"Not yet. Just snippets." She thought of the scene with her parents in the kitchen. A small smile crept across her face.

"So what are you saying? That God caused all this to happen?" Nick hobbled over to the plastic chair and sat down, grimacing as he did.

She shook her head. "No, not *caused,* but maybe *allowed.* I imagine that God gets blamed for a lot of things."

"I don't want to burst your bubble, but I don't think I believe in God. I don't see how anyone can."

"I don't see how anyone *can't,*" she countered.

"I guess I'm just a cynic, Lisa. I've seen too much, experienced too much."

"What does that mean?" she responded. "You don't really think that faith is just for those who lead sheltered lives, do you? That's absurd."

Nick brought a hand to his face and rubbed his eyes. His weariness was beginning to show. The unflappable facade was cracking. "Perhaps," he said. "Maybe I just don't understand such things."

"When I get my memory back, I'll do my best to explain what I know to be true."

"I'm glad you're feeling so confident," Nick said.

An awkward silence descended. Lisa could tell that the day's events had taken their toll on Nick. "I don't think I've said thank you for all that you've done," she said.

"Not necessary."

"I think it is. You may have been doing your job, but you risked your life and were injured on my behalf. That deserves some gratitude."

Nick laughed lightly. "Well, it has been an interesting day, hasn't it? Had I known that all of this was going to happen, I would have been better prepared. Maybe brought in the army or something."

"So what happens now, Nick?"

"What do you mean?"

"To me. What happens now?"

Nick straightened himself in the chair. "Well, the mission needs to be completed, and that means that whatever it was that you learned at Moyer Communications needs to come out. So I imagine that the first step is getting you well."

"So I'm to stay here for a while?"

"I doubt it. There are a few things that have to be worked out with the police. Our superiors will take care of that. I imagine that you will be transported to a larger, better equipped hospital until your memory returns."

"Nick," Lisa began. "Why didn't you tell me the truth?"

"About what?"

"About me. You knew my name, my occupation, and what happened to me on the road, but you lied to me — not once, but several times."

"I was instructed to do that. After I picked you up, it didn't take long for me to realize your memory was gone. After I had you safely tucked away in the Pretty Penny Motel, I called in. My supervisor told me to take it easy on you, that any further trauma could make things worse. We hoped that your memory would come back on its own."

"Is that why you took me to the house instead of to my own home or back to the office — wherever that may be?"

"Partly," Nick said.

"Is that house really yours?"

Nick nodded. "Yeah. The NSA has an office in southern California. Since I grew up in the area, it was natural for me to transfer there. It sure beats Washington, D.C. Anyway, I figured it was a safe place."

"What about my name? Lisa is my middle name, but you took it from the nametag of the McDonald's employee."

"That was coincidence," Nick admitted. "Massey was right about one thing: I hoped the familiar name might jog a few memories loose."

Lisa felt like an archeologist digging through the remains of a past civilization. What was she missing?

Chapter 22

Wednesday, 1:15 A.M.

The hospital was shaped like the letter U, with each wing forming one side of a courtyard. In front of the courtyard was a parking lot. Another, larger lot was situated at the rear. Massey had ascertained this by a systematic reconnoitering of the grounds that began with a slow drive around the block. From time to time, he would park and make mental notes of the facility. He studied the shape of the buildings, the lighting, the number of access points, the driveways, and to the best he could from a distance, he located the power supply and main phone lines.

The hospital was small, a simple community hospital, probably owned by a larger organization. It would be difficult for a man to enter such a small facility unnoticed. At a big hospital, he might be able to walk into the heavily used emergency room and get lost in the crowd. He also had to assume that a guard had been posted by the woman's door and had been given a description of Massey.

Already his plans had been changed and his life forever altered. Why did the woman have to be so belligerent? The woman was charmed, Massey decided. There was no other way to explain it. How else could she live through the auto accident, an attack by McCullers, and the assault in the motel room? How is it that the police showed up at just the right time? "Too many coincidences," he said under his breath. Charmed or blessed by fate, it no longer mattered. Robin Lisa Keller would die.

"So they're not picking you up until the morning?" Hobbs asked.

Tanner, who lay on the hospital bed in a room two doors down from Lisa's, replied, "That's right. I didn't see any reason for my wife to make the drive at this late hour. It's not like my life is in danger."

"I feel responsible," Hobbs said.

"Nonsense," Tanner countered quickly. "I'm a cop. Cops run the risk of getting shot every day. I came along on this investigation because I wanted to and because I wanted to know what happened in Mojave. You've got to admit, it's turned out to be an interesting case."

"It has certainly been that," Hobbs

agreed, nodding. "How long before you can return to active duty?"

"The bullet went clear through my leg, so I'll be off for a few weeks. They'll put me behind a desk for a while. That will be the worst part. I hate paperwork."

"Don't rush it, cowboy. Get well first."

"My wife will see to that," Tanner said with a smile. "How's the woman?"

"She's battered but safe. The doctor says her memory should return in seventy-two hours or so."

"She really has amnesia? I thought that just happened in novels."

Hobbs shook his head. "Not according to the doctor. He gave us a whole lecture on it."

"So she and Blanchard are NSA agents. I would never have thought that."

"That's confusing, all right. That's the problem with those government agent types. They play by different rules from the rest of us." The few times Hobbs had dealt with government agents there had been tension. It didn't matter if it was the FBI, INS, or ATF. The locals always resented the come-in-and-take-over attitude that some of the feds had, and the feds felt that the locals were provincial and uncooperative. "Maybe if he and NSA had brought us into the loop, we would have had fewer problems."

"That's for sure," Tanner agreed. "What do you plan to do now?"

"I need to hang around. The sheriff's department is going to have more questions for me about the shooting."

"The gunman is still on the loose?"

"Yeah," Hobbs said with frustration.

"It's just a matter of time before the locals catch him."

"I don't know," Hobbs admitted. He explained what Nick had told him. "In addition to that, I just got a report from the guys in the field. They found a couple of briefcases in the abandoned car that he was driving. There was some pretty sophisticated equipment in there."

"You don't think he'll come looking for the woman, do you? He has to be smarter than that."

"I hope so," Hobbs said. "Coming back would be about as dumb an act as a person could do."

"There's a guard by her door, isn't there?" Tanner asked.

"Yes. A local Ojai cop."

Tanner yawned. "I'm sorry," he said. "They gave me a pain reliever, and it's making me drowsy."

Hobbs smiled. "It's also the wee hours of the morning. I should let you get some sleep. I just thought you might want to know the situation."

"I'm glad you came by," Tanner said and yawned again. "Don't let me miss anything exciting. I want to know everything that goes on."

"You've earned that right, buddy. Now go to sleep. I don't want to have to answer to your wife."

To Massey, who sat in the stolen truck that he had again parked in the shopping center lot across the boulevard from the hospital, the situation seemed impossible, but he would not be deterred. His impulse was to simply walk in, find the woman, put a bullet in her head, and then make the best escape he could. But Massey knew that acting on impulse always led to failure.

He faced a couple of problems that he continued to mull over. One, he had no idea which room she was in. He thought of calling the hospital and asking for her, but he was certain that the switchboard would have been alerted to such calls. That would certainly be the case if he were in charge of her safety. Two, the police were there. How many were in the building he couldn't know, but he had to assume that there was at least one and maybe more. A frontal approach would be a disaster. He had only a few rounds left in the clip of his weapon. He would be facing better-armed men, and the uniformed officers would be wearing bulletproof vests. Even if he sacrificed his life for the cause, there was no guarantee that he would achieve his goal of killing the woman.

Massey needed another idea. Time was passing quickly, and every moment he wasted increased the chances of his being seen. Yet despite his keen intellect, his years of intelligence experience, and his overwhelming commitment to success, he could conceive of no way to enter the hospital undetected.

"If the obvious doesn't work," he finally told himself, "then look for the obscure." The wheels of his mind turned furiously. Then it happened. An idea surfaced unexpectedly, a gift from the gods. But to make it work, he would need a few things.

"Are you sure you wouldn't rather sleep?" Nick asked. "I know I'm exhausted."

"I'm too tired to sleep," Lisa replied.

"What? That doesn't make sense. How can you be too tired to sleep?"

"It's something my mother used to say."

Nick raised an eyebrow. "Really. You remember your mother?"

Lisa nodded slightly. "A little. I can't remember her name or where we lived, but I can see her face."

"Well, that is a step up, isn't it? Your memory really is coming back. What else do you recall?"

"Nothing, and you're changing the subject." Lisa had been pushing for an explanation. Some things about Nick and the events of the day bothered her, and she wanted answers. So far he had been evasive.

"No, I'm not. I'm genuinely happy that you're starting to remember things. I just think you're a little confused."

"Things don't add up, Nick. Your being an NSA agent answers some questions, like why you were on the scene of my accident and why you seemed like anything but a truck driver."

"What more is there?" Nick looked frustrated and weary. Lisa felt guilty about grilling him, but she needed answers.

"At your home," she said. "In your sister's bedroom, there was a radio alarm clock."

"That's not unusual," Nick protested. "Nearly every bedroom in the country has a radio alarm clock."

"But this one was just like the one I saw when I woke up in the Pretty Penny Motel."

"It's a common model."

"Perhaps so," Lisa persisted. "But everything in that motel room was old and battered. The alarm clock was new."

"So they're not much on renovation. Lisa, I don't see what this has to do with anything."

"It nags at me, Nick. Why does it nag at me?"

"Because you've had a very upsetting day."

"No, it's more than that. I know I'm being a pill about this, Nick, but I need to know that I can trust you. Hearing you say that you were something other than what you told me is upsetting. You've been lying to me all along."

"Only to protect you, Lisa. And that's the truth. You were in shock when I found you, and I didn't want to add to that."

"What about the dinner you fixed? You told me you had nothing in the house, but when I came downstairs, you were cooking up a storm."

"It was just huevos rancheros. How hard is that? Eggs, beans, tortillas, and sauce from a can. It's not a gourmet meal. It's one step removed from fast food."

"Then we ate outside, just in time to see the vapor trail of a rocket fired from Vandenberg Air Force Base. For some reason, seeing that shook me to the core. Were you using that to jog my memory?"

"And what if I was, Lisa?" Nick said defensively. "Don't you want your memory back? Don't you want your life back?"

"Why couldn't you tell me that?" Lisa asked with exasperation.

Nick shook his head. "I'm not an evil man, Lisa. I'm just a man with a job to do. I'm someone who wanted to help a woman in trouble, a colleague at that. We've been through a lot over the last twenty-four hours. Let's not turn on each other now."

"I'm right about the clock radios, aren't I?" Lisa asked.

"Why are you so fixated on that?"

"Because something caged in the back of my brain wants out, and I think that may be the key. I know it sounds strange, but I can't shake the feeling."

Nick didn't answer.

A thought popped into Lisa's mind. "It's a spy tool, isn't it?" She closed her eyes trying to get the innocuous, fleeting image in her mind to settle. "Surveillance cameras," she said flatly.

Nick remained silent.

"Hidden surveillance cameras," Lisa said. "Of course. You can buy them on the Internet, although I imagine yours are a little more sophisticated. They put cameras in everything now: wall clocks, smoke detectors, pictures." The crack in the dam of amnesia widened, and a few more memories leaked out.

"Ours," Nick corrected. "You work for the same organization I do. You know this stuff because you worked in the field."

"You had a hidden camera in the motel room and in your sister's room where I slept and changed."

"It's not what you think, Lisa. Your condition was fragile; I had to keep an eye on you. It was for your own protection. I placed the one in my sister's room to see if you had any distress. What if you passed out and fell to the floor? It could be hours before I came looking for you."

Lisa felt betrayed, manipulated. "And you just happened to have such a device at your home?"

"Yes. That's what I do, Lisa. That's my job. I spy on spies. I investigate the lowlifes who try to sell our country out. It's what I do, and it's what you do."

Can that be true? Lisa wondered. *Can I be the same kind of person as Nick? Is spying really my game?* She knew about the hidden surveillance cameras in the clock radio. Not many people would know such a thing. Her head began to pound, and she felt sick. There was too much to take in, too much to absorb.

Nick must have noticed because he said, "Hey, are you all right?"

"I want to be left alone," Lisa said, closing her eyes.

"I never meant to upset you, Lisa."

"Please, Nick. Just go. Let me sort these things out." She opened her eyes long enough to see Nick amble from the room on his crutch and close the door behind him. The sight of the wounded man broke her heart. He had fought gallantly for her, and she had just sent him packing. But he had lied to her, pulling her strings as if she were a marionette.

Closing her eyes again, she sighed deeply. Some of her memories were returning, but she felt no better about her situation. "Oh, Lord," she prayed. "What now? What do I do now? Whom do I trust? Where do I turn?"

Massey found what he needed less than a half-mile from the hospital. A pool supply store, which had been set up in a converted house, was situated off the main street in a quiet, oak-lined neighborhood. Locating the store had been easy. He simply looked in the yellow pages for the address. The small-town phone book had a complete map of the community. Ten minutes later he was driving away in the stolen truck, his newly acquired items in the back. The beauty of small towns, Massey thought, was that they were so trusting. The proprietor had not bothered to have an alarm installed. It took less than five minutes for him to lift the bathroom window out of its slide, climb in — which, because of his bulk, was the most difficult part — and find what he wanted. He then walked out the rear door and loaded the booty in the truck.

He smiled to himself. Years of desk work had not taken the edge off his cunning. He was beginning to enjoy the work again, something he was trying to avoid. He was above this now, no longer one to hide in the shadows, arrange secret meetings, and use force when he didn't get his way. But fate had dealt him this hand; he would play it through.

The hospital appeared on his right, and he headed in the drive to the rear parking lot. It was nearly deserted, populated only by a few cars that he assumed belonged to doctors and nurses.

Massey's earlier reconnoitering was paying off. He knew exactly where he wanted to park and every step that would come next. By his estimation, it would take five minutes for the setup and another five minutes to implement the plan. Less than fifteen minutes later, the Keller woman would be dead and he would be on his way out of town.

If things went well, he might even get away. But if he didn't, then he was prepared to pay the price of arrest. Somehow, someway, Moyer would get him out of jail and safely tucked away. He would have to begin a new life with a new identity, but he had done that before. He trusted Moyer completely.

It was all set. Moyer allowed himself the luxury of a moment's satisfaction. The satellite was in place and all its systems were operational. The process of uploading the software commands had been completed, and the on-board computers acknowledged their receipt. He was ready, the satellite was ready, and soon the world would be too.

The only thorn in it all was Massey. He had yet to call, and Moyer was fearful that he had failed. If he had, then everything was in jeopardy. If Massey had been arrested, he could be trusted to keep quiet, but if the woman was alive, if she spoke about what she knew . . . Moyer shivered and cursed Lisa Keller for her interference.

Chapter 23

Wednesday, 1:48 A.M.

Massey moved quickly but not hurriedly. The parking lot was empty of people, and the warm night air was filled with the sounds of machinery — sounds that were music to his ears. But before he could attend to those sounds, he had something else to do. The hospital had five exits, two at the rear of the building and three at the front. The rear exits were double, metal-clad doors, as were two of the ones at the street side of the building. The lobby exit was made of glass.

Using some nylon cord he had taken from the pool supply store, Massey tied the handles of one set of rear doors together, stringing the cord through the stainless-steel loops. He repeated the action with the other rear exit. He was unconcerned about the doors at the front.

The next part required more physical effort. Pulling the truck next to the rear wall, Massey climbed in the pickup's bed, removed two plastic pails and two large plastic bottles, and placed them on the roof of the vehicle. He then climbed on top of the cab. The tall truck enabled Massey to reach the hospital's parapet, which ran the perimeter of the flat roof, and he hoisted the buckets and bottles over its edge. Then, as quietly as possible, he scrambled onto the roof. The effort tired him. He was a large man who could hold his own with anyone, but hauling his bulk up was not something he did often. The task was more than difficult; it was painful. His arms were deeply bruised, and the effort made his injuries hurt all the more. He comforted himself with the thought that getting down would be easier. He derived even greater pleasure from the knowledge that his mission would be over in the next quarter-hour.

With deliberate steps he moved across the roof, stepping as quietly as possible on its gravel-and-tar surface and stopping at a four-foot-square sheet-metal box. It was one of four air-conditioning units. Crouching down, Massey circled the noisy device. A humming-whirring noise filled the night air.

Massey found the intake vent. He placed his hand near the vent and felt the air rush past. This was ideal. Setting the pail down by the grill, he opened the top of one bottle and emptied all of it into the pail. The powerful, pungent aroma of ammonia assaulted

Massey's nose, but he ignored it. Reaching into the second pail, he removed a cardboard box and extracted two three-inch tablets. He dropped them in the ammonia. Immediately a yellow-green gas bubbled out of the pail. The smell of ammonia was replaced with the thick, irritating mist of chlorine gas. Massey's eyes began to tear.

Chlorine gas, Massey recalled with satisfaction, was first used in gas warfare during World War I. It had been effective then, and it would be effective now. Quickly he moved to the second air-conditioning unit. He had only enough material for two of the four units, but that was all he needed. In fact, it was all he wanted. In moments an evacuation would begin, and Massey wanted everyone to move out the front of the building. Scores of people would soon emerge, but he was interested in only one of the throng. No, he decided, two. Blanchard needed to die also.

Without hesitation, Massey trotted to the edge of the roof over the stolen truck, sat on the parapet, swung his legs over the side, and then dropped to the roof of the cab. Seconds later he scrambled into the truck, started it, and drove to the front parking lot.

It was all just a matter of time now — a very short time.

* * *

"What are you doing out here?" Hobbs asked Nick. "What'd she do? Throw you out?" The look on Nick's face answered the question. "What happened?"

Nick frowned. "She has doubts about me."

Hobbs thought of saying, *Well, so do I, buddy,* but he decided against it. He didn't need a confrontation in the corridor of the hospital. Hobbs was too tired for that. "I was thinking of finding some coffee. How about joining me?"

"That depends. Are you going to grill me again?"

"Probably," Hobbs said, glancing at the silent Ojai policeman who stood guard. "It's part of my nature. But if it's any comfort, I'm out of questions for now."

"Okay, just remember: Ask me no questions; I'll tell you no lies."

Hobbs was about to respond when he caught sight of something out of the corner of his eye. A nurse shot out of a room at the end of the hall. She was holding a hand to her mouth. Hobbs watched as she raced by. Her eyes were wide with fright, and her skin was pale. "That can't be good," he said.

"Some patient must have taken an awful turn for the worse."

"Wait," Hobbs said, his face twisted into a display of puzzlement and disgust. "What's that smell?"

"I don't smell anyth—" Nick began then stopped abruptly. "Chlorine?"

Suddenly the hall filled with nurses, doctors, interns, and other hospital personnel.

"What's going on?" Hobbs called out to a passing man in a white coat.

"We're evacuating the hospital. We can use all the help we can get."

The sharp odor grew in intensity. "Chlorine gas," he said to himself, then exclaimed: "Chlorine gas. That stuff is deadly. We have to get these people out of here."

"You get your partner," Nick said decisively. "I'll get Lisa." Without waiting for Hobbs to respond, Nick turned and limped into Lisa's room.

"Go with him," Hobbs said to the policeman. "And stay with them. Also, make sure the fire department has been called."

"Got it," the man answered, but Hobbs was already headed down the corridor, crossing the short distance to Tanner's room in just a few steps.

Tanner was asleep on the bed. "Tanner!" Hobbs shouted. The man jerked awake in fright.

"What are you doing?" Tanner stopped and sniffed the air. "What is that?"

"No time to talk. We're out of here." Hobbs was already by the bedside pulling Tanner to a sitting position.

"I'm up. I'm up," Tanner protested as he slipped from the bed and stood unsteadily on his good leg. Hobbs stepped to his side, took Tanner's arm, and placed it around his shoulder.

"We need a wheelchair," Hobbs said.

"I'm fine. Let's go."

Outside the room a flood of patients poured by. Those who could walk did, some pushing wheeled IV stands in front of them. Most wore only a hospital gown. Hobbs was thankful that it was summer. At least they would be warm. Hacking and coughing filled the air. Those who could not walk were pushed in wheelchairs or rolled along in their hospital beds. In the panic, people stepped on others; bare feet were rolled over by wheels.

"Calmly. Don't panic." Someone was shouting.

"I can make it by myself," Tanner said. "See if anyone else needs help."

"You can't walk."

"Sure I can. I've got plenty of motivation. Now go. Don't worry about me." A lone woman in a wheelchair was trying to make her way through the morass of patients and having little luck. Tears of fear flowed down her cheeks. Tanner hopped on one leg and took hold of the wheelchair's handles. "Allow me, ma'am," he said. Hobbs watched as the ingenious CHP officer helped the frightened woman while providing support for himself. Hobbs decided that when everything was over, he was going to take this unique man out for the best dinner he could afford.

"Are there more patients back there?" the detective asked a passing nurse.

"Yes. Help us if you can."

"Use the rear exits," Hobbs shouted over the clatter of people.

"We can't. They won't open. Everyone has to go out the front."

The truth of the matter was suddenly clear: This was no accident.

It was like swimming up a waterfall, but Hobbs worked his way to the back of the corridor where it intersected another hall that ran to his right. The air was now thick with a yellow-green gas that was quickly settling to the floor. In high school chemistry, Hobbs had learned that chlorine gas was heavier than air. That was very bad news. There were only minutes left before the corridor and all the rooms would be filled with the toxic gas. Tears streamed down his face as the fumes irritated his eyes. The invasive gas burned his throat and lungs, and he began to cough. He checked rooms. The first few were empty. Hospital personnel were braving the deadly mist, valiantly trying to move every patient.

In the third room, Hobbs found a young child, a girl he judged to be only seven or eight, lying in the first bed. She was sound asleep. Without preamble he scooped her up in his arms and returned to the hall, moving as quickly as he could. Awakened by the sudden movement she opened her eyes and stared fearfully at Hobbs.

"It's all right, sweetheart," he said softly. "Just be still for another moment." He stopped suddenly. An elderly man had collapsed in front of him. The man was gagging, struggling for air. Hobbs dropped to a knee. He had to think quickly. He turned to the girl in his arms. "Does your daddy ever give you a piggyback ride?"

She nodded, then said. "The air smells bad. It hurts to breathe."

"I know, darling. I'm taking you to a place where you can breathe, okay?"

"Okay."

"I need to give you a piggyback ride, so I

can help this man. Can you hang on tight?"

"Yes."

"Okay then, hop on my back and put your arms around my neck and hold on tight. Hold your breath as long as you can," he added as it occurred to him that she would be nearer to the ceiling on his back and closer to where the deadly gas was pouring in.

The little girl crawled onto his back and wrapped her arms around his neck tight enough to choke him, but that didn't matter. Fresh air was a few steps away. He turned to the choking, gasping man. "You're coming with me, sir." Hobbs reached underneath the frail frame and took him in his arms. As he stood, the muscles in his back protested the strain. He ignored their protest. He had no other choice. Holding his breath, Hobbs raced toward the lobby. Rancid fumes clung to him as he charged through the cloud of death. In a few more minutes there would be no breathable air in the hospital. He could only hope that the others got outside safely.

There was a crowd at the lobby doors where the clutter of beds, wheelchairs, and people were trying to exit simultaneously. Panic had set in.

"Everyone STOP!" It was Tanner's

voice. He was still leaning on the back of the woman's wheelchair. He pointed to a young orderly who was pushing one of the rolling hospital beds. "You, go now." Miraculously, the others who were jammed next to the bed pulled back just enough for the young man to push through the opening. "Now you." Tanner ordered a nurse who was pushing a child in a wheelchair. She complied. "Now you. Now you." Tanner barked out orders with unmistakable authority. The strength of his voice had stopped the panic. One by one, the people emptied the lobby. Next Hobbs saw Tanner turn to him. "Out," he ordered. Hobbs didn't hesitate.

Once outside, Hobbs found an empty spot on the lawn that fronted the hospital and laid the elderly man down. As he crouched down, the little girl released her grip and slipped from his back. "Stay here, sir. Someone will be by to help you." He brought the little girl around to face him. She was frightened, and her cheeks were smeared with tears. "You're a brave little girl," Hobbs said with a smile. His voice was turning hoarse from breathing the gas.

"Thanks, mister," she said.

"And polite, too. You stand right here, okay?"

"Okay."

"What have you got here?" Hobbs rose and turned to see who was speaking. It was a man in a white coat. His eyes were red and watery. "I'm Dr. Lawrence. I'm setting up triage."

"I found the little girl in her room. She seems in pretty good shape. The elderly man fell in the corridor." The doctor bent down to examine the man. "Did everyone get out?" Hobbs asked.

"I think so," the doctor said. "Nurses and orderlies are going around the outside of the building looking in the windows to see if anyone was overlooked."

Sirens filled the air. "Help is on its way."

"We need it. I don't know how this could have happened." The doctor stood.

Hobbs had an idea of how it had happened, and he didn't like the idea one bit. Keller? Where was Lisa Keller? Nick was supposed to be with her. Hobbs scanned the crowd but in the scores of patients and medical personnel he couldn't locate her. The smell of chlorine escaped the confines of the hospital through the open doors of the lobby and wafted into the night air.

"Air conditioners," Hobbs said. He turned back to the doctor who was starting to walk away, continuing his triage evaluation. "Hang on, Doc. Where are your air-conditioning units?"

"What?"

"The air-conditioning units. Are they on the roof or at the back of the building?"

"The HVAC system is on the roof."

Hobbs turned and looked up. He saw nothing. *No,* he told himself. *He wouldn't attack from the roof; there would be no exit. Nick said that Massey was a smart man.* What then? The rear exits didn't work. Massey must have blocked them somehow. He wanted people to come out the front. That had to be it.

Pushing his way through the crowd, he began looking for Lisa. "Ms. Keller," he called and then listened. Nothing. He called out again. Still nothing. There was too much noise. Too many people were coughing and talking, and the more frightened ones were weeping. Medical personnel were calling out instructions and information to each other as they attended the sick.

"What's wrong?" It was Tanner.

"I think the attacker is back," Hobbs said. "This whole thing was a way to flush the woman out."

"Are you sure?" Tanner asked.

"As sure as I can be. The rear exit doors were blocked, and the gas came in through the vents. How do you get chlorine gas into a ventilation system unless someone puts it there?"

"I saw Blanchard and the woman make it outside," Tanner said. "They were ahead of me, then things got backed up at the lobby."

"That means that they were among the first ones out. Where's our guard?"

"Over there," Tanner motioned with his head. "He got several lungfuls of the gas. The guy went back in to pull more patients out. He's a hero."

Looking at the police officer, Hobbs saw that he was out of commission. The man was on his hands and knees gulping air. A nurse stepped up to the downed officer. "I have to find her," Hobbs said with desperation. He began pushing through the crowd.

This time there would be no talking, Massey decided. No banter, no questions, no answers. Just a simple approach, raise the gun, pull the trigger, and walk away. If anyone tried to intervene, he would die too. Simplicity was the key to success. It had always been so. In those cases when a foreign agent needed to be neutralized, Massey had always insisted that a direct approach be taken. The attempts by the CIA to kill Castro in the sixties had proven that fancy plans lead to embarrassing results. To

Massey, schemes were like machines. The fewer the parts, the fewer things there were to fail.

He had weighed the options. At first he thought he would sit in the stolen truck, wait for Lisa Keller to appear, then take his shot. But Massey soon dismissed the idea. It was unlikely that she would get close enough to the parking lot for him to make a sure-kill shot. He was sure that he could hit her, but not so sure that he could kill her. Nothing would be solved.

No, a more direct approach was required. There were, however, problems with that scheme. Nick Blanchard and the presence of the police. A close kill would mean that Blanchard might confront him. Not that he feared the man. Killing the NSA agent would be a bonus and might solve some future problems. Still, it was a risk. And if a guard was with him, he would have to make three kills. He counted the ammunition he had left: three rounds. More ammunition would have been the answer, but he couldn't purchase any at this hour of the night and stealing some was far more risky than breaking into a pool supply store. Gun shops usually had bars on the windows and sophisticated alarm systems. If he had more time, he might have tried it.

After starting the gas on the rooftop, Massey had returned to the truck and parked in the front lot. There he had waited. It took less than two minutes for enough gas to fill the ductwork to be noticed. Nurses and others began to appear out the front lobby door. In the confusion, Massey had exited the truck and walked toward the front of the building. No one paid any attention to him. Standing to the side of the courtyard in the shadows, he waited for the only person in the hospital he cared to see. The smell of chlorine filled the air. To him it was like perfume.

"My eyes," Lisa complained. "They feel like they're on fire."

"Mine, too," Nick agreed. "I suppose all the eye drops are back in the hospital."

"Is that a joke?"

"A weak one, admittedly."

Lisa blinked back the tears and looked around her. Nick had her by the arm and had unceremoniously pulled her from the hospital bed and propelled her down the corridor before she could ask what was going on. A few seconds later she had no need to ask. The hall was packed with frightened, choking people, and the powerful smell of chlorine provided all the answers she needed.

With Nick's help she was in the first group to explode from the lobby into the fresh air. Nick had carried his crutch with him, not bothering to spare his leg the pain of supporting his weight. He still hobbled, but he pressed on. Lisa understood that his pain took a backseat to immediate, suffocating death.

"What happened?" Lisa asked.

"I'm not sure. A gas leak perhaps." Nick was now leaning on the crutch again and holding his foot off the ground.

"Gas leak? What does a hospital use chlorine gas for?" Lisa was puzzled. "That doesn't make sense."

The expression on Nick's face changed from weariness and pain to alarm. "Oh no," he said.

"What?"

"Massey. This must be Massey's doing."

Lisa's heart slammed hard in her chest. Frantically she scanned the area, trying to look at each face, hoping that he wasn't there, praying that Nick was wrong, but she knew that he must be right. The man was obsessed enough to do this. She had seen it in his eyes, heard it in his voice. She glanced back at Nick, who was scanning the area too.

"I need to get you to a safe place," Nick said.

"Where? There is no safe place."

"In the crowd." He took her by the arm and started to pull her with him, but she jerked her arm free. "What's wrong?"

"I'm not going to use other people as a shield. That could put their lives in danger."

"He's after *you*, Lisa, no one else."

"And he just gassed an entire hospital. I don't think he would let the fact that a few people were between us stand in his way."

"It's the only chance we have."

"No. It can't be."

"Name another." Nick was angry, and he reached for her arm again. He was too slow, and she started to move away. "What are you doing?"

"I'm going to find him," Lisa said with a stern determination. "I'm not going to wait around here until he makes his move. Someone else could get hurt."

"Lisa!" Nick called. "Wait!"

But she didn't.

When Hobbs heard Nick's voice call out Lisa's name, he snapped his head around. It sounded like it came from the front of the crowd, the side closest to the parking lot —

the worst possible place. He was on the move a second later, weaving his way through the forest of people, adrenaline coursing through his veins.

He saw her when he reached the edge of the crowd. Her tousled black hair shimmered under the moonlight; her face appeared pale under the parking lot lamps. Sirens continued to wail as police and fire units rushed to the scene. They would not arrive in time to save Lisa if that madman got there first.

Hobbs reached for his gun and withdrew it on the fly. A few people saw it and gasped. As he reached the edge of the crowd, he saw Lisa walking twenty-five feet away, followed closely by Nick, who hopped more than walked.

He saw something else: a movement in the shadows near the south wing of the hospital. A man was emerging, a man in a dark, rumpled, three-piece suit, with a dark metallic object in his right hand. He walked calmly, with purpose, straight for Lisa. Nick and Lisa had their backs turned to him. They had no idea he was there.

"Lisa, wait," Nick shouted, struggling to keep up. "This is crazy."

What is she doing? Hobbs wondered.

The man from the shadows moved closer

and then raised his gun.

"Gun!" Hobbs shouted as loudly as he could. "Down! Get down!"

The man turned briefly and looked at Hobbs, then returned his gaze back to Lisa, who had spun on her heels sharply. Nick turned toward Hobbs, who was raising his weapon. Hobbs saw Nick follow the direction of his aim.

"No!" Nick shouted as he pivoted on his good foot and threw himself at Lisa.

A loud bang echoed through the predawn blackness. Then another as Hobbs fired. He missed. Massey had dropped to the ground as he fired, landing on his side, his gun now pointing at Hobbs. Hobbs adjusted his aim. He saw the muzzle flash of Massey's weapon.

An explosion went off by Hobbs's ear, and his face began to sting. Massey's shot had struck the stucco corner of the hospital, blasting sharp pieces of tiny shrapnel into the air. Several pieces hit Hobbs, whose face was less than a foot away. Instinctively he flinched, raising his gun hand to shield his face. His eyes slammed shut. When he opened them again he saw the gunman scramble to his feet and rush toward the startled and screaming crowd of patients.

* * *

Lisa fell to the ground like a toppled statue. She had heard Hobbs yell "Gun!" and Nick scream "No!" The next sensation was an amalgam of alarm, pain, and confusion. Her legs felt heavy, immovable, and she was having difficulty breathing. It took another second for her to realize that someone was lying on top of her. She started to fight back when she realized it was Nick. He wasn't moving. Lisa had seen him jump before she heard the report of the pistol. He had interposed his own body in front of hers.

"Nick?"

Silence.

"Nick?" Lisa struggled to get out from under his weight. "Nick. Talk to me, Nick." But Nick said nothing. Mustering her strength and ignoring her pain, she rolled Nick's body off her own.

He groaned. Blood oozed from the side of his head, not from a hole, but from a gash. The bullet had grazed his skull. He was unconscious but alive.

"Thank you, God," she said softly, and a sudden sense of relief raced through her. He was alive. But the relief was fleeting. Massey was still there. She saw him disappear into the crowd only to appear a moment later with something in his arms. When Lisa recognized it, her terror intensified beyond anything she had experienced.

Massey held a child in his arms, a young blond girl, and he had the barrel of his gun pressed against her small head. The young girl wailed in fright, and Lisa's heart sank like a stone.

"Don't do it, buddy," a voice said.

Hobbs looked to his left and saw Tanner shakily standing on one leg and holding a service revolver in front of him. He must have taken the downed officer's weapon, Hobbs reasoned. He was barefoot, with a heavily bandaged leg, and like all the other patients, wearing only a hospital gown. In any other setting, the sight would be comical, but to Hobbs it was a scene of bravery. With Tanner's help, there were now two guns aimed at Massey — but neither could shoot.

The girl was familiar to Hobbs. She was the same one he had helped out of the hospital.

"It's time to put this to rest," Tanner continued. "No need to hurt a little girl."

"Shut up!" Massey screamed. "Or this time it won't be your leg that gets shot."

Hobbs knew that Tanner had not seen his

assailant before, but he had put the pieces together.

"It's over, Massey," Hobbs said firmly, ignoring the blood that trickled down his face. "It's been a lousy day for everybody. Let's just call it quits, and no one will hurt you."

"You think I'm worried about being hurt?" Massey laughed. "Pain means nothing. I have a job to do, and I'm going to do it."

"There are more cops on the way," Hobbs said. "In another minute or two they're going to be all over the place. You'll have no place to run."

"I don't care," Massey said. "If anyone moves without my say-so, then this little girl dies. Is that clear?"

"Crystal," Hobbs said. "So how do we do this without anyone getting killed?" *Time,* Hobbs reminded himself, *Eat up some time. Delay him until help comes.*

"Mommy!" The little girl screamed. "I want my mommy!"

"Shut up!" Massey pressed the gun harder into her head. The child cried out with pain.

Hobbs moved beyond fear into rage. Only his training and his concern for the girl restrained him.

"Here I am." Lisa walked slowly toward the gunman.

The terror was gone now, the pain just a faint shadow of a time past. Her assailant, her stalker, stood staring at her as she approached. Peace fell upon her like the roaring cascade of a waterfall.

"Here I am," Lisa repeated boldly.

The expression on Massey's face was the antithesis of the peace that Lisa felt. His eyes were filled with demonic rage, his mouth pulled tight in anger.

"Lisa, get back," Hobbs called.

Lisa ignored the detective, keeping her eyes fixed on Massey. "You don't need the girl, Mr. Massey." Her tone was firm but even, speaking just loud enough to be heard over the coughing and frightened mumbling of the crowd. "It's me you want, not her."

Massey fell silent, his eyes darting from Lisa to Hobbs to Tanner and then back to Lisa. The gun in his hand remained pressed against the child's head.

"It's been a long day, Mr. Massey," Lisa said calmly. "You've been hunting me without rest. You're tired. I'm tired. Let's get this over with. Let the girl go."

"Lisa, get back!" Hobbs shouted again.

"No," she said. "I'm not going to let a

child die because of me."

"You have caused me a great deal of trouble, Ms. Keller," Massey growled. "You have no idea how much trouble."

Lisa walked toward him until she stood between him and the line of fire of Hobbs and Tanner. She imagined that her action was driving Hobbs mad, but she had to do it. "I'm here," she said. "They can't shoot you with me standing in front of you. Let the girl go and use me as a hostage."

Massey's eyes flickered.

"Let's not waste any more time, Mr. Massey," she said forcefully. "In a few seconds, both the police and the fire department will be here. I know you don't care about a bunch of firemen, but I'm sure you have some concerns about having an additional fifteen or twenty officers around. The longer you wait, the greater the danger."

A police car rolled into the parking lot, bathing the area in red-and-blue light. The policeman exited the car, saw the situation, pulled his weapon, and leveled it at Massey.

"No!" Lisa shouted, raising her hand in the direction of the officer. To the gunman she said, "Time is gone. We have to do this now. This is between you and me. Let the girl go and take me." Lisa took another step closer and reached for the girl. The child looked up at her, her cheeks wet with tears, her eyes wide as saucers. Her lower lip quivered. "Now, Mr. Massey. Give me the child now, and you can take me as your hostage."

Massey hesitated for a moment, and Lisa took another step forward, slipping her hands under the girl's arms. *Please God,* she prayed. *Please make him release her.* He loosened his grip, and Lisa took the child from him.

In a rapid move that was almost impossible to see, Massey reached forward with his free hand and grabbed Lisa by the hair. She dropped the child to the ground as he pulled her close to him. She felt the gun press into her cheekbone. A sharp stab of pain ran through her head and neck as he pressed the gun home. Lisa involuntarily closed her eyes and then forced them open again. She saw the little girl scamper toward the crowd where a nurse grabbed her, picked her up, and disappeared into the mass of patients. "Thank you," she whispered.

"Don't thank me, Ms. Keller," Massey spat. "Nothing has changed between us. You still die tonight."

I wasn't talking to you, she thought silently as he spun her around, placing his thick forearm around her throat. The gun was now mashed into her temple. The pain was nauseating.

"Giving your life for another might be noble, Ms. Keller, but it was also stupid. I'm impressed, but unmoved."

"Someone did it for me a long time ago."

"Let's not do anything stupid," Hobbs called out. "We can talk this over."

"Right," Massey spat out. "And while we talk, SWAT marksmen are planning on using my head for target practice."

"Release her and no one will hurt you," Hobbs said with authority.

"You just don't get it, do you?" Massey said. "I'm not afraid of being hurt." Then to Lisa he said in a venomous whisper, "Let's go." He began to walk backward, keeping Lisa pressed against his body and interposed between him and the police.

More sirens, more lights.

Lisa offered no resistance; she wanted to be as far from the bystanders as possible. Step followed backward step. Suddenly the ground changed elevation, and Lisa stumbled slightly. They had stepped off the curb and onto the pavement of the front parking lot. Hobbs and Tanner followed, keeping the same distance between themselves and Massey. Hobbs was staring deep into Lisa's eyes, as if trying to communicate with her.

She wondered how Massey was going to get into a car with her in front of him. At some point, he would have to release her or at least allow them to separate enough to open the car door.

An idea struck Lisa. It was risky, but no more so than what she faced if her captor found a way to escape with her as his hostage. He was smart enough to do it, so she had to assume that he had a plan for just such a contingency as this.

It was time to act.

As they continued moving backward through the parking lot, Lisa fixed her attention on Hobbs, staring into his eyes just as he had been doing to her. With only the slightest of motions she pointed at her chest with her right index finger, then pointed down to the ground. She repeated the sign several times. Hobbs nodded slightly. The concern on his face intensified. She watched his lips move and assumed that he had whispered something to Tanner. Tanner cut a quick look at Hobbs and then returned his gaze to Lisa and Massey. His face remained unchanged, as if it had been chiseled in stone, but he seemed to tense slightly.

Lisa swallowed hard. Then, using the same hand, held three fingers against her chest. She closed her eyes and folded one finger under leaving only two extended. She did the same with her middle finger as she continued the silent countdown.

Her heart pounded so hard she could hear it in her ears.

"Okay," Massey said. "This is how we're going to do this. You're going to open the door to the truck and —"

Lisa pulled the last finger in and went limp. She felt herself drop, and the gun barrel scraped along her head. Massey's arm was still around her, but the unexpected dead weight of her body pulled it down. Lisa's eyes were clamped shut as she waited for a bullet to enter her brain.

There was a popping and banging that sounded to her like cannons being fired. Lisa hit the pavement, and as she did, she curled into a ball, covering her head with her hands.

The shooting stopped, but Lisa remained still. She didn't want to move. Didn't want to open her eyes and see what carnage was there.

"Lisa? Lisa!" The voice was familiar.

There were more sirens, and she could hear footsteps around her.

"Come on, Lisa," Hobbs was saying. "Let's get you out of here." He reached down and helped her to her feet.

Lisa opened her eyes. She was facing the hospital. The crowd was staring at her, many with their hands to their mouths. She started to turn, but Hobbs restrained her. "No need to look back," he said. "Massey's dead. He'll never bother you again."

Hobbs walked her back toward the others, but she veered off. "Nick. I need to check on Nick."

He was still on the ground, unmoving. Two people, a man and a woman, each wearing a doctor's smock, were crouched over him. Fearing the worst, afraid that he might have died while she was away, Lisa felt a strong sense of remorse. She had been rough on him earlier, challenging everything he'd said, doubting every explanation, calling into question every statement. He was a man of mystery, but he had once again thrust himself into danger to save her life.

One of the doctors looked up. He smiled. "He's conscious now. There's a deep scalp wound, but that's all. The bullet grazed his skull. He's going to be all right." Nick groaned and raised a hand to his head. "Lie still, sir," the doctor said. "We'll have you in an ambulance and on your way to a hospital in Ventura."

"I'm going with him," Lisa said as she

knelt by his side. "I owe you so much. Thank you."

"Who . . . who are you?" Nick said and then smiled a moment later. "Just kidding." He laughed and then groaned loudly.

"What? I should hurt you for that."

He chuckled. "Please don't. I don't think I have any parts left that haven't been damaged." He looked deep into her eyes. "Tell me that you're all right."

"I'm fine," Lisa said. A tear ran down her face.

Chapter 24

Thursday, three weeks later, 1:48 P.M.

"That's quite a story, Ms. Keller," Senator Kilgallen said. "It's almost too hard to believe."

"Believe me, Senator, it is even harder to forget," Lisa replied. Her tone was professional, diplomatic, and no-nonsense.

"This is a grave matter that you bring us, Ms. Keller. It not only involves at least one of our fellow senators, but also one of the richest and most influential men in the world." Kilgallen leaned back in his leather chair and chewed on the end of his pen. There were six other senators with him in the private hearing, each a high-ranking member of the Senate, and each was sworn to secrecy. Lisa had been answering questions for two hours, and she knew that Nick had gone through the same thing. Next, the assistant director of NSA would enter the wood-paneled conference room to answer questions.

"How long did you work undercover at Moyer Communications?"

"Six months, Senator. I was hired as a security specialist charged with upgrading building security."

"And it was in that capacity that you learned of Mr. Moyer's . . . dealings?"

The senator can't bring himself to say it, she thought. She could not blame him. "Yes sir."

He sighed and rubbed his eyes. "I must admit, I find this all very hard to comprehend."

"And rightly so," Lisa said. "I'm an expert in the field, and I have trouble believing it myself. But it is important that we start seeing and believing these things. Our country faces several crucial decisions in the future about these matters, and I think it is best that those charged with creating and maintaining the laws of this land be as fully informed as possible."

"Your contentions seem so outlandish," the senator rebutted.

"With all due respect, sir, everything in my report, as well as everything I've said in testimony, is truth deeply rooted in fact."

"But the satellite, Ms. Keller, what device could do that?"

Lisa knew that most of the senators on the panel would balk at that revelation, but she was surprised at Kilgallen's disbelief. He sat on several key committees that dealt with military intelligence and operation. She cleared her throat and shifted uncomfortably in her chair. Most of her injuries had healed in the intervening weeks between the culmination of events in Ojai and her appearance before the Senate panel, but her ribs were still tender and sitting for extended periods was uncomfortable. "Senator Kilgallen," Lisa began, "technology has been a boon to society. In the last twenty-five years we have seen our technological prowess grow at an astounding rate. The general populace, the people we serve, are aware of only a small measure of it. You, as well as many of your colleagues, are more aware of that than most, but even you are left in the dark about many matters.

"It has always been assumed that the military leads the way in the creation of new intelligence operations and devices —"

"And the intelligence community," Kilgallen interjected.

"Agreed," Lisa responded quickly. "But such is not the case. Many, indeed most, of the significant advances in technology have come out of the private sector — a sector, I might add, which is much harder to police. Megacompanies can be as secretive as any foreign government. They can also be as self-protective. This is understandable, and megacorporations have the right to privacy, as do individuals. But at times the rights of the individual come in conflict with the rights of the corporation."

"You're saying that Moyer Communications crossed the line."

"I am indeed. And there are other such companies that have done the same."

"What are the specifics, Ms. Keller?" the senator asked. "What did Moyer Communications do that drew the keen interest of the NSA?"

"As you and your distinguished colleagues may know, Moyer Communications designed and built many of the electronic devices used by the military. Over the years, they have greatly enhanced radio communications between fighter aircraft and ground troops. But their real claim to fame, at least with the military and intelligence communities, is the network of spy satellites they have designed. Such satellites were used over Iraq during the Gulf War and the subsequent skirmishes that followed, as well as over Kosovo.

"For years," Lisa continued, "those satellites have intercepted messages, tracked electronics, and photographed military installations. Moyer Communications has advanced the science of digital optics by a decade, and their satellites are now sophisticated enough to read a sales flyer left on the windshield of a car."

"They have provided a great service to our country and spared the lives of many of our young soldiers."

"Yes sir, that is true, but things have changed."

"How so?" the senator asked.

Lisa shifted in her seat again. "In 1949 George Orwell wrote *1984*, a book about totalitarian control. Ever since, it has been assumed that the greatest danger to individual privacy was from the government. He called it Big Brother, but we now know that we have less to fear from the government than we do from private industry, from Little Brother — except Little Brother isn't so little."

"And this leads us where?"

"Panopticon."

"Panopticon? I'm not familiar with the term."

"It's from two Greek words that mean to see all. Gregory Moyer and his company have designed a spy satellite that can track individuals or groups."

"Individuals or groups? You mean a single individual?"

"Yes," Lisa said. "The idea was sold to the military, which funded the research and development through its black-ops budgets. With this device and others like it, an individual could be tracked wherever he went in the world."

"That's unbelievable," the senator countered. "How could such a device work?"

"The electronics is beyond me, sir, but this much I know. In phase one of the project, a satellite was placed into orbit over the United States. This was the test vehicle. The optics are superior to anything that has preceded it. In principle, subsequent satellites would be placed in strategic orbit around the globe, forming a network of surveillance. Ideally it was to be used to track leaders of unfriendly nations, activity at foreign military bases, supply movements, and even to find downed airmen."

"All noble goals."

"Left at that, yes. But Moyer had other plans. With such a device, information could be gathered on Americans without their knowledge. Already several states have used photographs from spy satellites to hunt for property improvements that may have been made without county permits. Other government agencies have used such photographs to catch farmers who water their fields without irrigation permits or to monitor tree cutting by lumber companies. On the surface, these are not necessarily bad, and society as a whole benefits, but what could happen if a private corporation begins gathering information on individuals that might be an invasion of personal privacy?

"What if," Lisa added, "a corporation paid Moyer Communications to spy on its competition, giving it an unfair advantage? The possibilities are enormous and frightening."

"Those were the reasons that caused NSA to send in an undercover agent?"

"Only partly, Senator. We began to suspect that Moyer might sell some of his information beyond the borders of the United States. While there are laws on the books that control the sale of technology to foreign countries, it would be difficult to stop the selling of information. Not long ago, such information had to be passed by hand or through encrypted messages. Today all someone like Moyer has to do is place a receiver in the hands of a client and let him or her receive whatever information is available. Satellite receivers are relatively easy to build. Some can be purchased over the Internet. All that needs to be changed is the frequency it receives. A high school student could do that. Frankly, that part of the chain is old technology. Moyer would need to provide the codes to unscramble the satellite's signal. That could be done with a phone call or over a sheltered site on the Internet."

"And your investigation found all this to be true?"

"And much more. It was Gregory Moyer's plan to sell, not information about our military bases and research, but his services to other countries. Not all countries in the world experience the freedom we do. We are blessed; some nations seem to be cursed. With Moyer's devices one could track undesirable groups. Imagine a country bent on ethnic cleansing, such as Rwanda or Yugoslavia or even China. How much more powerful and effective would a despot be if he knew where his enemies gathered, when they moved, and what their resources were? That is just the beginning of the nightmare. For me, the most chilling revelation was an agreement I discovered between Moyer and several Third World countries. It was an agreement for which he was receiving a great deal of advance money."

"And just what did they want from Moyer Communications?"

Lisa paused. The thought chilled her

more than anything that had ever entered her mind. After swallowing hard she said: "Senator, I am a person of faith. By that, I mean I am a Christian. My faith is central to my life. As a Christian in the United States, I live in a society that allows me to worship whenever I want and without interference. Such is not the case for Christians in many countries. Countries like the Sudan, China, Burma, Pakistan, North Korea, Egypt, and many others have made it a goal to drive Christianity from their land. Many horrible acts often sanctioned by the government have taken place. What I discovered was this: Greg Moyer had made deals to locate the meeting places and hiding places of Christians in some of these countries. His new MC2-SDS satellite would make it impossible for these people to evade detection by those who wish to seek them out and slaughter them."

"Do you really believe that Moyer is that evil?"

"I do. He is not the first; he will not be the last. His kind has a lineage that extends back through the centuries. He cared nothing for how the information was gathered or would be used, just as long as it was lucrative."

"Do you know where Greg Moyer is

now?" the senator asked.

"No," Lisa said sadly. "The news media carried the events that culminated in the shooting at the hospital in Ojai. We assume that Moyer saw a report and realized that his empire was about to be brought down. We think he fled the country, but we can't be sure."

"Is there any hope of finding him?"

"He is a clever man with tremendous resources. I'm sure the search will go on, but he could be anywhere in the world."

"At least his plot was foiled."

"Maybe," Lisa said softly.

"Maybe?"

Lisa took a moment to look each of the seven senators in the eye. "The satellite is still up there, gentlemen, and who knows what contingency plans Moyer had at the ready. It's not over. I'm afraid it's not close to being over."

Epilogue

Sunday, noon

The summer sun shone through a crystal blue sky and radiated off the black pavement. The sound of people chatting filled the air. A crowd of 150 had gathered to share in the dedication ceremonies on the grounds of the soon to be Fillmore Community Church. No one was allowed in the building that had so captured Lisa's attention nearly a month earlier, but that would soon change. Renovation would begin tomorrow.

"It was a nice service," Nick said. He held a small paper plate piled high with finger foods. "It was a great idea to have an outdoor worship service."

"Thanks for coming," Lisa said. "The contractor told me it would take about two months to bring the building up to code and make it safe. We plan to have services in it as soon as possible."

"We?" Nick asked. He and Lisa were sitting at a folding table that had been situated in the middle of the lot. Seated with them were Bill Hobbs and Jay Tanner.

"I plan to come back for the first service. This place is important to me."

"That's a long trip from Washington, D.C.," Nick said.

"Well, I made it here today."

"I'm glad you did," Nick said. "I miss you."

"Be careful what you wish for," she said with a broad smile. "I've asked for a transfer, and I think they're going to give it to me. I may be working out of the same office as you. Then you'll see more of me than you can stand."

"Wonderful," Nick exclaimed. "If you need help moving, just call. I know where I can get a truck."

"Very funny," Lisa said. "Last time I rode in that truck I had a really bad day."

"You and me both."

"If you don't mind my asking," Hobbs said, "where is the money coming from for the renovations?"

"Various contributions and supporters," Lisa said. "I've made some calls and asked for some help. There were several senators and congressmen who were glad to contribute."

"Did you raise enough money?" Tanner asked. "I might like to contribute."

"All contributions are cheerfully accepted," Lisa said. "There's enough for the renovation, so we're now collecting money to bring a pastor to the church. We hope to have enough money to pay for two years' salary. By that time the church should be self-supporting."

Hobbs nodded in approval. "You've done a wonderful thing, Lisa. I think we all have a lot to be thankful for. I'm the only one who got away uninjured."

"I'm glad you were there," Lisa said. "Things might have been a lot different if you hadn't been."

"I'm still in the dark about what started all this, and Nick there won't tell me anything. I assume that there are still secrets to maintain."

"Yes," Lisa said sadly. "Nick is a mystery man, but that's the nature of the work. I can tell you, however, that you did your country a service."

"She trusts me now," Nick said with a broad smile.

"Not entirely," Lisa responded quickly. "I'm still a little put out with you because you kept me in the dark so long."

"It was for your own good," Nick said. "I did what I thought was right."

"How is your memory?" Tanner asked.

"Back and operating as well as it ever has.

Of course, there are a few things I would like to forget, but I guess our brains don't work that way."

"So what now?" Hobbs asked.

"It's back to work," Lisa replied. "It's still a scary world."

"That's true," Hobbs said, and then he raised his glass of iced tea. "Enough of the past. To the future."

The others joined him. "To the future."

After sipping his tea, Nick turned to Lisa. "When they hold the first service here, let me know. I think I'd like to attend."

"I will," Lisa said, warmed by the comment. "Then you can buy me lunch."

"I know a great place across the street," Nick said.

"Oh no you don't," Lisa retorted. "This time I want to go to a restaurant with menus you can hold."

High above the earth the MC2-SDS received a signal and slowly turned its optical eye a few degrees to the east. In response to its electronic orders, it began to focus on a small town in California, pulling the image tighter and tighter until a small gathering of people at an outdoor luncheon could be seen.

It transmitted the image back to earth.